To Frank —
With the Pablo —
[signature]
Nov 04.

© Copyright 2004 Sean Lyons. All rights reserved.

No part of this publication may be reproduced, stored in a retrieval system, or transmitted, in any form or by any means, electronic, mechanical, photocopying, recording, or otherwise, without the written prior permission of the author.

Printed in Victoria, Canada

Note for Librarians: a cataloguing record for this book that includes Dewey Classification and US Library of Congress numbers is available from the National Library of Canada. The complete cataloguing record can be obtained from the National Library's online database at:
www.nlc-bnc.ca/amicus/index-e.html
ISBN 1-4120-2418-8

TRAFFORD

This book was published on-demand in cooperation with Trafford Publishing.
On-demand publishing is a unique process and service of making a book available for retail sale to the public taking advantage of on-demand manufacturing and Internet marketing. On-demand publishing includes promotions, retail sales, manufacturing, order fulfilment, accounting and collecting royalties on behalf of the author.

Suite 6E, 2333 Government St., Victoria, B.C. V8T 4P4, CANADA
Phone 250-383-6864   Toll-free 1-888-232-4444 (Canada & US)
Fax 250-383-6804   E-mail sales@trafford.com   Web site www.trafford.com
TRAFFORD PUBLISHING IS A DIVISION OF TRAFFORD HOLDINGS LTD.
Trafford Catalogue #04-0246   www.trafford.com/robots/04-0246.html

10   9   8   7   6   5   4   3   2

CHAPTER 1

As parties of that type go, it was fairly standard. A fiftieth birthday for a mid level manager does not hold out great hopes of any excessive enjoyment. For Malachy, it was a useful way to meet people from the company. He had already been there nearly four months but the demands of a rapidly expanding company in a booming economy, even in a provincial town, were severe. The social life seemed exciting but he found it very difficult as an outsider to make any inroads. There was a golf club, sailing club, rugby club and all sorts of other clubs locally but again he sensed that he had to spend a period of social purgatory and isolation before he was accepted into the paradise of inclusion and membership.

He had been headhunted by the company for his accounting skills, especially in the field of international taxation, and once he had been shown his office and how to turn on his computer, he was left entirely alone. He found the work rewarding, if not very challenging, and the people at the plant seemed pleasant enough but there had not been a chance to make any real friends or even decent acquaintances. He had been hoping that the party might provide one or the other.

The birthday boy had greeted him heartily on the way in and had ignored him from that point on. Other colleagues had done the same but at least he was matching faces and names. His romantic notions took a serious nosedive when he realised that the only unaccompanied woman was well over seventy, and she was the widowed mother-in-law of his boss. Years of socialising all over the world had made Malachy very comfortable in this type of situation so when he found himself standing by the lady in question, he slipped effortlessly into his ideal son in law mode. He had developed several of these personae over time. As well as the every mother's son in law one, he had the charming devil, the sound rugby man, the sympathetic counsellor and a few others besides.

When he called the woman 'Ma'am', she cringed and insisted that he call her Nora. She was interested in his travels and had done a fair share herself. She told Malachy of holidays spent in luxury resorts which he too had visited, of which airlines had the best service and which hotels the best chefs. She obviously had that hard to describe quality called class and did little to hide her disdain for most of the other guests, observing them with the raised nose and pinched lips of the unrepentant snob. Obviously warming to Malachy, she told him that she had gone to Switzerland skiing when most of these people's families had been lucky to have a week in a caravan in Inniscrone or Lahinch. While these would be socialites had been growing up in draughty houses, sons and daughters of labourers and shopkeepers, she had had servants and gardeners. Malachy played his part well, and allowed her to waffle on.

Malachy was long enough around, even before doing an MBA in California, to appreciate that in the workplace, knowledge is power and these tit bits of information could come in useful. He was also shrewd enough to realise that keeping the mother in law entertained would not go unnoticed. In the course of his career to date, he had worked in several multinational companies in facilities and offices all over the world. The same games were played in them all. The same petty politics and empire building and back stabbing. He was not above playing along if it suited so the time spent listening to Nora was an investment, what he once heard referred to in a management training seminar as 'Quality Face Time.'

Nora eventually looked at her watch and said, 'Well, that's my duty nearly done. Another ten minutes and I can go home, take off my shoes and watch the Late Late Show. Let me get you a drink before I go.'

Malachy said he wouldn't hear of it but she said it was a small price to pay for a bit of pleasant company. 'When you get to my age Malachy, you know well that little pleasure in life is free.'

'Pleasure is always more enjoyable when it's free, Nora.'

'Don't patronise me with some dinner party banter, young man. You're a nice man but you'll be as bad as the rest of them after a while. One of these jumped up nouveau riche families will have you marrying their over educated daughters and then you'll be golfing and yachting with the quality as if you were born to it. Speaking of which, where are you from?'

'I was born and raised in Castlecarraig, County Mayo.'

Nora smiled, patted him on the arm and got up to leave.

'I should have known, Castlecarraig. The soft voice and charming manners. God Almighty, some things never change. Have you still got family there?'

'Not really, a few cousins I haven't seen for years and one or two uncles and aunts that wouldn't recognise me if I met them. Do you know the place?'

'Where do you think I learned that pleasure has a price? Good night Malachy, I've enjoyed my self no end.'

With another grin and a shake of her immaculately groomed head, she left.

Malachy sat in confused silence. What was going on, or more appropriately, what had gone on? Blessed with his mother's curiosity, he decided to find out.

He sought out his boss and complimented him on his choice of mother in law.

'I suppose you could do worse,' the boss said, swaying slightly and wafting warm brandy breath. 'But don't be fooled by the tough exterior. As they say, beneath that false steely exterior, there lies a real steely nature. Our Nora came up the hard way and she'd cut the knackers of any man who crossed her. What was she on about anyway?'

'Well,' Malachy replied, 'she started to tell me something about my home town but never finished.'

'Never mind, Malachy, it'll keep. Come over here now because there are a few people you need to meet.'

Malachy spent the rest of the party meeting a few people. He and they bought a few drinks for each other and he ended up the night singing a duet of Kevin Barry with his boss. The two of them were the last of the party goers to leave the bar and the boss insisted that Malachy share a taxi to his house for a night-cap, 'Jus' a l'l brandy, jus' the wan, ould stock.' A taxi was duly arranged and in less than ten minutes, Malachy was supporting his boss as he vomited all over his driveway. The security light came on as the front door opened and there stood Nora, stern, regal and disapproving.

'Thank you Malachy,' she said in a voice that would chill a vindaloo. 'Try to get him onto the couch in the sitting room without waking the few remaining people in a five mile radius who are not already awake. You can sleep on the settee in the study until it's bright enough to walk home.' She glanced at her watch. 'About three hours. Good morning.'

Malachy dragged the retching, drink stained mess that was his boss inside. He parked him on the couch, placing him on his side to avoid a tasteless and messy death through regurgitated stout and sausage rolls. When he located the kitchen, he found a basin and spare cloths under the sink. These he placed strategically around the couch, in hope rather than confidence that any stray projectiles would be accurately aimed. He then found the study.

He took off his shoes and lay down but by this time all sleep had deserted him. Turning on the reading lamp on the desk, he looked around the room. The desk itself was stacked high with files and reports. Malachy smiled ruefully. The company paid well but certainly extracted its' kilo of flesh from the employees. The walls were bare except for a huge wedding portrait of the boss and entourage. Though the picture by Malachy's reckoning was about twenty or twenty five years old, the boss had aged a lot more, and a lot worse, than the photo. On his wedding day, thick black wavy hair curled where now as the poet might have said, there were a last few wisps of sad grey hair. A footballer's build had thickened, especially around the waist and the square jawed handsome features had softened and lined. 'There but for the grace of God go I in a few years,' thought Malachy. The bride in the picture looked suitably radiant, and bar a few delicate wrinkles, had barely changed, except her hair was now blacker. Nora stood beside her daughter. Though she must have been in her late fifties when the picture was taken, she looked almost stunningly attractive. She wore a short skirt and high heels and her head was held in such a way that the photographer had caught her in full smile, the wide rim of her wedding hat failing to obscure her beauty. The rest of the wedding ensemble looked dull and uninteresting beside her.

Sensing rather than hearing a presence behind him, Malachy turned around.

'Are you interested in photography, young man?' Nora had that half smile he had seen as she left the party.

'I used to have an interest but it never developed. I suppose I was too negative.'

'God it's so true what I said earlier. Whatever is in the water in Castlecarraig, you have the soft talk. Come in to the kitchen and I'll make you a cup of coffee.'

'I'm not being smarmy Nora, but you were a remarkably handsome woman, and you know we never lie in Mayo.'

'Before we go into the kitchen, Malachy, look closely at that picture. In that group you'll see one of the most decent men that ever lived and I don't mean that heaving lump inside. You'll also see the most beautiful daughter in the world who deserves every happiness. Now we'll have coffee.'

They sat with their cups of instant coffee in the conservatory. Hints of dawn streaked the sky and the vague outlines of the mountains beyond the bay edged the horizon. Malachy was in that dreadful state between drunk and sober. The effects of the alcohol were wearing off and his nerves were frayed. In his younger days, he would have gone on the batter again but his good sense and poor liver dictated otherwise.

Nora regarded him with a mixture of amusement and puzzlement.

'Well, Malachy, will you ever drink again?'

'Never. I've said it before and I'll say it again, never.'

'I'm over seventy years of age and I've given up the booze many times. It was actually in bloody Castlecarraig that I began to drink among other things.'

'God, Nora, my head is tender, don't give me a hard time, please, I haven't lived there for nearly thirty years.'

'I only lived there for a few months and it turned my life upside down. I'm going to tell you a story, Malachy, about my time in your home town. I'm telling you because you'll be back there sometime and you'll start asking questions about the boss's mother in law and no doubt there's one or two old ones who'll be only too glad to tell you what they remember. But, Malachy, if I ever hear that the story got back to my daughter, I will see to it that you never work in this county or even this country again if I can help it. Is that fair enough?'

'Sound's fair, Nora.'

CHAPTER 2

Ireland in the late 1940's was a strange and dour place. Nora was born into fading gentry in County Wicklow, but fading or not, connections were still connections and family was still family. A relation in business in Mayo had a 'position' which would suit the youngest daughter of the house. Mayo was still an outpost and to go from the relative modernity of the East coast to the bogs of the West was a major decision. But times were hard so Nora boarded the train in her small village, changed at Dublin, changed several times more through the midlands and eventually, near midnight one late Summers night, disembarked onto a low platform and into a new world.

The smell was the first thing to strike her. Her nostrils filled with the soon to be familiar odour of cow dung, mingled with smoke from turf fires. The station was strangely quiet for the number of people milling about as most of them seemed intent on getting away as quickly as possible after the long and tedious journey. Porters unloaded wooden boxes onto trolleys while the driver leaned against the side of the great engine, puffing an oversized pipe almost in time with the belching machine behind him.

Through the door of the station, Nora could see a few cars and several horse drawn traps, though most people seemed to be making their way towards the town on foot. Before long, the train had left and Nora still stood on the platform, alone but for one remaining passenger. He spoke to her and, like the smell of the cow dung, she was soon to become used to the soft accent of the locality with which he spoke.

'Are you to be met, miss?'

In the dim light of the station she saw him to be a slim and serious looking young man, a little older than herself. Nora had never stood in male company on her own before, let alone late at night in a strange place. The man sensed her nervousness.

'My name is Myles Walsh; my father should be along soon to collect me. We live about two miles outside of town. If we can oblige you at all, please feel free to ask.'

As he finished speaking, a car noisily stopped outside. A dapper man in pinstripes and bowler hat came rushing in.

'My dear Nora! You poor girl, please forgive me, I was delayed. You must be exhausted. I am your Uncle Thomas, please let me get your bags. Young man, perhaps you would be so kind?'

Myles was thus drafted in to help load Nora's bags to her uncle's car, which was shuddering seriously and belching blue smoke into the bovine scented air.

'Good man, good man, put the big one in the boot, well done, now, Nora, we'll be home in ten minutes, thank you, young man.'

Nora waved to Myles as her uncle ground the gears of the car and it grudgingly and slowly moved away. Myles raised his hat in salute and the lights of the car lit up a handsome face and fine mop of black hair.

'So Nora,' he uncle continued his monologue, 'welcome to Castlecarraig. Quite a change no doubt from the east coast and the city but you'll get used to it. The people are pleasant and the ordinary folk keep to themselves. That young man seemed fairly typical actually, helpful if asked and well mannered. So, how was the journey?'

Nora was watching the town pass as they drove. Narrow streets were unlit and candle light flickered from some windows. There were few cars. As they entered what seemed to be the main street of the town, every second house seemed to be a tavern and every second one of them seemed to be doing well.

'I beg your pardon, Uncle Thomas?'

'Please, call me Thomas, I asked how was your journey? I go to the city twice a year and I know how tiring it is.'

'It certainly is tiring, I seem to have been travelling forever. But as you said, the people were very courteous and helpful. I am looking forward to a nice sleep in a comfortable bed.'

As she spoke, her uncle stopped the car outside a large two- storey house.

'This is Mrs Browne's, you'll be stopping here. She was widowed in the Great War and sometimes lets a room to single girls. If they are vouched for, of course.'

Nora had believed that she would be lodging with her uncle and said so.

'Dear me, young lady, I am a bachelor and we could not have that, not in a small town, even if we are related, if only by marriage. Tongues would wag and no doubt the Vicar would remark on it. And God alone knows what the priests would make of it. You must bear in mind, Nora, that this is not a big place. We are in the minority here, have been for years, so we must be seen to be above reproach. I spent half my life here as a subject of the British Empire and the last half as a citizen of their Free State. We are different but we are part of the community. We must keep and maintain the highest standards in everything we do. Never forget that, dear girl. Now, let's meet Mrs Browne.'

Mrs Browne greeted Nora formally but with affection. She dismissed Thomas with hardly a glance and provided her new lodger with warm, sweet tea and biscuits. She then led Nora upstairs and showed her to her room. Exhausted, Nora undressed to her slip, crawled under the hand crocheted bedspread and slept.

CHAPTER 3

Nora awakened for the first time to the sounds of the country. She heard birds singing, cows lowing, the neigh of horses and the clip clop of their hooves on the street. She heard the braying of donkeys and the shouts of men. Opening the curtain, she looked down at her new environment. It was another sunny day and, glancing at the clock on her mantelpiece, she saw it was past ten o 'clock. Dressing quickly, she went downstairs.

Mrs Browne was standing at the open hall door. She was buying eggs and butter from an old woman wrapped in a black shawl. Hearing Nora on the stairs, she closed the door and smiled at her.

'Special treat for you on your first morning, dear, eggs fresh from the farm, freshly churned butter and I even baked fresh bread.' Sure enough, the odour of baking wafted from the kitchen and before long Nora was sampling the tastiest breakfast she had ever had. Mrs Browne sat with her and seemed to enjoy the youth and energy she brought to the house.

'Tell me about your family,' she said.

'Papa still works in the mill, but his health is not good. I have two brothers older than I, and they both work in London. They send what they can so Papa may soon be able to retire. I am of course the youngest and Uncle Thomas was kind enough to offer me a position in his shop.'

'When did you mother pass away? Thomas told me she died during the war.'

'Yes, poor Mama was killed during a bombing raid in England. She was in fact visiting her sister in Coventry to arrange for her family to move to Ireland and safety. The shelter they were all in was hit directly by a German bomb and dozens of people died.'

'My own dear husband died at Mons. For King and Country. Now the King is dead and the country he served is gone and here we are. War is men's business and we won't talk of it again. Freshen up now and I will take you to your uncle in the shop.'

The two women walked side by side from Mrs Browne's house to the shop. On the way, they were greeted by the townspeople with a mixture of deference and friendliness. Nora's smart new suit was in stark contrast to the women they met. They were wearing well washed and worn clothes, a lot of which were patched. Older women wore shawls. All the men wore hats and nearly all seemed to be smoking cigarettes or pipes. She was struck by the mixture of smell. Despite the warmth of the day, turf smoke clung acridly to the air. Horse and donkey dung spotted the road and the few cars and vans that passed belched petrol and diesel fumes. Several of the shops had large slabs of fish and bacon hanging outside.

There were few young people. Nora asked her companion why this was.

"Emigration, quite simply. A lot of young men left to fight in the war of course but DeValera's neutrality was widely heeded here. Usually most young men and women leave here for England or America. You see, they were so eager to get their independence that they didn't really think through the consequences. Now, the old enemy England is their refuge. The men are rebuilding the cities and the women nursing the sick.

"There are two small factories here, one making shoes and the other producing bacon. Those are both owned by English people but that doesn't seem to bother our nationalist brethren. Here we are."

They had stopped outside a large shop. Over the door was the name: 'B Williams and Co Ltd.'. Under the name was a description of the trade: 'Suppliers of finest meats, teas, animal feeds, hardware, imported goods etc.'

"The 'B' is for Bill, Thomas's grandfather who started the business," explained Mrs Brown, as she opened the door to allow Nora to enter the shop.

The interior was dark, lit only by a few electric light bulbs. Dust swirled thickly in the brightness. Nora was struck by the size. The shop stretched back a long way, on three different levels, each level reached by a short flight of steps. Counters ran along each side. Bulging canvas bags were stacked along the counters while behind them, shelves climbed from floor to ceiling. Nora had never seen such a mix of items under one roof. One corner was stacked with farm tool, rakes, forks, shovels of all shapes and sizes. As sales were made, the assistant would place the money and docket into a small container. This was then attached to a cable stretching across the ceiling. The assistant pulled a little lever and the container flew across the ceiling by means of the cable, landing in a small booth. From the window of this, she saw her uncle watching her. He waved and came to meet her.

"My dear child, how lovely to see you. Thank you Mrs Browne for escorting her. Are you exhausted, dear Nora?"

"Not at all. My room is so lovely and Mrs Browne gave me the best breakfast I have ever had so I am ready and willing to start."

"Not today, surely, Thomas," Mrs Browne said. "The poor girl must find her feet and get to know the place. Everything is so different for her here, away from family and friends, knowing not a soul."

Just then, Nora saw a familiar figure at the counter.

"Ah, but I do know some people, like both of you and that young man at the food counter was at the station last night. I must speak to him to express my thanks."

Not noticing the exchange of glances between her companions and the pursed lips of her landlady, Nora crossed the shop.

"Myles, isn't it, you were on the train last night."

Myles appeared surprised and somewhat flustered by her greeting.

"Of course, Miss…"

"Fortune, but please call me Nora. I am sorry if I was not very polite to you last night but thank you for your kindness. I was quite distracted by all the activity as it was my first time ever to set foot in Castlecarraig."

"Well I hope your stay will be a happy one. We don't get many strangers here, especially young beautiful women like yourself." Myles face reddened and eyes blinked. "Forgive me, I did not mean to be so rude."

"Where I come from, Myles, it is not considered rude to pay a girl a compliment. I have a lot to learn about Castlecarraig so thank you for starting my education."

Myles and Nora stood in silence. She saw a darkly handsome face, green eyes that held understanding and she also saw in herself a stirring of feelings that were new and strange. Myles too felt sensations that were not only new but to him were sinful.

Thomas watched them both. He noticed their stances and the way they smiled. He felt jealousy and also resentment for the generation that separated him from the couple. He crossed the floor and touched Nora's elbow.

"Yes, well, the young man from the station, I know you now. How is your father? Well, I trust. Nora, if I may, I'd like to show you around the shop. Good day, young Walsh."

As Nora allowed herself to be escorted away, she smiled at Myles and he bowed awkwardly.

"Now, Nora," Thomas spoke as he led her through the shop. " First of all, I would be obliged if you would stop this 'uncle' nonsense. It makes me feel quite the grand old man. Officially, I am your mother's cousin, by marriage indeed, so we may be on first name terms. Please call me Thomas. Is that alright?"

"Why, of course, Thomas, I would be far more relaxed and delighted to call you by whatever you wish. My mother told me so much about you. And your kindness in taking me when things are not quite going as well as we wish.."

"I am not doing you any charity, I assure you, Nora. I need someone here that I can trust to look after my books. We have built up a substantial business as you shall see and you will have your work cut out I can assure you. This is your post, through this door."

He led her up a flight of four steps to a small cubicle that overlooked the shop floor. A woman, a little older than Nora, sat at a cramped table, surrounded by piles of ledgers and account books. Money lay on the desk in coin and paper and the woman was counting that and recording into the ledgers. Against the far wall stood a large safe.

Thomas cleared his throat and the woman turned to face them. Nora was surprised to see that she was in fact only slightly older than herself. In spite of the stooped shoulders.

"This is Miss Tracey, our present accounts clerk. She will soon be Mrs. so of course will be leaving our employ. We shall of course miss her but her duties are clear. Miss Tracey, please meet your replacement, Miss Fortune."

"Very pleased to meet you, Miss Fortune."

Nora was struck by the softness of her voice and gentleness of her accent. She took her hand in hers.

"My congratulations, Miss Tracey. How exciting for you. When will you be getting married?"

The clerk glanced at Thomas, as if seeking permission to reply. He frowned but nodded tightly.

"Our banns have been called and we will be married at month's end."

Nora clapped her hands. "I've never been at a wedding! Surely Thomas we will go to see Miss Tracey become Mrs…Mrs what will you be?

Again the exchange, except this time the pause was longer and the frown deeper, the nod tighter.

"Mrs O Murchu, Mrs Seamus O Murchu." the clerk said with a touch of defiance. She then went back to her work.

"Quite. Now, Nora, you will have one week with Miss Tracey before she leaves. She will teach you how to keep everything in order. Meanwhile, Mrs Browne will be wondering where we have got to."

Before Nora could speak again, he ushered her out.

Mrs Browne was studying the labels on packets of tea when they found her.

"Thomas," she said, "you look quite agitated."

"Yes, quite. I wonder if you would care to join us in my office for a cup of tea."

On the way through the shop, Nora looked for Myles but could not see him.

Thomas led them into his office and busied himself making tea. The office was as neat and tidy as himself. More ledgers lined the shelves and there were rows of order books, docket books, invoice books and many other books stacked on the floor. There was a small window which looked into the shop. Thomas drew a curtain over this then set a tray on his desk. The tea was poured into china cups. As Thomas stirred his tea, he looked seriously at Nora.

"Nora," he said, "I must speak very seriously to you. Mrs Browne, I am sure will agree with what I say."

Nora looked from one to the other, completely at a loss.

"Life in the West of Ireland," he continued, "is very different to where you have lived. I am not just talking about the size of the town or the poverty or indeed the people. The people we live among are by and large decent God fearing folk. Indeed, many of them are old and dear friends. We do, however, come from different worlds, even though we live cheek by jowl as it were. Take Miss Tracey, for instance. A fine woman, a good and honest worker. However, you will no doubt have noted the Gaelic name of her intended. While your relations and Mrs Brownes were fighting Nazis to keep Europe free, her young man was interned in the Curragh for the duration of the war because he is a rebel. A member of a secret army, as they like to call it. Several of them were strung up for their treason but if you ask me, a lot more should have joined them."

Nora's hand shook as she placed her cup and saucer on the table.

"Oh my Lord."

"Oh my Lord, indeed! From all of that, it is of course obvious that she, Miss Tracey, that is, is a Roman Catholic. One does not attend weddings of the other side, and that is their choice quite as much as ours. If one of their priests were to find Miss Tracey in our chapel, I am sure she would be regarded as an outcast."

"I never thought...." Nora stammered.

"One must always think, Nora." This time it was Mrs Browne who spoke. "Take that young man you were talking to. Young Walsh."

"Is he a member of this army too?"

Thomas and Mrs Browne both laughed softly.

"A rather different army, I am afraid," Mrs Brown replied. "Did you notice how he was dressed?"

Nora's brow creased in concentration.

"I did notice his clothes were, well, rather worn, but clean. Is that what you mean?"

"What about the colour of his clothes?"

"The colour?" Nora thought some more, "black, I think."

"Black indeed!" Thomas said triumphantly.

"Whatever does that mean?" Nora was puzzled.

"Young Myles is in a seminary my dear." It was Mrs Browne who spoke. "In a few short years he will be the Reverend Father Walsh, a priest of the Roman Catholic Church."

CHAPTER 4

Nora and Malachy sat in silence. The sun had long risen and the day held promise of warmth and a chance to go outdoors.

Malachy spoke. 'I think I can see where the story is going, Nora. You fell for the man of the cloth, I suppose.'

'Oh, you suppose right, Malachy, but as Oscar Wilde said, "The truth is never plain and rarely simple". Myles was the most handsome man I had ever seen and I've not met any more handsome since. Have you ever been swept off your feet, by the way?'

'I was on a yacht of the Great Barrier Reef once and I slipped on some coleslaw. I nearly fell over the side.'

'Now, now, young man. I am telling you things nobody knows, and nobody but you will know. So, have you ever been besotted?'

'I drank too much sake in Kyoto at a wedding and I was blottto. On the love side, though, in all honesty, since I left school, I've never really been that lucky, or otherwise.'

"What about at school?'

'I spent most days as horny as a young bull. I used to think I had a problem because I fancied every thing female. At discos, I'd be afraid I'd trip on the floor in case I'd pole vault through the amplifiers. I was mad about a particular girl. Breege. She was gorgeous. I used to dance with her at the socials and I'd talk to her on the street and walk to school with her.'

"Did you ever tell her how you felt?'

'Every time I bumped into her or she glanced at the front of my trousers she knew how I felt. One night, I was determined I was going to tell her and ask her out. I knew she went to the girl's sodality the first Sunday of every month. It sounds a bit stage Irish but the nights of the sodalities and the pilgrimages to Knock were great times to shift the women.

'Anyway, this Sunday, I waited outside the church, with the rest of the frustrated lads, committing sins of impurity in our minds. Breege was first out. She spotted me and ran over. I still remember the two lumps I had, one in my throat. Before I could say a word, she piped up: "Is John Joyce here? Maggie Flynn says he fancies me."

Nora laughed. 'You still look a little hurt after all these years. Did you really fancy her that much?

'Well, you guys look like you are having a good time. Have you been up all night?' Nora's daughter Felicity stood at the door of the conservatory. Although she had only had a few hours sleep and had not put on any make up or even so much as dragged a brush or comb through her hair, she looked beautiful. "I haven't heard you laugh so much for a long time Mother. Obviously sleepless nights agree with you.'

Nora went over to her and hugged her.

'This young man was telling me a story about his courting days in Castlecarraig. It's hard to believe when you look at his handsome countenance now that he was an awkward, pimply school boy once.'

'I never mentioned the pimples,' Malachy protested. 'Anyway, I'd squeezed the worst of the blackheads before I went out. The pimples we had to do before we went to bed, putting boiling water on cotton wool and trying to draw the badness out. I can tell you both now that teen aged boys suffered as much for their looks as any super model, between squeezing blackheads and bursting pimples.'

'I was going to fry up a few eggs and rashers', Felicity said,' but I am afraid I might lose my appetite if this conversation keeps going.'

'You make some nice bacon sandwiches, like a good girl. I want to hear the rest of poor Malachy's tale of woe.'

Felicity went smiling into the kitchen and Malachy continued.

CHAPTER 5

Only twenty years had passed between Nora's arrival in Castlecarraig and Malachy's heartbreak at the church. Both events occurred in the gentle evening sunshine of a summer's day, both events involved emotions but, whereas one was to prove a life changing turning point, the other was only a blip on the road of sexual awakening.

Malachy stood there and said,' What?"

'Maggie Flynn was talking to Joe Murray. He told her that he heard that John fancied me. Did you hear that too?'

Malachy felt the lava of humiliation in his gut. The empty spaces on his face, recently vacated by blackheads, pained him like pin pricks. Other pricks shrivelled at the despair of the moment. His courage deserted him with his pride and he heard himself say yes he had heard that John Joyce fancied her.

Breege looked around her excitedly.

'Should I say something, Malachy, or will I wait for him to make a move? What do you think Malachy?'

What Malachy thought was, 'John, you BASTARD! You horrible slimy, lucky bastard. And you, you bitch, I could give you pure love that would last forever and all you want is that arrogant pain in the arse foot-balling skinny BASTARD!'

What Malachy said was, 'Come on so and we'll find him.'

Breege grabbed his arm and said, 'You are a great friend Malachy. All the girls think you're the nicest of them all'

Malachy wanted to shake himself free and scream, 'Feic off you patronising Jezebel, you bitch. Nice! No teenaged lad wants to be nice. I want you to think I'm sexy and threatening and want to rub against me. That's what I want, not nice!'

John Joyce was standing at the edge of the footpath.

He was wearing his older brother's black leather jacket and was affecting a Jimmy Dean look, chin tucked in, hair fringe flopping over his forehead. He had even stolen Malachy's idea and put on his vest backwards so the rim showed around his neck, under a dark shirt, giving him a hard man look. He pretended not to notice Malachy and Breege coming towards him, keeping his hands stuck in the back pockets of his corduroy trousers.

'Look at him now,' Malachy thought, 'with his hand me down clothes and scratching his arse and his underwear back to front. Look at me Breege!'

Breege greeted John with a cheerful smile and fawn like eyes, he greeted her and looked at Malachy the way a bullock looks over the side of a trailer, all expectation.

'Breege and myself were going for a walk, John, would you like to come along, for the craic like?' Malachy nearly choked on the words.

'Sound so,' John replied and the three of them fell into step away from the church. Breege and John did not so much as steal glances at each other as plunder lecherous stares and leers. Eventually, Malachy felt obliged to make an excuse and leave. The couple were so bound in the thrall of lust and infatuation that they made no pretence at wanting him to stay.

Malachy walked on his own towards the local park but as soon as he was inside the gate, he stopped and peered through a space in the wall. He watched John and Breege turn towards the soccer pitch. It was still bright so he allowed them to get a little ahead of him and then he followed.

He could not believe the turn the night had taken. It had begun with him on a cloud of expectation and love and now he was reduced to a frustrated and rejected peeping tom, sneaking along a lane to spy on his friend and true love.

When he spied, he had to choke back a shout of anger and jealousy. Breege was standing against the lone advertising hoarding on the sideline of the soccer field. Her back was between the words 'Murray's' and 'Bread' and John was up against her, arms locked around her, lips to hers, both sets of hips moving in the classic samba of the dry ride, while Breege's glorious buttocks moved rhythmically from the apostrophe s to the capital B. Malachy was hypnotised and shamed, aroused and embarrassed. Then he saw Breege look at her watch over John's shoulder and push him gently away.

'Even whores have curfews,' thought Malachy.

John was not in any hurry to break the embrace. Even when they had separated, he lingered, leaning casually against the M of Murray's. Malachy knew why he was delaying. He knew John could not walk without a limp for a few minutes, as his trousers held a beater that could drive an ass up the side of Neiphin Mountain. It gave Malachy time to escape and skulk back home.

The next morning at school, John sought out Malachy at break time. They went behind the shed with the smokers.

'Mighty night last night, Malachy.'

'Did you do any good?'

'That'd be telling.'

'Blasht you, did you get a court?'

'Shtop.'

'Did you or didn't you?'

'I got the hand and a mighty shift.'

'Did you get the full hand now or just outside the knickers?'

'The full hand. I'll be dug out of that one, I'm telling you, she's a good thing.'

'Are you taking her out again?'

'We're going to the pictures Friday night.'

'What's on?'

'Matther a shite to me pal, I'll be in the back row with me tongue in her throat and me hand in me knickers. You'll have to do me a favour though.'

'Do you want me to put my hand in her knickers for you? I will if you want since you're my best friend.'

'You can shag off, that's one knickers you'll never get your hand into, boy. The problem is, Breege won't be allowed to the pictures unless she goes with her friend. I can fix you up with the friend and we'll both be right then.'

Malachy knew why John was not looking him in the eye while he spoke, it was because he knew who this friend was.

'I presume we are talking about Marian Waters,' he said.

'We are indeed.'

'Better known as Marian the Wagon Walters, the Four Wheeler.'

'Some call her that.'

'So do you, you bollocks. You are the one that said to me not two weeks ago that if we were ever attacked by Apaches, we could circle her to keep them out.'

'That was only a bit of craic.'

'Bit of craic my arse! She has no diddies, a bald spot and no chin either.'

'She's supposed to be a mighty court and you don't look at the

mantle piece when you're poking the fire, Malachy.'

'You have to look at the shagging mantle piece when you're finished poking the shagging fire though.'

Just then, the bell rang and they went to their religion class. As the Brother read from the life of a saint, Malachy's mind was full of unwanted but nurtured images. He saw himself and Breege lying in fields, on beaches, by streams but his images kept being nudged out by that of John and Breege dry humping against Murray's bread.

The week passed slowly. As Leaving Cert students, they had supervised study every night. They sat from five til seven, while a Brother sat watching. Different Brothers had different styles of supervising. The Hopper moved constantly as he apparently had chronic varicose veins. He was well liked because he treated the lads with respect, unless the veins were at him and he'd throw a duster at someone who annoyed him. The Lizard was a devious, cruel man. He loved to catch boys copying homework or arriving late. He would try to humiliate them by making snide references to their family circumstances, or by pulling the locks of hair under the ears. Monkey Man looked like a monkey plain and simple while Snakey was a pervert, impure and complex. He would stand too close to young pupils, and often his hand would be making strange movements under his cassock. He had a dreadful and dreaded habit of putting his hand under boys' shirts and caressing their flesh. He was always distracted on Thursdays in Summer, however. The study hall looked out on the football field. Players used to tog out and off in a crudely made shelter near the school building. Older players would be aware when Snakey was on supervision and pause half dressed or bend over and tie their laces with their togs at half mast. Snakey would stand at the window, red faced, while his cassock shook like the waves beating Bertra beach.

The Lizard was on duty this particular day. At six o'clock on the button, he would go outside and smoke a Gold Flake cigarette. The sweet addictive smell of the burning tobacco and assorted cancer inducing chemicals wafted through the study hall, driving the smokers wild with longing. Smoking, however, was one of the few vices Malachy did not have to bring to Confessions.

While the Lizard was outside the door, John Joyce leaned over from his seat and whispered to Malachy.

'Are you on for Friday night?'

'Do I have a choice?'

'There's always a choice, Malachy, either you take Marian to the pictures or I'll beat seven colours of shite out of you. And I'll tell your mother what you did in the holy water font in Knock.'

'I'll look forward to seeing you all Friday night so.'

A loud voice boomed from the door at the back of the hall.

'Malachyeah!' The lizard had snuck back into the room. 'Back here to meah Malachyeh!'

The Lizard was a Kerryman with the habit of putting an eah sound at the end of any word that ended in e or y. Hence, every time he called Malachy, it came out as 'Malachyeah!'

'Malachyeah! Fwat were oo and John Joyce tawking about? Well, Malachyeah!?'

'Nothing, Brother.'

'Nawtin! And how do oo tawk about nawtin, Malachyeah!?'

'I don't know, Brother.'

'Oo don't know, Malachyeah!? Well. Faith and I don't know either, by! Have oo finished oor Latin translations for meah for tomorrow, have oo?'

'Yes, Brother.'

'Well, oo can write them out again, Malachyeah!, so the next time I ask oo fwat oo were tawkin' about, oo will tell meah, am I making my self perfectlyeah clear to oo, Malachyeah!? Do oo understand meah, Malachyeah!?'

'Yes, Brother.'

'Go back to oor seat now, by, and not a peep out of oo, are oo listening to meah, Malachyeah!?

'Thank you, Brother.'

As Malachy passed John on the way back to his seat, he muttered to him under his breath: 'She'd better be a bloody good court.'

And within certain parameters she was. As soon as he and Marian sat in the dim back row of the cinema, she stuck her face in his. Her tongue was already out and she ground her lips to his. Her tongue remained unmoving in his mouth for most of the first feature, which was a short documentary on life in the Galapagos islands. Marian's tongue seemed to have the same leathery texture as the skin of the giant turtles. Malachy tried to follow the narration but the lapping of wet lips and the occasional breaking of the airlock between his mouth and Marians made it difficult.

The court itself was not totally unsatisfactory but Malachy felt he was making most of the effort as Marians tongue refused to budge and sat inside his mouth like a half inflated furry balloon. She smelt of Lux soap and talcum powder. Now and again, Malachy was able to manoeuvre her head to the side and over her bald patch he could see Breege and John. She was coiled like a languorous reptile around the front of his body. Her lips moved slowly and sexily, no doubt her tongue was writhing and teasing inside his mouth. Every now and again, Breege would nuzzle John's ear and whisper sweet somethings, causing him to giggle and look about him as if looking for someone to share the lechery with. Marian only broke the tongue lock occasionally during the main feature, a violent Western called the Wild Bunch. Once to say breathlessly, 'Chrisht, Malachy, you're a horrid sexy kisser,' several times to unwrap and eat a chocolate and toffee sweet, Oatfield Coleen Selection, and a number of times to gawk around at John and Breege, after which she would nudge Malachy mightily in the ribs and wink. She moved with such speed at times, that she would have her tongue back in his throat while still half way through the wink.

Eventually, the movie finished, Malachy watched the credits roll while trying to breathe past a mouthful of Oatfield Coleen Selection flavoured and unyielding gristle. Soon, the Irish flag fluttered across the screen and a scratchy brass rendition of the national anthem rolled through the cinema, deserted now except for two couples, one still lost in the throes of teenage hormonal passion, the other only half so. Malachy burst from the attentions of his shift like a swimmer emerging from an over long spell under water. He went and shook John's shoulder.

'Come on, let's go.'

'The picture isn't over yet,' John replied, his voice muffled by sex and a set of beautiful, pearl like teeth, chewing on his lower lip. Then he glanced around at the empty seats and blinked at the lights.

'Oops, Breege, time to go.'

They both went down the stairs of the balcony, giggling like the guilty school kids they were. Malachy looked at the calf eyes of his date and smiled like the cowardly hypocrite he was.

CHAPTER 6

Felicity cleared away the breakfast plates, empty bar a few bits of crust and bacon rind. Nora, despite being the oldest, looked the chirpiest. Malachy was feeling that sense of disorientation that comes from missing a lot of sleep after consuming a lot of alcohol. The coffee had added a dimension of stimulation to his overall exhaustion so he was beginning to feel the irritability of the half baked hang over.

'That's enough true confessions for one morning,' he said through a yawn.

'But what ever happened Breege and John and poor Marian?' Nora wanted to know. Felicity had come back.

'I think you were very cruel to the poor girl,' she said.

'The "poor" girl actually matured into a beautiful woman. Hair grew on the bald patch, she developed a model's body and a charming personality. She got a rake of honours in her Leaving Cert and ended up as a doctor. She married a Yank and she is now one of the top paediatricians in the Los Angeles area. I actually met her there a few years ago. I was doing a stint in Silicon Valley. I got her address in Santa Barbara and went for a visit. She's got it made. A mansion of a house on a hill, overlooking the Pacific, swimming pool, four cars in the garage.

'The husband is a typical Californian, every thing is "goood!". He has a strong jaw, a firm handshake and great teeth. She has two lovely kids.

'She organised a cook out for me.

'We laughed about the old days and when I was leaving, she put her arm around me. Stuck her tongue in my mouth, and then she laughed and said I was still a horrid sexy kisser. I watched her in the rear view mirror as I drove away. The husband had his arm around her, the kids were holding her hands, the mansion, the money, the success. She could have had me.'

'And John and Breege?'

'They went their separate ways.'

Malachy drained the last drops of cold coffee from his mug and got up to leave.

'I just realised that I left my car at the hotel. Can I call a taxi?'

Nora got up.

'There's no need to call a taxi. I'll drop you down town. I have a few things to get anyway. Felicity, I'll see you this afternoon. God knows when we'll see that husband of yours.'

Felicity smiled. 'He will be so sick and so guilty when he gets up. I'll send him off for a swim and a sauna and hopefully that will sweat the badness out of him. Then a steak dinner and he'll be himself again.'

'Unfortunately,' snorted Nora, but she said it gently and with a hint of affection.

As she drove Malachy back towards town, she seemed distracted. She was quiet, which suited Malachy, whose head was aching and there was a pounding behind his right eye. He tried to alleviate this by half closing the eye but when he caught a glimpse of himself in the wing mirror of the Merc, he realised that he looked like a fool. He closed his eyes and the warmth of the sun through the tinted windows, along with the soft hum of the engine, made him drowsy.

'Malachy.' A voice came to him. 'Malachy.' He woke and sat upright too quickly. His brain seemed to slide forward and beat against his skull. He realised he was still in the passenger seat of Nora's car, with the seat reclined totally. Nora was looking at him from the driver's side. She pushed a button and his seated glided into the upright position.

'What time of day is it?'

'It is just gone three in the afternoon, you have been out cold for nearly three hours. Here.'

She handed him a bottle of mineral water and the sour taste in his mouth abated a little. Although he felt a little stiff, he felt better overall.

Looking out the window, he noticed they were parked overlooking a beach he recognised.

'Come on,' Nora commanded. 'A long walk in the fresh air and you'll be fine.'

'A long walk in the fresh air and I'll be dead,' Malachy replied but he climbed out of the car and fell into step beside the woman.

'How come you never married?' she asked.

'An old bachelor friend of mine used to say why make one woman unhappy when you can make hundreds happy. As he got older, he changed his position a little and said why should he take another man's daughter into his house and feed her and keep her for life.'

'So why didn't you get married?'

'For the first while, I was too busy travelling around the world having a good time, then I got lazy. After that I lost interest and at this stage now, I'm too set in my ways. I'll be celebrating my fiftieth in a year or two but I'm afraid it will be a much more low key affair than last night's do.'

They walked in silence. The Atlantic air was clearing Malachy's head and the physical exercise was improving his humour. They came to a small group of rocks and Nora sat on one. He sat beside her, to her left and slightly higher. The afternoon sun was warm and the crash and hiss of the foaming tide provided a relaxing backdrop.

Without looking in her direction, Malachy asked, 'Whatever happened to you priesheen in Mayo?

CHAPTER 7

Nora was not entirely sure how to react when she heard Myles was a seminarian. Her knowledge of the Roman faith was limited though she did know that priests were not allowed to marry.

'So, Nora,' Thomas said, 'the ways of a small town are strange and it takes a while to get to know them but you shall in time, you shall in time. Now, Mrs Browne and I must rush off to meet our esteemed vicar. Another financial crisis I'm afraid. With so few of us on the ground as it were, money is always a problem. Still, one does what one can. Shall we Mrs Browne?'

Mrs Browne spoke to Nora. Her tone was not unkind.

' A young and beautiful girl like you will have many admirers wherever she goes, Nora. Try not to let your heart rule your head. A woman has a place here in this society and a Protestant woman has an even smaller place. Now, I've left some nice cold beef for your supper in case you are home before me. It is a lovely evening so why don't you take a stroll around on your way to the house. The park is beautiful now, the chestnut trees are especially attractive. It used to be the landlord's cricket ground in the good old days. Some Summer evenings, Thomas and I walk around it and I try to describe to him what it was like in its heyday. The soldiers in their uniforms, the ladies and gentlemen in their finery, the cheers of the crowd for the batsmen. Imagine it for yourself as you stroll around. And then, consider what's in it's place.'

Nora went back to her little work cubicle to get her coat. Miss Tracey was checking the last few figures of the day and smiled at her.

'I am just about finished, Nora, will you lock up or shall I?'

'I'll do it, Eileen. I have some time to spare. Mrs Browne and Thomas are gone on some errand or other so I am going to take a stroll when I leave.'

'It's such a lovely evening, I'll join you if you don't mind.'

Soon, the two young women were strolling along the main thoroughfare of the town. The late Summer shadows made it a cool evening. They were greeted by most people, the men tipping their caps, the women nodding briefly. A few cars lined the footpath. Several carts were being pulled by ponies and a few by donkeys. Some shop keepers were sweeping in front of their premises. Eileen had words for each of them and most of them in turn wished her well in her coming marriage and asked after her fiancée.

'Miss Joyce, will you take a walk around the park with me?' Nora asked.

''I would be delighted, Miss Fortune,' replied Eileen, linking her arm.

Giggling happily at their daring intimacy, they entered the local park.

A group of boys played football, using mounds of the recently cut grass as goal posts.

Old men sat on benches, smoking pipes, while women in groups of two and three walked casually along the paths that ran around the inside of the park.

Nora and Eileen walked in silence, enjoying each others company. A man's voice called from behind them.

'Eileen!'

They turned and a man in his late twenties, with a serious face and dark eyes approached them.

'Seamus, this is a surprise. I thought you were on overtime all week.'

'There was a problem with the chill room. Again. So we had to stop killing early. Who's the stranger?'

'This is Nora Fortune that I've been telling you all about.'

'Indeed, she has not stopped talking about you for weeks, Nora. I'm Seamus O Murchu, as you may have gathered.'

Nora looked into the dark eyes of a rebel for the first time. Automatically, she took his outstretched hand and returned his greeting.

'How are you settling in Castlecarraig, Nora?' he asked.

'Fine thank you, everyone is very kind.'

'Do you like our park? It's steeped in history you know.'

'Yes, Mrs Browne tells me it used to be a cricket ground.'

Seamus threw his head back and laughed loudly.

'A cricket ground indeed! Indeed it was. Not too long ago, from where we are standing, you could see the lords and ladies decked out in their finery, watching the redcoats and the RIC at play, swinging their cricket bats and fielding and catching and the devil knows what. But do you know what else you could see, Nora?'

'Shh, now Seamus.' Eileen could see the change in his eyes, the glint of fanaticism that at times frightened her.

'What do you mean, Seamus, what else?' Nora asked. She too sensed a change in the atmosphere. Though she felt a thrill of dread, she also felt a tinge of excitement and quickening interest.

Seamus looked at her, his face a mixture of amusement and anger.

'Over there, Nora, there was the hanging tree. During the rebellion of 98, rebels and priests were strung up there, without trial, judge or jury. Their bodies were thrown in unmarked graves. There was a bounty on the priests heads too. Twenty pounds for a bishop, ten pounds for a Jesuit, a fiver for the rest. Behind that spot, where the fire station is now, was the local barracks. During the War of Independence, my own uncle was gunned down inside those walls. This park has it's ghosts alright, for your Mrs Browne they might be ghosts of cricket playing gentry. For the people of this town, though, they are ghosts of rebels and croppies.'

Nora was stunned by this speech, delivered with such heat and passion. Eileen stood between her and Seamus, totally at a loss to know what to do.

Seamus allowed his face to relax into a smile.

'Welcome to the republican politics of the West of Ireland, Miss Nora,' he said with surprising gentleness.

'I really do have a lot to learn. That's what Mrs Browne told me today. You and her seem to have that much in common, anyway, Seamus.'

Seamus laughed again.

'Actually, she and I have about as much in common as the poor pigs I slaughtered today have in common with the thoroughbred stallions of the cavalry that trotted across this park on parade a generation ago. At least the pigs will feed the natives.'

'Whereas the natives fed the thoroughbreds,' Nora teased.

'Oh, Eileen, we have a frisky filly here. Mr Thomas will be kept on his toes now. He'll rue the day you got married and left him with this lady.'

'If the rebels were hanged, was that not because they had rebelled against the king?' Nora demanded. 'If the peasants of Sussex or the people of Glasgow had rebelled, they would have suffered the same fate. Treason is treason, whether you agree with the government or not,'

Eileen looked nervously at her companions. She grasped Nora's elbow and tried to lighten the mood.

'Don't spoil a lovely evening walk now with talk of politics and execution and horrible things like that. Come over here and look at the beautiful horse chestnut trees. I always think they are the nicest trees in the park.' She looked at Seamus, expecting him to react furiously to Nora's words.

Instead, he shook his head slightly and gave a small grin.

'Nora,' he said quietly, ' this country was occupied for eight hundred years. Part of it still is. While some people accepted that and grew rich on the backs of a suffering people, others have fought and died to get rid of the invader. They tried to destroy our faith, our culture, our language, our freedom. They didn't succeed and will not succeed. You have a very one sided view of Irish history so maybe you would do well to look at the other side.'

'Maybe you could do the same yourself, Seamus,' Nora retorted.

The humour had left his eyes. In it's place was a coldness that made Nora feel uneasy. When he spoke, there was intensity to his words.

'The blood of my family stained this land. That sacrifice was not in vain. I lost my freedom at the hands of traitors and Free Staters in the cause. The cause is sacred. Anybody who stands in the way of the cause is my enemy. The time is coming when everybody is going to have to make a choice. We would have made it thirty years ago if we were not sold out. It might take another thirty years and thirty years after that but Ireland will be a free and sovereign thirty two county nation , not a bastard twenty six county Free State, ruled for England's convenience by traitors and turn coats. It might take the guts of this century to do it, but the twenty first century will dawn on a free country."

Seamus turned on his heel and walked away.

'I'm sorry, Eileen,' Nora said, 'I should have been more discreet.'

'Not at all, Nora. I've heard that speech so many times I could recite it myself. I've been to a few meetings with Seamus and I've met some very shady characters but most of them just like to talk. I worry about Seamus but he's set in his ways. Anyway, Nora, if you want to make a man happy, don't try to change his opinions on politics, religion or his mother.'

'What's his mother like?'

'There's nobody like her Seamus and nobody is good enough for him, especially me. The way she talks about him, you'd think he was an accountant instead of someone who spent his day splitting pigs bellies in the bacon factory.'

'Are you sure about marrying him?'

This time it was Eileen who laughed out loud.

'Oh I'm sure all right. He is a good worker and not a drunkard like most of the men around here. Even his poor uncle that was shot in the barracks was a roaring alcoholic who only went into the place because he was fluthered. He tried to grab a gun from a Black and Tan. The poor Tan I heard tried his best to send him home but Uncle Dan tripped and the gun went off by accident. The bullet went through his backside and ripped into his lungs and heart. By the time the local boys had the story, Dan had been shot in cold blood while trying to break in to the armoury and steal guns for the movement. My own father often says Dan must be the only man in history to have cold blood in his arse.'

Nora was shocked both by the story and Eileen's language. Eileen, however, was laughing so infectiously that she was soon giggling along with her.

As they walked arm in arm, laughing and enjoying the evening, Thomas was also in the park. He had been watching them for a while ,seated on a bench, concealed by the shadow of a large oak tree. He saw the exchange with Seamus, though he was too far away to hear what was being said. He saw the carefree strides and tossing heads of the two young women and felt a sadness and anger that he was not, and could not, be part of it.

Since Nora had arrived, Thomas had felt a deep emotion that was alien to him. He knew it though to be infatuation. Thomas had known nothing like this before. An only child, both his parents had passed away while he was at boarding school. From school, he had gone straight to the family business. His capacity for hard work and eye for business opportunities had seen him prosper and now he was a man of considerable wealth. He had begun to wonder about the future but there were no eligible marriage partners in the area, at least until now. Now there was Nora and she seemed to have more time for priests and rebels than she had for him.

As if to mock him, Nora and Eileen had stopped to speak to another man. By his clothes, Thomas could see that it was none other than Myles, the would be priest.

The two women were indeed in conversation with Myles.

Nora was forthright as usual.

'I would never have thought a man like you would be a priest,' she said.

Eileen was not very comfortable with the conversation. She was more than a little in awe of the clergy.

'You mustn't talk like that, Nora. Myles will make a fine priest.'

'I will certainly do my best to do the Lord's will, wherever it takes me,' Myles said shyly.

'I have to say that I am very ignorant about the whole business of priesthood. Perhaps, Myles, if you have a few minutes, you could walk with me and Eileen and tell us all the secrets.'

'I'm afraid that I will have to miss this sermon,' Eileen said. 'I have to get home and feed my brothers and sisters. My mother will kill me if I am too late. Still, it's only a few more weeks and then it will be Seamus giving out to me instead of my Mammy! I'll see you tomorrow, Nora. Goodbye, Myles.'

Myles and Nora stood awkwardly for a few moments.

'You do realise,' he then said breaking the awkward silence, ' that you are now an occasion of sin.'

'A what?'

'The rules of the seminary forbid me from being alone with a member of the opposite sex.'

Nora looked around at the people still ambling and sitting around the park.

'We are hardly alone, Myles. If I promise not to grab you or molest you in any way, will you walk with me, just for one round of the park?'

With a definite glint in his eye Myles replied, 'Only if you promise.'

'I promise.'

Together, they walked slowly beneath the canopies of the great horse chest nuts and oak trees. The once noble elms looked tired. Nora asked Myles if he knew why this was so.

'These trees represent so much of this town's history,' he told her. 'I am sure you know some of that history at this stage. Indeed, between Mrs Browne and the bauld Seamus you probably have heard quite a bit. But these poor elms won't see much more of the town's life. There's a disease that is wiping out the species all over Europe and these lovely trees are to be destroyed before they infect the others. I'm sure you remember a few years ago when there was a disease called foot and mouth across the water and all those animals had to be destroyed so the infection would not spread. The elms will be gone before Autumn.'

'Maybe that's why you're not supposed to mix with the likes of me.' Nora said with a smile, but with wistfulness as well. 'In case I'd infect you with heretical ideas.'

Myles gave a short laugh.

'Indeed and you might not be too far away from the truth there. Both of us will ask God to lead us not into temptation next Sunday.'

Again, they drifted into silence. The night was, as Nora often heard the people remark, 'drawing in', and it would soon be dark, too dark for any unattached couple to be seen walking out, much less a single Protestant girl and a student priest.

'How long will you be in Castlecarraig, Nora?'

The question surprised her.

'I honestly don't know. I came here for a position but there are no plans for the future that I am aware of. Why do you ask?'

'I have only a few weeks before I go back to the seminary. I was thinking about the elms these past few minutes. I know little of your faith and you know little about mine. I wonder if we could meet and talk, under appropriate circumstances. I think what you said is correct, there is a fear that we will infect each other if we mingle. That has been the cause of so much pain and suffering in this country for so long. Maybe now is the time to change things before we have to cut something down..'

'I'm only here to do the books in a shop,' Nora replied. 'I don't think I am some kind of scholar who can change the whole country.'

'I'll be the scholar for both of us,' Myles joked. 'You can be the philosopher.'

Before the conversation could develop, Nora recognised the figure seated under the oak. She felt embarrassed, as if caught in a forbidden and private act.

'Th..Thomas,' she stuttered. 'You gave me a start.'

'I do apologise, Nora, I was sitting here taking the evening air, as is my custom on these pleasant days. I often mull over the problems and worries of business here and then head home for a good night's sleep. And how is young Myles?'

'Very well, Mr Williams.' Myles was no longer the relaxed and smiling companion of a few moments ago. Now he too looked like a guilty party, unable to meet the older man's eyes.

'And how much longer before your ordination then, no doubt your parents are very proud?'

'I have one more year before I am fully ordained, Mr Williams. My parents are very much looking forward to it.'

'And then you'll be off to some foreign parts no doubt, converting heathens and the like, what?'

'Actually, I will be posted to the American missions, probably the New York diocese.'

'New York! No shortage of heathens there, I'll bet. Skyscrapers, big cars and lots of sin. Sounds like you'll have your work cut out for you. Now, Nora, Mrs Browne has been home for ages. She may well be worried about you. You're a big girl now but she still takes responsibility for her lodgers so, come along and I'll escort you to her door, goodbye Myles. Good luck with your priestly duties.'

With that, he virtually whisked Nora away, grasping her elbow firmly. She had time only for a backward smile at Myles, who stood watching them leave.

When they were out of earshot, Nora tried to shake her elbow free from his grasp.

'Please, Tomas, you are hurting me.'

Thomas refused to release her.

'Have you forgotten so quickly everything Mrs Browne and I told you? There are certain things we can and cannot do. That young man himself has just scandalised his entire family by walking unescorted with you. I'll warrant the parish priest will hear of it and don't be surprised if he is hauled back to the seminary quick smart.'

'Thomas, please, let me go.'

Thomas relented and he and Nora stood facing each other. Nora had expected to see anger or fury in his eyes and was surprised to see gentleness instead.

'Nora, please believe me when I say that I wish to protect you. Your family expect no less. You are in a strange place at a strange time. This state is only a couple of years old. Only thirty years ago, this land ran red with blood. I remember as a young boy seeing the lorries full of troops going through the streets. I remember my own relations staying with us because their houses had been burned down by the insurgents. I was ten years of age in 1916 and when the leaders of that rebellion were shot for their treason, these very streets were filled with angry mobs screaming for revenge. We were threatened and reviled. Only for my father and his father were decent men who looked after the townspeople, God alone knows what would have happened. There are those around still today talking of revolution. We might not be so lucky next time. Nora, dear sweet child, we must stick with our own and stand together.'

Nora bowed her head. Standing beneath a condemned elm, she meekly took his arm and together they walked to Mrs Brownes'. She cast one backward glance and in the distance, she could see Myles still watching her.

CHAPTER 8

Nora fell silent. Her thoughts were far away and still long ago. Malachy let the silence linger. A stray cloud obscured the sun and the air turned cold. The beach was still deserted. Nora turned toward Malachy and regarded him for a moment with a strange, questioning look.

'Have you any plans for the rest of the weekend?' she asked him.

'I have a date tonight with a Chinese take away and I promised some dirty laundry I'd wash it tomorrow. Otherwise, I have a pretty empty diary. Why do you ask?'

'Who have you left up in Castlecarraig?'

'Nobody really, a few cousins and uncles and aunts. Once again, why do you ask?'

'What do you say we take a trip up, a quick run, up and down?'

'Just the two of us?'

'Just the two of us.'

'I don't know, it could turn awkward.'

'How could it turn awkward?'

'It's just that, if you fall in love with me and we get married, my boss will be my son in law and my step daughter will be older than me.'

'Don't flatter, yourself, Malachy, you're too old for my taste and I like my men to be thick on top and thin in the middle, not the other way around. What do you say, will we go?'

'Only if you promise to respect me on the morning.'

'Feic you, I don't respect you now, will you come with me? Just for a second, forget that you are a Mayo man and give me a straight answer. Yes or no?'

'Sure, let the last day be the worst and the last hour be the hardest, and God be with you Louisburg, fair enough!'

'Which means…….?'

'Let's do it, we'll be dead long enough.'

'One more thing, Malachy.'

'Yes, Nora?'

'You will stop talking funny when we are on the road, won't you?'

'Only if you're sure you want me to.'

They walked back to the Merc in silence. As Nora started the car and reversed onto the road, she outlined her plan.

'It's a four hour drive. It's just gone five now. If I drop you at your car, you go home and get organised and meet me at Felicity's at, say, what time?'

'I suppose by the time I have a shower, a shave and a shoe shine it will be about half six.'

'God, I'll be ready before that myself and look at the damage I have to repair.'

'Those are laughter lines, Nora.'

'Nothing's that funny, believe me. Seriously, Felicity's at a quarter past six. We can take turns driving. I'll book a couple of rooms in a nice hotel in Galway, my treat. I'll make sure there are no adjoining doors in case you get all passionate during the night.'

'If I do, I'll bring a bottle of champagne in one hand, two glasses in the other and still be able to knock at the door.'

'Yes, well. Oh, Malachy, this is the maddest thing I've done for years! I feel great. Which is your car?'

They had arrived at the hotel where the party had been held the night before.

Malachy pointed out his sporty little Alfa Romeo and Nora dropped him off. A few minutes later, he was in his own apartment. He stripped and headed for the bathroom.

He regarded himself in the mirror.

'Well, Malachy' he said aloud to his own reflection, 'you've done well with your life. Saturday night and you biggest decision is whether to have a shite or a shower first.' He hated it when his funniest lines occurred to him when he was alone.

Forty five minutes later, he was parking outside his boss's house and wondering what he had let himself in for.

Felicity was in the garden, looking very inch the suburban housewife, with floral gloves and secateurs, doing a token bit of work while the gardener was off.

'What's this I hear about you and Mummy heading off for a dirty weekend?'

'It's more of a dirty night really, Felicity, I don't think even a gasur like myself would have the energy for an entire weekend with herself.'

'Isn't she gas all the same? She hasn't spoken about that place for years and had no interest in it, now she's off like a spring chicken. What's it all about, Malachy?'

She seemed to be worried despite the banter.

Just then, the boss appeared at the front door.

'Good man Malachy!' When he got nearer, he said in a stage whisper, 'I won't forget this, taking the old battle axe off on my birthday. I reckon I'm on a promise tonight,' He wrapped his wife in a bear hug.

'If you get the grass finished out the back and the stink of alcohol off your breath, you'd never know your luck,' Felicity said, pushing him away and heading for the front door. 'I'll tell Mummy you're here, Malachy.'

Just as she reached the door, it opened and Nora appeared. She had two overnight cases and was beaming.

'I feel like a school girl going on her first date. Come on, Malachy, let's ride off into the sunset.'

'Enjoy your ride, Malachy,' the boss whispered, leering suggestively.

Malachy smiled and him and went obediently to the Merc.

As they were driving out the gate, Nora called Felicity.

'Don't worry, sweetheart. I'm doing something I have wanted to do for years but didn't have the courage. And don't worry about Malachy either, if he tries anything funny, I'll simply rip his testicles off.'

'Enjoy, Malachy!' the boss roared through the laughter.

Nora drove through the thin traffic of the town and they were soon on the open road.

'Scenic route or good road, Malachy?' she enquired.

'We'll do the scenic in our way back tomorrow. Right now, let's get where we are going so we can have a night's sleep.'

'Good choice. Felicity is worried about me heading off like this. She thinks I'm too old to be heading off on wild goose chases. She said I should forget about it and take life easy.'

'She gets my vote on that,' Malachy answered. 'You should be enjoying the Autumn of your years, sipping Complan and watching telly in your dressing gown instead of chasing some ghosts in Mayo.'

'Do you really think that's what we are doing?'

Malachy thought for a moment before he replied.

'I spent six months working in an office in Sydney a few years ago. The office was right in the middle of the city, on the second floor of an office block. There was a big shopping centre across the street called the Queen Victoria Building, with a statue of herself parked right in front of it. The statue used to stand outside the parliament house in Dublin before we drove out the invader eight hundred years after he came in. Anyway, I used to have my lunch each day on a bench beside this statue and watch the world go by. Each day, I used to see a little old English lady pass by. She'd nod at a few people she knew and you could tell by her voice that she hadn't lost a bit of the Home Counties accent. But I noticed that she always carried a shopping bag from Harrods of London. She held it in such a way that everybody who looked could see where she was from and what she stood for. Old England. John Bull. Rule Britannia and all the rest of it. But I always thought it looked pathetic. I wanted to tell her to forget it, it was gone. Harrods was owned by an Egyptian and Britannia ruled shag all, except a rock in the Mediterranean and a few more rocks off Argentina. And some parts of Northern Ireland.

'One of the guys in the office brought me to his house a couple of times. He lived in a beautiful spot in the south of the city, about ten minutes from the beach. He had neighbours from England as well. They had rose bushes and lawn out the back. They worked against nature to keep the roses blooming and they poured water on the lawn by the gallon to keep it green. We'd be sitting under a pergola drinking cold beer and sweating like stuck pigs and these poor Brits would be there nursing the bloody roses.'

'So you think they should just have let them die?'

'The Brits or the roses?'

'The roses, you idiot.'

'I think they shouldn't have planted them in the first place. Take what you get I always say. If you get a rain soaked garden in Keighley, grow roses or ferns or daffodils but if you are stuck on the driest land in the world, grow cactus or palms or whatever. Memories are the same when you think about it.'

'How do you mean, memories are the same? That's very profound.'

'Well, here we are, driving to a town that has memories for both of us. If you spent countless hours of your life watering those memories with, with, with..I don't know, the water of daydreams, then it's like the roses. It really is not worth the effort. If, on the other hand, you were like me and let the memories turn into dry old cactuses and plant new memories every place you were, then you would be much happier.'

Malachy sat back in his seat, delighted with his analogy. He looked towards Nora for approval. Instead, she gunned the engine and the Merc moved forward at over eighty miles an hour.

'You pompous little man!' Nora snorted. 'Have you become so cynical about life that you think you can throw away the past like a piece of garbage some cretin might leave on a beach?'

Before Malachy had a chance to tell her to slow down, the road narrowed and bends appeared like magic, forcing her to lessen the pace. She did not, however, lessen the pace of her attack on him.

'You are so smug. Your parents worked so hard to send the likes of you to college. I saw what it was like when your parents and their generation got married and spawned the likes of you. They lived in small houses and didn't have running water or electric cookers and still they managed to send people like you off to University. And there you sit, with your 'I've been to Australia' and you 'poor old English lady with her Harrods bag' and your big job. You really make me want to throw up, the lot of you. I see my own grandchildren and they're even worse. Off to Lanzerotte for the mid term! Disneyland when they were two years old and Eurodisney for the weekend. I knew this country in the bad times and your parents as well. When the bad times come again, and come they will, it will be easy talk to smug bastards like you and the rest of them.'

'So,' Malachy said, 'are we having fun yet?'

'Don't try the funny man, Malachy. Do you really value the past so lightly? Have you no wish to keep the past alive in your heart?'

'God, Nora, you're gone fierce serious all of a sudden.'

'Because this is important to me, Malachy. I know I don't have a lot of time left. I'm not terminally ill or anything but I'm getting older, not younger. Every year something else stops working or needs a tube or pill to keep it working. I take pills for diabetes, arthritis and blood pressure. I have to wear three different types of glasses depending on what I'm doing. In a few months I'm going to my apartment in Spain for a while and I hope to spend Christmas in South Africa with some friends but this trip is my shaking a stick at old age. Cocking a snoot at my body's fading state. Humour me, Malachy, I'm as alive now as I was then.'

'OK, Nora, I'll share a memory with you.'

CHAPTER 9

Malachy watched with envy and resignation as John and Breege became an item. They met each day after school and spent most of the weekends together. They became more and more physical, even in public. One balmy evening, he sat with them on a park bench. At first, the three of them spoke about music and records. Soon, John and Breege were stuck into each other again.

'I think we'll go for a stroll,' John said, extricating himself from Breege's embrace and taking her by the hand.

Malachy knew exactly where they were going so, as soon as they were out of sight, he took off briskly to get there before them. They would go through the graveyard to get to the little woods by the lake shore for their court. He could sprint around the school and race along the near shore and get into place before them. How often he had imagined himself in this situation with Breege, lying on the grass, slowly opening the buttons of her blouse, expertly undoing her bra with one hand, while the other hand delicately grazed her soft thighs, bending the downy blonde hairs until his fingers reached the hem of her knickers. Here, his imagination had to work harder because he was not really sure what exactly he would find after that and what he should do when he found it but he had heard enough of the lads talk about dropping the hand to know that it must be something bordering on mystic so he allowed the rest of his fantasy to occur in blurred shades of ecstasy.

He had reached the spot in the woods that he wanted. He lay on the ground. He was covered from view by the low branches of the pine trees but had a perfect view of the small clearing where Breege and John were headed. He did not have long to wait before he saw them.

They had their arms around each others waists. As they got closer, they kissed deeply. John's mouth was open very wide and Malachy could make out the sheen of spit that glistened around Breege's mouth. Malachy squeezed his thighs together, grinding his crotch into the soft earth.

John and Breege were sitting on the ground. He was unbuttoning her blouse. With one hand! Soon, the blouse was spreading it's wings like an erotic butterfly and Malachy gazed at the reality of the bra that had been his fantasy for so long. Then Breege reached behind and opened it herself. Malachy wanted to scream at her to let John do it, the lazy bastard, but he was already lying back in the pine needles, gazing at twin peaks of heaven while Malachy gazed at a scene from teenage hell, as the object of his lust and love ran her hand along his friends crotch. He saw her pop the buttons one by one and place her hand, her gorgeous lily white and virgin hand into the opened trousers. Both he and John shook and spasmed at that exact moment but John and Breege laughed together while Malachy bit his lip alone. He now faced two problems. One was to sneak away alone and unobserved, a slinking pervert and broken hearted lover. The second was to get the stains out of his drawers before he put them in the wash. His mother might seem to believe his story about blowing his nose in the sheets but even she would not accept that he blew his nose in his underpants.

He slunk away through the bushes and made his way to the short cut through the grave yard. He was still languishing in the vision of Breege's semi nakedness when a voice called from behind him.

'Malachyeh!'

The bloody Lizard!

Malachy waited for him.

'Fwat are oo doing here, Malachyeah!?,

'Nothing, Brother.'

'Nawting! Well. Oo're a great man for doing nawting, Malachyeah! Did oo say a prayer for the martyred dead inself, by?'

The Lizard was using his umbrella to point at the Republican plot, a large grave which held Castlecarraig's full quota of rebel dead, all three of them. The outsize Celtic cross gravestone towered high over the wilting wreaths which had been placed there over Easter as part of the town's commemoration of the 1916 rebellion. This commemoration had fallen very much by the wayside until the Civil Rights marches had begun in the North a couple of years before. The Brothers had since been on a serious recruiting drive for new martyrs to enter the plot and be shaded by the giant Celtic cross and pissed upon by passing drunken teen aged revellers. The plot was occupied by the rotting corpses of two men who crashed a stolen car as they were driving to Dublin to fight in the GPO in 1916. Apparently, the car stalled on a railway track at a level crossing in Roscommon. A train happened along at the same time and swept the pair to their martyred glory. Fortunately the train was carrying a regiment of Welsh Guards going to Dublin to reinforce the forces of the crown. Their presence on the train ensured that the rebels had died in action, even though the train driver was a returned Yank, originally from Belmullet. The third corpse was a genuine martyr as he had been shot in action against the Tans.

'I'll walk a bit of the way wit oo, Malachyeah!'

Malachy did not have much choice and so fell into step beside the long legged Brother dressed in black.

'I've been watching oo, Malachyeah!'

'Oh, Christ,' thought Malachy. 'Really, Brother,' he said aloud.

'Indeed I hov. And so hov others. Oo seeah, everyeah generation God cawls certain young min to serve Him. Tis a great challenge to give up awl worldly pleasures and follow the vows of charityeah, chastityeah and celibacyeah. Have oo ever tawt that God is calling you, Malachyeah!?'

'I must say, Brother, the thought did cross my mind.' Malachy knew the best way out of this situation was to lie, even about God and risk an eternity in Hell, just to get over the next few minutes.

'I noo it!' the Lizard exclaimed. 'I said it just last night at supper in the Monasteryeah! We were discussing possible candidates for vocations and says I, "Malachyeah! Lydon and John Joyce," says I, dem bys will hear the call to the priesthood." And I was right! Do oo think John feels the same way.?'

'He might, Brother.'

'He's a good by, but a biteen shtiff at times, do oo think?'

'At times, indeed.'

'Shtill, he hos spunk, and thot's what it takes, am I right, Malachyeah!?'

'You are indeed, Brother.'

'If he is handled the right way, John will come good. Oo can count on that.'

They had reached the park. Malachy made a hasty farewell and rushed away while the Lizard strolled onwards, dreaming of pupils led in the path of righteousness to martyrdom or chastityeah.

Malachy walked disconsolately through the park. He sat on a bench and allowed himself to experience a sense of loss and depression. His mind wandered again to the scene he had just witnessed. He felt himself become excited and thought for a moment he might have to give his drawers a second rinse. Looking back along the path, he saw John and Breege walking towards him. John had recently taken up smoking and had a cigarette hanging from the corner of his mouth. His mouth was set in a grin, like, as Malachy's father might say, "a turkey in stubble."

His arm was draped around Breege's shoulder and she was looking at him with nothing short of admiration. John had the look of a man who has been to the mountain top and seen and felt the promised land.

'There's Malachy, the auld bollix,' was his cheerful greeting. 'How's the craic? Wide open!' he laughed at his own crude, predictable humour and Breege, appropriately, tittered. She had left one middle button of her blouse undone and by leaning slightly to his right and moving a little on the bench, Malachy could see her beautiful left breast against the white of her bra.

She and John sat beside Malachy.

'What are you still doing here all on your own, pal?' John asked.

'Nothing really.'

'Nothing! How do you do that?' He said this with a smirk at Breege, who responded with a simper of admiration.

'Jayzez, you're worse than the bloody lizard. He met me at .' Malachy had to check himself.

'At what?' Breege asked.

'At the corner over there and asked me what I was doing and when I said "nothing", I got his standard "How do oo do nawtin?" lecture. By the way, he reckons me and you are ideal candidates for the religious life. Apparently we were the topic of conversation over supper at the monastreyeah!'

John beamed at Breege who obligingly simpered again.

'By Jayzez, me and you as priests! That's some idea, hah? What do you reckon, Breege, am I cut out for the priestly life?'

'Whatever about you, Marian reckons Malachy has other ideas. Is that right, Malachy?'

'Where is she tonight anyway?' Malachy asked.

'Ooooh, is somebody interested?'

'No, somebody is being polite. Somebody really couldn't give a curse but somebody is making conversation.' Malachy knew he sounded like a prick but in his mind he heard the song's refrain, "you always hurt the one you love." Oh, he thought, I'll hurt you alright, you bitch.

''Well excuse me,' Breege said, 'but if you must know, she is at home stuck in the books. Her parents drive her very hard, and she says she won't be let out again until after the Leaving. So you won't be doing any more courting, Malachy.'

Malachy was surprised at this coarseness from Breege.

'There's plenty more fish in the sea,' he muttered.

'Not with your bait, pal!' John roared. He and Breege fell about the bench at this, grabbing and squeezing each other.

'Speaking of exams and future careers,' Malachy said, ' have either of you thought of what you're going to do after?'

'I suppose it'll depend on the results,' John muttered. 'I know my auld fellah and auld lady are expecting me to get the four honours for the grant. I'll go to Galway I suppose and do something, maybe History or medicine.'

'What about you, Breege?' Malachy asked, 'you did fierce well in the Inter.'

'Mammy was talking about me doing medicine as well. Wouldn't that be gas if me and John were both doing the same thing? We could qualify at the same time and work together. I'd love to go to America and live there. My cousins were here last Summer from New York and they said I'd get on great.'

'So would I,' John interrupted,' I always get on well with the Yanks. When I caddy for them at the golf links they're always saying what a charming boy I am. Remember those two big lads from California last Summer, Malachy? They asked me out to San Francisco to visit. They were nice lads, though I was a bit worried by them wanting me to hold the towels while they were in the shower. They said the caddies always took showers in San Francisco but I suppose it's the heat. They were great tippers too. Maybe we could go to San Francisco Breege. Isn't that where the flower power is, Malachy?'

'That's where it is, pal, peace and free love. They reckon they do nothing but pole from one end of the day to the other.'

Now it was Breege's turn to look shocked.

'Malachy! And all the girls saying you are such a gentleman. What will you do after the Leaving?'

'I'd love to do something different, feic off to Australia maybe and get a job in a newspaper. Or go to South Africa and work in a gold mine. I'd hate to be stuck in an office for the rest of my life, working for someone else. I see the auld fellah off to the garage each morning and home in the evening, then out for a few pints. God, I'd hate to be stuck in a rut like that.'

'I know,' John said, 'that's why I reckon medicine would be good because you could feic off anywhere at all. What do you reckon Marian'll do after?'

Breege shrugged.

'She's a real home bird. I'd say she'll do secretarial and get a comfy job with a solicitor or dentist and settle down for life. Maybe with you, Malachy.'

'She could do worse,' John said, digging Malachy in the ribs while sneaking a feel of Breege's thigh at the same time.

'I heard there's supposed to be a big American factory to be built in town. I wouldn't fancy that though,' Malachy tried to keep the subject alive but Breege had other ideas.

'She said she really likes you Malachy. It'd be lovely if you brought her out again. She said she had a great time at the pictures with you.'

She looked up at the church clock in the distance. 'I'd better go or I'll be killed again I'll see you tomorrow, John.' She left with a smirk at him and a wave at Malachy. 'I'll tell Marian you were asking for her.'

John and Malachy sat a few minutes in silence.

'Going well, is it, John?'

'Mighty.'

'Are you serious about Galway?'

'Kind of.'

'Would you really do medicine and stay with Breege after you were finished?'

'Maybe, I don't know.'

'She seems to have it all worked out.'

'It's like this, Malachy, Breege is the finest court I ever had, she's red hot, I reckon if I play my cards right, I'll get the full whack there. That's why I'm playing along with this auld guff about going off after Uni. I've no intention of sticking with one woman at Uni, sure there'll be women there from all over looing for it. I was talking to Tommy Murphy over Easter and he said the girls from the North were fierce mad for it altogether. He reckoned he could get a ride every night of the week if he wanted.'

'So why doesn't he?'

'Why doesn't he what?'

'Get a feicin ride every night. If he can. Jayzez, I would if I had that kind of chance.'

'I suppose you get used to it, like once the novelty wears off.'

'I suppose. Tell us more about Breege anyway.' Malachy was torn between hearing sordid and salacious details to fuel his secret fantasies and not wanting to hear anything dirty about the woman he loved.

'Oh she's a flyer. We had a mighty court above at the lake this evening.'

'Go away now, you're only making that up. The lake is a bit public for a court during the daylight.'

'Not if you know where to go it isn't.'

'So tell us about this great court.'

'I got the hand, top and bottom.'

'Go away. Serious?'

'Serious is the word. We were at it hammer and tongs for ages. She ran out of steam and sure I was only starting. I tell you, pal, I'll be dug out of that one.'

There was another silence, this time fraught with hormones, John reflecting on what might have happened, Malachy vividly recalling every detail of what did.

John broke the silence.

'I have an idea, Malachy. My sister and the husband are going to Dublin in two weeks. I have a spare key of the house that no one knows about. If you get Marian out for a while, I might do the trick with Breege in the house.'

'Why don't you do it up the lake?'

'Because there's thistles and nettles the size of shagging Mount Everest there, that's why. Imagine doing the job and your arse going like a fiddlers elbow and next thing a thistle gets wrapped around you ballens? Or your elbow sticks into a lump of cow shite?'

'That might spoil the mood alright,' Malachy agreed. 'But two weeks time is awful near the exams.'

'There's still three weeks or more after that. We'll say we're swotting. We won't be telling lies either because we'll be studying anatomy by Braille.'

'I don't know, John. Marian is grand but she's a wagon.'

'One night, Malachy, that's all. I reckon I'll be on board if I get the chance. After that, we'll say goodbye to Marian.'

'And what about Breege?'

'I'll get a few more rattles out of her.'

Malachy shook his head and smiled.

'What's the joke?' John wanted to know.

'I was just wondering. When the landlords and the gentry played cricket on this spot, did they ever think the day would come when two peasants like ourselves would be planning a ride and a university career over their dead bodies?'

'Yerrah feic them. I only want to do to Breege what they did to the country for eight hundred years.'

Malachy was once again torn between conflicting loyalties. He was loyal to his friend John and loyal to his fantasy of watching Breege's body again, even if it was not himself that was groping her.

'So what's the plan?'

John leaned forward excitedly. Malachy could tell by the way he adjusted his crotch as he leaned that he was already excited.

''I reckon Marian's parents won't let her out at night, good nor bad. We'll organise for a little get together for Saturday afternoon. We'll bring the girls to the house. You and Marian can have the sitting room and I'll get Breege into the bedroom.'

'Do you really think she'll give you the jaunt?'

'I'll be on deck in five minutes flat.'

'What about if she gets into trouble?'

'There won't be any trouble. Sure they'll be home by six o clock.'

'I don't mean that, I mean suppose she gets snigged?'

'Oh yeah, the last thing I want is to put her up the pole. Still, I thought of that'

. 'How do you mean, you thought of that, what will you do?'

'You know them long balloons, the ones that look like sausages when you blow them up?'

'I do but I thought it was just going to be the four of us.'

'What are you on about?'

'Why do we need balloons if it's only the four of us, if it's not a party?'

'I'm only talking about one balloon. For me. To put over me lad while I'm on the job.'

Malachy knew little about contraception so he could not really question the validity of the plan.

'I'll put it on before the girls arrive so when we're at it we don't have to stop.'

'Supposing you want to have a slash, though, will that not make it a biteen awkward?'

'All worked out, Malachy. I won't take a drink after the dinner. Empty bladders and full liathroidi. A recipe for a happy man.'

'Maybe your right. But one thing sure, and that is that after you get your shift, I don't have to touch the other wagon again. I know she's a lovely girl but there's only so long a man can keep his eyes closed and pretend she's someone else.'

'That's a good trick, Malachy. Who do you pretend she is?'

Again, Malachy felt a lie was justified.

'Remember that one we saw in the James Bond film, Ursula Andress? That's who I pretend she is, so I do.'

'Jaysus, Malachy, you must have a great imagination. How in the name of God could you transform the four wheeler into a beauty like your one Andress?'

'All you have to do is change the head, the hair, the body and the legs. The arms are grand.'

John and Malachy fell about the bench laughing at this.

A figure approached them along the path.

'Ah, no,' John said under his breath, 'it's that bloody O Murchu, don't mention the North whatever you do.'

'Well, lads, I suppose you heard the latest from above?' O Murchu greeted them.

'I was telling Malachy about the craic in Galway, Peadar, with the women,' John replied, trying to keep the subject of Northern Ireland buried. It was well known that Peadar had followed the family tradition of violent nationalism. Though only a couple of years older than Malachy and John, he reflected a seriousness beyond his years.

'Never mind that, lads. There's more important things in life now.'

'What could be more important than the bit of waski?' John tried again.

'I'll tell you what's more important. Irishmen and their families are being burnt out of their homes night after night in the North. That's more important. You and the rest of the lads should be prepared to do something about it.'

'But I have to be home by eleven,' Malachy said.

'Don't try your auld shite with me, Malachy. The time is coming when people will have to make a stand. They're'll be people swinging from the hanging tree in this park again, and they'll be wondering why they're swinging but they'll be swinging anyway! Do you know the problem with this country? It's not the orange and the green on the flag that's the problem, it's the streak of yellow down the middle.'

With that, he strode away, leaving the two lads in an uncomfortable silence. After a few minutes, John spoke.

'I suppose in one way he's right.'

'About what?' Malachy asked.

'The ride is still important.'

'I'm not sure I heard him say that. But to get back to your balloon ride, have you thought it through all the way? I mean, like, will you take Breege into a room and sing " Would you like to ride on my beautiful balloon?"'

John thought this was hilarious.

'That's a good one or maybe I could say "do you want to do the Hucklebuck or something that sounds like it?"'

'Or you could put a cinema ticket into it and tell her you've got a ticket to ride.'

'Help.'

'She loves you, yeah, yeah, yeah.'

The two lads found all this hilarious and were falling around the bench laughing. When they began to compose themselves, they noticed the small figure of an old lady approaching.

'Here's auld Mrs Browne,' John remarked. 'Jawzez, she must be nearly a hundred years old. Maybe she used a balloon and that's why she has no kids.'

This brought further gales of laughing and spluttering from the pair. Mrs Browne stopped beside them and regarded them with a small smile.

'It's so nice to hear the young people enjoy themselves. I've lived near this park for many years and I always loved to hear the sound of laughter. Would you share your joke with an old woman?'

The two boys looked at the ground, giggling.

'Well, Mrs Browne, ' John eventually managed to say, ' believe it or not, we were talking about balloons!' Once again, he and Malachy exploded into guffaws and hoops, wiping tears from their eyes as Mrs Browne walked away shaking her head at the immaturity of youth.

'Do you reckon that one ever did the gig?' John mused after she had gone out of ear shot.

'They reckon the husband died in some war, the Boer or First World War or someplace.'

'Could be the Battle of Clontarf, she's old enough.'

'So, John, you're all organised for your first whang?'

'All I need is the balloon and Breege's attention distracted for a minute and I'm away for slates.'

'I'll see you tomorrow so.'

The boys went their separate ways, each to his own room to commit mortal sins of various hues, mental and physical.

CHAPTER 10

Nora and Thomas walked the short distance to Mrs Brownes in silence. Nora felt guilty but more for having been caught and the way she had abandoned Myles than for anything else. She knew she felt attracted to Myles. She had had her share of girlish crushes in her home town but the strictness of her parents had ensured that they never went beyond that. She had had one furtive meeting with a boy when she was seventeen but they had both been so petrified in each other's company that they had barely uttered three words to each other during an embarrassing hour together.

She knew one girl at school that had not returned after a Christmas holiday. Word was whispered that she had 'fallen' and it had taken Nora a few years to realise that this meant more that a trip and fall. She knew what it meant to be an unmarried mother as she had often passed the laundries in Dublin where such women worked. Her mother would point them out and cluck about the poor unfortunates and stress that 'nobody in our family has ever let the side down in such a way' and glare meaningfully at Nora.

Mrs Browne was in her small front garden when they arrived. She had a pair of gardening gloves on and was pruning a decorative shrub that had begun to overhang the wall, onto the street,

'I sometimes think these plants are worse than children,' she greeted them. 'If I take my eyes off them for a second they go all over the place. Nora, where have you been? I was expecting you home earlier.'

Nora glanced at Thomas but he was busy examining a shrub. She was grateful he was not going to make a fuss.

'I had the most pleasant walk in the park with Eileen from the shop. The time flew. We just gossiped and chatted about her wedding.'

'She is a respectable girl but I do wish she was not involved with that O Murchu fellow. He is trouble, like all his family, I knew them and he is just the same.'

'We actually met him,' Nora said.

'You met the rebel?' Mrs Browne seemed surprised. 'And when can we expect the next uprising? I gather he is cut out of the same violent cloth as his father and uncles.'

'I did find him quite frightening, I have to say. He spoke very seriously about history and did not seem pleased when I questioned his view of the world.'

Thomas and Mrs Browne looked at her.

'We should not interfere, Nora, it's not really our business,' Thomas said, looking at Mrs Browne for approval.

'Tosh and poppycock, Thomas!' she said with a beam of delight. 'Well done, Nora. These upstarts need the wind taken from their sails and by a woman, no less.

Thomas, we can be a part of this society but we must never become too quiet for our own good. Come inside, my dear Nora. I'll fix supper and I want to hear every detail about your meeting with our Mr O Murchu.'

As they moved to the door, Thomas called, 'In all conscience, Nora, I will be able to tell your family you are in safe hands. Goodnight to you both.' With that, he gave a cheerful wave and strolled away.

While Nora was eating her meal, Mrs Browne questioned her at length about her encounter in the park. She laughed aloud and poured a constant supply of tea for them both.

After supper, she invited Nora to join her in her small sitting room. This room looked out on a large back garden. At the back of the garden was a graveyard and behind that a small lake. Several apple trees grew outside the house.

It was now late in the evening but a full moon and cloudless sky ensured a good view through the window. There were several photographs of Mrs Browne's late husband hung on the walls. In all of them, he was in uniform. A small glass case held a selection of military medals. There was a small fireplace, with a comfortable armchair on either side of it.

Mrs Browne sat on one of these and indicated that Nora should sit on the other.

The only light, apart from the moonlight through the window, came from an ornate standard lamp in one corner.

The older woman pointed at the largest of the photographs. This one showed Captain Browne in the full dress regalia of the Connaught Rangers.

'He was a handsome man, wasn't he?' she asked.

Nora had to agree. The captain stood with one hand on the hilt of his sword, the other clutching his helmet to his side. He was dark haired, with piercing eyes. He had a handlebar moustache in the fashion of the time and stood tall and proud.

'He was twenty five years old when that photograph was taken. One month and three days later, he was dead. One of those medals is the Victoria Cross. My Monty died a hero's death. A platoon of soldiers was trapped in no man's land after one more doomed assault on the enemy line. They were being picked off one by one by German snipers and machine gunners. Monty, it seems, crawled through half a mile of corpses and barbed wire and managed to kill enough of the enemy to allow a few dozen men to escape back to their own lines. He almost made it back himself but he heard the groans of a man trapped in barbed wire. He went back and freed him. He carried him to safety but he was hit several times as he carried him. He died ten days later from his wounds.

'The battle he took part in was in a place called Mons. They even have a street called after it in town here because so many local people fought there. It was said that an angel appeared during that battle but even an angel could not stop the slaughter. I hate all war. It destroys goodness as well as people. It destroyed my Monty.'

The room was silent. Nora could think of nothing to say but she was pleased that she was here for Mrs Browne in her pain.

'The men my husband saved were Irish to a man. The man he carried to safety lives not two miles from here. That is what O Murchu and his ilk fail to see. Every family has it's martyrs in this country, they have just been sacrificed at different altars. Are you tired?'

Nora was surprised by the question.

'Not at all, did you want to go to bed?'

'No, but if you would allow me, I would be very grateful to read you a couple of letters that Monty wrote to me.'

'I would be honoured to hear them.'

Without leaving her chair, Mrs Browne reached to retrieve a box from the mantle piece. It was yellow tin box that had once held cigarettes.

'Monty's one indulgence,' she said affectionately. 'He loved to sit here on evenings like this and smoke cigarettes and watch the swans that used to live on the lake. A simple man really. They sent this very box home with his……..remains.'

She opened the box reverently and extracted a small sheaf of papers, thin and faded, covered in small, neat writing.

'Poor Monty had to dictate these few words to a nurse. An Irish nurse. She was very kind to them all, I have been told. Monty was a very quiet and reserved man. Many evenings, sitting here, we would exchange only a few words. He loved the silence.

'He only wrote a few letters. I honestly did not expect any more. This one was written soon after his injury. He starts off by asking for some people, your own relations included. He was very fond of Thomas. Then he goes all romantic.'

Mrs Browne's face was lit slightly by the fading sunlight. Nora could see a sad, affectionate smile that made the older woman much softer looking and vulnerable.

'The medicine they are giving me takes most of the pain away,' she read. 'From where I lie, beside a window, I can see trees. My nurse denies it but we casualties believe that those who have least hope of recovery are given the best views. She is smiling as she writes. She is kind, Flora, kind like you and makes this sad place more bearable.

The trees remind me of Castlecarraig. I am sorry I did not spend more time sitting beneath them with you. I am sorry we did not walk more often by the shore of the lake, around the ruined castle. Remember the day I asked for your hand? It was in the shadow of that castle. There was a bird perched in the ivy. You were so beautiful, so young. Every man should experience the happiness I had with you. We made plans that day, Flora. We named all our children, can you remember those names? Can you remember how each one looked, as we dreamed our dreams? I can. Maybe we will make those dreams a reality. If they move me to a different bed, away from the window, I will allow myself to dream.

'My angel nurse has sat for so long to write this. I fall asleep and when I wake she is there, ready. These are the things I fought for. Her kindness, your love, our children.'

'The nurse signed his name. He was, I suppose too weak. He was a wonderful man, Nora. It is over thirty years since he wrote that and I can still see him every day, sitting there, smoking his cigarettes, watching the trees.'

Nora was touched that Mrs Browne had shared these things.

'I hope I meet someone some day to love me like that.'

'I have no doubt, Nora, but you will have your choice. But make the right choice. I never had the chance to fulfil my life with Monty. We never had the children, the dreams never came true for us, we never did sit under the trees again.'

'You said there was another letter,' Nora reminded her gently.

Mrs Browne took another thin sheaf and read quietly:

'My own dear Flora,

It will not be long now. I sleep and wake and do not seem to know which is which. Just now I was walking by the lake with you again. I could feel the softest of breezes on my face. I even heard the sounds of insects in the bushes and whins. Most of all, I felt your hand in mine.

'I've slept again. The dream this time was about you again. Our wedding. You so beautiful. My comrades in their uniforms, the artillery men, the dragoons. But I thought I saw you cry. I do not want you to cry, Flora. My sacrifice will not be in vain. I have served my King. I have saved the lives of fine men. I have loved a beautiful woman. That is as much as any man can pray for.

'The pain is all gone now. The trees outside are greener than before, they remind me of your eyes. My faithful nurse is writing still. She will tell you all when this is over. I will sleep. I will dream of you. I will always be yours. Plant more apple trees. Tell everyone that I thought of them all these last days. Gentle, gentle Flora, goodbye. I will always love you.'

Nora and Mrs Browne sat quietly. Eventually, the older woman broke the silence.

'Each year, I plant an apple tree for him. Each year, the local boys sneak in and steal the fruit. I pretend to be cross but it is now almost a ritual. Every child I see in the garden makes me think what might have been if Monty had lived. He would have been a wonderful father. Come, walk with me in the garden. I want to share one more secret with you.'

Intrigued, Nora followed the older woman through the house and out the back door. When they reached the apple trees, Mrs Browne looked furtively about her. Then, from the sleeve of her cardigan, she took a packet of cigarettes and a box of matches.

'This is my secret vice. Every night, I sneak out here and smoke a cigarette or two. Thomas is such an old fuss pot he'd be disgusted at me letting the side down. He thinks it's not lady like. I have to go to the other side of town to buy my supply every week. Still, it's just a bit of fun.'

Nora was looking out over the lake. She could understand how it held such romantic memories. The Moon seemed to be sitting precariously on a conical mountain in the distance. The night sky was full of stars and the ruined castle on the far shore added a touch of mystery. She pictured the young couple, Flora and Monty, walking arm in arm, making plans. Soon, she began to see herself walking with Myles, sharing thoughts and dreams. She was surprised at the feelings that stirred in her.

'What are you thinking, my dear?' Mrs Brownes voice startled her. 'You seem far away.'

Nora felt herself blushing. Looking into the wise, kind eyes of her companion, she just shook her head and smiled.

'I was imagining you and Monty walking along the shore. Then, I wondered when I might be so lucky as to stroll with someone who cared for me in the same way he cared for you.'

Mrs Browne drew deeply on her cigarette and then extinguished it against an apple tree, before throwing it into the long grass behind the wall.

'Love comes to us all, Nora. Some, like me, receive a fleeting visit. Others, like Thomas, have to wait and hope and others are blinded by their passion and mistake other feelings for love. Some, again like me, may only love once and never again while others have the pain of choosing from more than one.'

'How can that be painful?' Nora asked. 'Surely we can love one person and then meet someone we love more and move on. I hope to fall in love many times.'

Mrs Browne took Nora's arm and guided her gently back towards the house.

'Trust me, child, love hurts more people than hate ever did.'

Nora gently released herself from her companion's grip.

'I'd like a few minutes more to stroll around. You go ahead and I'll follow and lock up.' The older lady smiled and went inside. Nora walked again to the end of the garden. Gazing over the lake, she tried to identify the emotions she was feeling. First she thought of Monty. She pictured the dashing young officer, heading off to war, and then she pictured the broken, dying man, dreaming of his young bride. She felt a great sadness as she thought of that young bride, standing alone at her door, receiving the news of her lover's death. She cried as she imagined that young woman reading his letters time and time again, trying to recapture the images of their time together.

Then, Monty's face faded and in it's place she saw Myles. She pictured his dark eyes and wondered what it would be like to feel his arms around her. She felt her face grow warm, with a strange tingling and also with some guilt and embarrassment. She glanced around her, as if afraid that someone might be watching and realise the thoughts that were racing through her mind.

With one last glance at the ruined castle, she went back to the house, a small smile on her lips.

CHAPTER 11

The day of the seduction finally arrived. It was another sunny day and it was still warm when Malachy met John at the end of his sister's street. It was a short street, more of an alley off the main thoroughfare of the town. The house itself was small but as John pointed out, 'The brother in law hasn't managed to land the bag of fertiliser on the box of the sister's eggs yet.'

On cue, Breege and Marian arrived as John was opening the door with a key he had pilfered from his sister's purse.

The girls had a bundle of books each but the look in their eyes was not one of academia. They giggled and nudged each other as they went in the door.

John led them into a tiny sitting room. There was a sofa and an arm chair and the rest of the room was taken up by a huge television set, on top of which stood an equally huge radio.

'Let ye sit here, girls, for a minute. Me and Malachy will make a pot of tea.' John looked strained as he said this. 'Come in to the kitchen, Malachy.'

'I have to be home in an hour, John, so don't be long,' Breege fluttered her eyelashes as she flirted with him. Malachy felt a mad surge of jealousy.

'I have to be home in an hour, too, Malachy,' Marian said in a voice that he presumed was meant to be husky but in fact sounded like she was holding in a belch, Malachy thought.

John grabbed his sleeve and dragged him into the kitchen. There was not enough room for the two of them to fit comfortably so John squeezed against Malachy and dragged the sliding door shut behind him.

'I'm dying for a slash,' he gasped. 'What'll I do?'

'What's stopping you?' Malachy asked.

'Do you not remember the plan? Look!'

In the small space between them, John unbuttoned his trousers and pulled down his string drawers. Malachy looked with horror at the sight of the contents of his friends underwear. John's penis was swollen and purple.

'It's fuckin' purple!'

'That's the only colour balloons they had in O Reilly's. But it's killing me. It's cutting me lad off.'

Malachy reluctantly looked closer.

'True enough,' he said, trying not to breathe too deeply of the offensive odour of cheap rubber and talcum powder mixed with pubic sweat. 'The nozzley bit of your knob doesn't look too healthy. The band at the back seems to be cutting of the circulation to your mickey. There's a lot of the balloon not used as well.'

'Feic that, I need to squirt in the worse possible way but if I take this yoke off I'll never get it back on. Look at the way it's cutting into me foreskin.'

'If you don't get it off quick, you'll have a feicin five skin and six skin, John. On me solemn, I never saw anything so out of shape.' Malachy was crouching to get a better look when the sliding door opened slightly.

Marian peeped through the crack.

'What are you doing? Breege, get out here quick.'

John pushed his weapon back into his trousers but the action caused him such pain that he cried out .The door slid all the way across and the two girls stood looking at the boys in horror. Malachy had tried to straighten up too quickly and bumped his head on the corner of a shelf. John was holding the flaps of his trousers together, as tears of pain and frustration filled his eyes, which bulged in his blood red face.

'I told ye to wait outside, girls,' he moaned through the pain.

'John, are you sure you're ok? Remember we have to go soon,' Breege said nervously.

All John could do was gesture with his head towards Malachy, pleading with half closed eyes to do something.

'We'll be out in a minute girls. John is having trouble with the flex. Of the kettle.'

The girls went reluctantly away from the door.

'It's no good, Malachy,' John groaned. 'The feicin' thing is going to have to go.'

Malachy was surprised to see that John had taken out his balloon encased penis again.

'Jaysus, John,' he said, 'I've never seen any bar me own and a few photos but there's something fierce wrong with your lad there. The lot seems to be going purple at this stage.'

John was short of breath and very red in the face.

'See if there's a scissors in one of the drawers, Malachy. Either the balloon goes or me mickey goes.' Malachy found a sharp knife in the top drawer.

'Cut the tight bit, Malachy, there where the foreskin is swollen.'

'I'm not cutting it, John. I'd have to hold it steady and that wouldn't be right. The Lizard reckons we'll go to Hell if we touch our own, never mind anybody else's'

'Isn't there a shagging balloon over it? I don't want you to blow it up, just cut the feicin' thing.'

Malachy delicately lifted the tip of the balloon. The veins running along John's penis had swollen to look like leeches, throbbing and blood filled, and the skin was an unhealthy dark purple. Malachy placed the tip of the knife under the rim of the balloon. John gasped as the steel touched his body.

'Careful, it's not a bloody lamb chop,' he warned.

Breege's voice came through the door.

'I'm not hanging around all day, lads. Marian and I have more important things to do. Bye.'

As the front door slammed behind the girls, Malachy felt a sense of guilty relief that his idolised woman would not be ravished by a man with a balloon on his wire. Even though he was holding his friend's prick in one hand at that moment and a bread knife in the other, he felt happy. The tip of the bread knife was under the ring of rubber.

John turned on Malachy.

'Well, blast you, Malachy, why didn't you cut the bloody thing quicker?' John shouted angrily.

'Why didn't I cut it? Why did you put a balloon on your bollocks in the first place? Why didn't you have a slash and strain your kidneys before you put rubber all over your budley? If you had to put a balloon on your willy, why did you get one that was too long and too narrow?' With that, Malachy snipped the rubber band holding the balloon in place. John attempted to run towards the toilet but Malachy was still holding the tip of the balloon. With a final wrench of strength, act of will, gasp of pain and cloud of talcum powder, John managed to free himself. Seconds later, Malachy heard the splash as a massive jet of water met water and John groaned with a relief equal to any he would have felt if the purple balloon had served it's prophylactic purpose.

When he joined Malachy in the sitting room, John looked pale.

'I think I might have done myself damage.'

'I know I'll never eat black pudding or sausages again,' Malachy said. 'Do you ever wash it? There's a smell off of it like a used sewer rod.'

'I'll be having a bath tonight. How are we going to sort this out, Malachy?'

'I like the "we" bit, John. You're the one so desperate to house it that you'll wrap it in purple.'

'I reckon we both have a bit of explaining to do.'

'Why's that?'

'Well, what's your story going to be if the girls tell the lads and lassies that they saw you looking at my mickey in the kitchen?'

Malachy was stunned.

'You better explain to Breege before she tells anyone anything so,' he said nervously

'If I get them back, will you run up to Reilly's and get another balloon?'

John knew Malachy was not a violent man so he was surprised when he grabbed him by the lapels of his jacket.

'Listen, now, John. I couldn't give a tinker's curse if you never got your end away as long as you live. If you ever want to stick your doodle into a party balloon or Christmas decoration itself again, that's up to you. Don't get me involved. But I'll tell you one thing, if you let them girls go around telling people stories about me being some kind of reverse in and I'll load you merchant, friend or no friend, I'll knock seven colours of shite out of you.'

'Settle down, Malachy, settle down. I'll bet the pair of them are above in the snack bar having a lemonade and giving out now. We'll trot up the pair of us and you watch the master at work. I'll have her eating out of my hand in five minutes.'

'If you don't take more care of your personal hygiene, she certainly won't be eating out of any place else. Come on so and we'll find them.'

John had recovered his pride and scrotal comfort as he sauntered up the street, hands stuck in the back pockets of his cord trousers. When they reached the snack bar, they could see the two girls inside. Breege noticed them looking in the window and looked away immediately. Marian saw them and waved.

The boys sat at the table beside Breege and Marian.

'Well, girls,' John began, 'it's amazing, you know how people get the wrong end of the stick.' Malachy , remembering what he had been holding a few minute previously, thought that this was an unfortunate choice of phrase but said nothing. 'The thing is, like, that , you know the way you girls do swap clothes?'

Breege and Marian looked puzzled. Malachy felt a terrible sense of dread that things were about to get worse.

'Me and Malachy were wondering whether we might do the same thing. You see, when we finish the exams, we'll be doing interviews and things and instead of wearing the same clothes to all the things, we were thinking of maybe sharing clothes.'

'So why was he looking at your privates?' Breege asked, scowling at Malachy.

'He was not, would you have some sense. He was checking the size of my trousers so he was to see if it was the same as his.'

'And was it?' Marian asked.

'Was it what?' John said.

'Is yours the same size as his?' Both girls giggled at this. 'Well, Malachy,' Marian continued, 'did you see anything you liked?'

Malachy smiled as best he could. 'Me and John have become very close. When we head off to the priesthood, I'm going to make sure we get the same bishopric.'

Marian was the only one to appreciate the ecclesiastical pun. Breege had already begun to throw calf eyes at John, who was gesturing at her with his eyebrows. Without a word, just a giggle, she got up. John did likewise and, hand in hand, they left.

Marian gazed after them.

'They make a lovely couple,' she said.

'They do that,' Malachy agreed.

'Malachy, I know you only hang around with me because Breege is head over heels in love, or thinks she is. Don't deny it. And another thing, Malachy, have you studied your Leaving Cert Shakespeare much?'

He was surprised by the turn on the conversation.

'Not really. I'm concentrating more on the Maths and Science.'

'Lady Macbeth is talking to her husband at one stage. She tells him his face is like a book where men can read strange matters. I can read your face every time Breege is within a mile of you.'

'What are you talking about? Breege is a very good friend, that's all.'

'Yeah, and I'm the image of Liz Taylor. Malachy, she is cracked about John. I actually worry about her because she would do anything for him. Don't waste your life pining after her. I'd be delighted to be your girl friend, really, but I know I'm not your type. I don't seem to be anyone's type in this town, except for half an hour after the socials. That's one of the reasons I swot my backside off. I want to get away, to make something of myself.'

'I think you're a lovely girl, Marian, in all fairness.'

'And how would you feel, Malachy, if Breege treated you like you treat me, like I don't exist and then sat here and said to you, "In all fairness, you're a lovely boy, Malachy," how would you feel?'

Malachy could not look her in the eye. He knew she was right and that he had treated her badly. He still didn't fancy her, though.

'Nothing to say Malachy?' Marian got up and smiled at him. 'When you grow up, give me a shout. In the meantime, enjoy yourself in John's trousers because as sure a hell, you'll never get into Breege's.'

CHAPTER 12

The miles slipped away as the Summer sun slipped into the Atlantic.

'Poor Marian. She really had it bad for you,' Nora said.

'Yerrah, wasn't she better off as it happened? She has her big house and big Yank and big boobs now. I could never have given her any of that. Well, maybe the big house.' Malachy looked out the window. They were travelling the coast road. 'She's the far side of that pond now. Given the time difference, it's about lunch time in California. It's Saturday so the family is probably sitting outside, the kids home from college, with Mom and Pop for the weekend. Pop will pick some lemons and squeeze some fresh lemonade while Mom lies back to take the sun. They'll have steaks in the icebox for the cook out tonight, and I suppose a couple of bottles of Californian Chablis on ice. Or maybe they're gone to the log cabin for the weekend, skiing. And here am I, travelling through the feicing bogs of Ireland with a woman old enough to be my mother, Jesus, where did it all go wrong?'

'Malachy,' Nora said gently, ' believe me. You are better off without her. Any woman who would drink Chablis with steak is beneath you.'

Both of them found this hilarious. The lights of a country pub appeared on the roadside ahead of them.

'What do you reckon, Nora?' Malachy asked. 'May as well be hung for a sheep as a sheep. Pull in here and we'll have the famous wan.'

Nora parked in the almost deserted car park across the road from the pub. Inside, the place was dimly lit and smelt of disinfectant. Three men sat along the bar, which was being tended by a sour faced woman. Customers and barmaid alike were watching a quiz show on the T.V. in the corner of the bar Not being a very committed television viewer, Malachy was surprised at the ease at which the contestants clocked up large amounts of money.

'What will you have?' he asked Nora as they moved towards a small table.

'Probably an embarrassing infection by the time I use the toilet,' she remarked, ' but a cup of tea in the meantime.'

Malachy went to the bar to order. The woman did not seem pleased at being dragged away from her quiz. Malachy assumed the regulars timed their orders to coincide with commercial breaks.

'A cup of tea please and a pint,' he ordered.

'We don't do tea after seven.' A burst of applause from the TV audience caused her head around towards the set.

'What happened there, Jamsie? What happened?'

One of the men took a pipe from his mouth and replied without looking at her.

'The stout lady with the hair do is after winning a car so she is.'

'Isn't she the one that said she couldn't drive at the beginning ?'

'That's the craic, you see, that's why your man is laughing.'

'I hope she doesn't win the big money, that wan. She's a bit full of herself. The man on the end with the seven children deserves it.'

'So long as the single mother doesn't get it. She's too cocky altogether, if you ask me.'

Fortunately for Malachy, the ads came on so the lady of the house began filling pints.

'What will you have instead of the tea so?' she asked Malachy.

'Coffee?' he said.

'No coffee either after seven.'

Malachy decided to argue with her.

'There's a sign outside that says tea and coffee served. There's a kettle behind you.'

'That's for hot whiskey. Now what else do you want with the pint?'

'A smile would be nice.'

'Do you know what you can do with your tea and smile and smart arse? The woman said with a sneer. 'Yourself and that auld bitch can shag off out of here and go to some fancy hotel where you'll meet your own kind of stuck up snobs. Feic off out of here, the pair of you.'

Malachy looked at the men along the bar, and noticed they were all smirking into their pints. He beckoned Nora over and told her what had happened.

'We are not wanted here, sweetheart,' he said. 'My parents told me this marriage would be difficult but I did not expect it to be so difficult to get a drink on our honeymoon.' He took Nora by the hand and swept her toward the door. As they were leaving, she turned and shouted back towards the bar, 'The condom machine in the ladies is empty. I hope your boyfriends their brought their own.'

Howling with delight, she and Malachy got back into the car.

'Ireland of the welcomes my arse,' he said when they eventually calmed down. 'When they built all these Irish pubs around the world with bicycles hanging from the ceiling and sowing machines beside the tills, they forgot to install the frustrated bitch behind the counter. Did you ever see the likes of that? Yourself and your cup of tea! At ten to nine at night, you stuck up snob.'

'I do believe that's the first time I've ever been refused a drink in my life! Wait til I tell the ladies at the golf club about this. You are definitely a bad influence, Malachy. We may as well keep going as far as the hotel at this stage. At least my friend will give me a cup of tea without making me feel like an undesirable element.'

Malachy agreed.

'We should be there in about an hour or so, I suppose,' he said. 'You still haven't told me what happened your prieshteen.'

'My prieshteen, God bless him.' Nora smiled. 'When I think of poor Monty Browne dying for freedom and the rebels dying for Ireland. And all so that sour faced bitch can refuse to make a cup of tea. It was a high price to pay.'

'All I hope,' Malachy said, 'is that the single mother wins the jackpot.'

CHAPTER 13

Nora's days took on a pleasant routine. The shop was busy and she and Mrs Browne walked each night. Thomas called to visit regularly and often strolled home with her after the shop closed. She enjoyed his company and took pleasure from the courteous way he treated her.

She was disappointed when Eileen announced one morning that it was her last day at work.

'Don't look so sad, Nora, ' Eileen teased her. 'I'm going to a better place, Matrimony.'

'I'm sure you will be so happy. And you'll have loads of children and be a doting mother.'

''I would be so happy if you could come to the wedding, Nora. I know old stuffy Uncle Thomas wouldn't allow it but it would be great.'

Nora thought of Mrs Browne's words about taking whatever opportunities came along. Looking over her shoulder to make sure they were alone, she spoke to Eileen in a whisper.

'What if I was to go along after the Church? I have to see you in you bridal finery.'

'Thomas will hear if you come along, no matter what time it is Nora. Do you want to take that chance?'

'I think I do.'

'Well, next Saturday, I'm getting married in the local church. From there we go to the Royal Hotel for the wedding breakfast. Then we have a hooley and after that, me and my man go back to his house for the honeymoon.'

'His house?' Nora was surprised.

'His mother is moving out to one of the sisters for a few days. She doesn't want to be under the same roof when her little boy consummates his marriage and I do my woman's duty.'

Just then, the door of the office opened and Thomas came in. He cleared his throat and addressed Eileen.

'Now, well, Miss, em, Eileen, that is. As we all know, I believe, this is, in fact your last day here. In my employ as it were. I of course wish you well and I am sure you will make a fine, a fine…wife. You have given honest and loyal service and I am considerably saddened to see you, as it were, leave the shop. Nora will no doubt prove more than capable I am sure but you will be a loss to us, that is us in the shop. I have taken the liberty of bringing your final wages to you, with a small token of our appreciation contained. I must go to Galway soon today so I will not be here as you depart, that is as employee, but obviously, we hope you will grace us with your custom. We have some excellent items of children's clothing, ha, ha.'

Eileen seemed touched by this speech. She smiled at Thomas, who was looking everywhere but at the two women.

'That is very generous of you, sir,' she said. 'I am sure when the time comes for bay's clothes and the rest of it, we'll do business. I'll be looking for a discount after my years of loyal service.'

Thomas laughed with genuine amusement.

'Discount, you say, well indeed. You know, several of my staff are farmers. Next thing, if I give you discount, they'll be looking for cheaper chicken feed every time their hens lay eggs.'

Nora was delighted to see him in such good form. He actually was, she noticed, a handsome man in his own way. Even though he was over twice her age, he held himself erect and his abstemious lifestyle lent him a certain vigour. He left the small office, still chuckling at the banter he had exchanged with Eileen.

'He is a charming man, Nora, is he not?' Eileen asked.

'Perfectly, Eileen. I wonder why he never got married?'

'The same reason that has brought so much sadness and loneliness into this country for so long. Religion. Thomas is old money, new religion. There are plenty of eligible poor and papist around the place but he's stuck in the same rut as the rest of us. There are expectations, Nora.'

Nora nodded. She had come to regard the older woman as a trusted advisor and knew when she spoke, it was wise to listen.

Eileen continued. 'If Thomas was a Catholic, he would be married for years now, with a brood of children. At least one son would be a priest, one daughter a nun and probably a few alcoholics mixed in with the rest. But it's not easy for him. You've seen it yourself the short time you've been here. Half the people in this place live in the past and the other half are not living at all. If there was a third half, they'd probably be fighting with the others. All I'm saying to you, Nora, and because I'm from where I'm from I can't really say it straight, is, Thomas and you have more in common than you seem to think.

'Now, this is my last day so I'm going to work. I want to go to every counter and check up on them. I also want to remind them about the arrangements for Saturday. And even if Uncle Tom is feeling cheery, it won't stop him rearing up on me if he thinks I'm not making an effort. I'll talk to you later.'

When she had left, Nora found it hard to concentrate. There was a ledger in front of her and it had to be balanced but the figures became blurred every time she tried to work on them. She kept thinking of Eileen's strange speech. Was it a warning, she wondered, or advice? She thought too of Myles. No matter how hard she tried, she kept imagining his eyes and the way she felt around him. She knew she had to meet him again. She decided to find out if he would be at the wedding. If he was to attend, she would too. And not just for the sake of meeting Myles. Eileen was the closest she had to a friend in this town, a place that was still strange to her. Eileen helped her not just with her work but with making sense of the local ways and dialects. Each day, she heard a different accent. Just the day before, she had overheard one customer say to his companion; 'Did ya lave hersel abow?' The reply was, 'Shtop. Hersel wouldn't stir til the quare detail landed.' Eileen translated that one man asked if his friend had left his wife at home and had been informed that he had and that she would not join him until her mother arrived.

Having made her mind up, Nora was able to concentrate on her work. The morning passed quickly as she efficiently balanced the cash and stock for the previous week. Eileen popped in and out of the office regularly, collecting invoices and receipts and it was lunch time before Nora had a chance to talk to her again. Whenever they could, they liked to have their break together in the small shed behind the shop that the tea was stored in. Nora and Eileen would spread out their food on a tea chest and share what they had. Nora usually had a sandwich made of the leftovers from supper the previous night, with a piece of fruit. Eileen's lunch consisted of slabs of home made soda bread, with chunks of bacon or ham. She also brought along a bottle of tea, milky and sweet, which she had kept wrapped in a towel so it was pleasantly warm by lunch time.

Each day, they chatted about the business, the customers and staff. This day, they were quiet. Eileen was obviously distracted by her impending departure. Nora was anxious about having to find out about Myles. After ten minutes silence, both women spoke at the same time.

'Eileen, I wanted to…'

'Nora, I have to tell….'

Both laughed and Eileen insisted Nora tell her whatever it was she wanted. Nora found it hard to look straight at her companion. With her fingers, she traced patterns in the fine dust on top of the tea chest.

'You know I'll miss you. I know, I know, you will be in and out but it won't be the same.'

'That's not what you wanted to say now, is it?' Eileen asked gently.

Nora stopped tracing and drew a deep breath. She looked at her friend and smiled.'

'See? That's one of the things I'll miss. You know me so well.'

'Maybe better than you think, but go on, get it out.'

'I really want to be part of the celebrations at the wedding. But there's another reason I want to go.'

Again she paused but this time her friend remained silent.

'God, Eileen, I am so jealous of you sometimes. You seem so mature and content. How do you know if you are in love?'

'Nora, Nora. I am jealous of you too, you know. You are so delicate and beautiful while I'm what they call a horse of a girl. Now, don't try to tell me different. Look at the two of us. You with your beautiful fair hair, me with rats tails on my head. You with your beautiful slim body, me with a set of hips for breeding and a pair of shoulders for lifting bags of turf.'

With her eyes gleaming with tears and a voice full of gentleness, she took Nora's hands in hers.

'You with your beautiful, soft hands, me with two rough old gammons for hands. You can and will love a man but for the likes of myself, it's convenience. Himself is a decent man, I'll not want for anything and, please God, we'll have a squad of lovely children. You, you are so different to me. You can marry for love. When you look around you, you see life and hope and joy and happiness. I look around and I see emigration, drunkards, hard work. You have everything a girl could want. Will I tell you what you are going to ask me?'

Nora could only nod.

'You are in love. I may not be the most romantic at heart but I am a woman. I can tell by the look in your eye when a certain name is mentioned. I can tell by the way your voice changes when you say a certain name. But the man you love is not available for you or for any other woman. Myles Walsh is going to be a priest. Have you any idea at all of what that means to him and to his family?

'To be a priest is to give up all kinds of contact with women. Me, I'll never understand it but that's the way it is. I could never live without the feel of a man's arm around me or the bit of human contact. And the bauld Seamus is like a buck goat waiting for next week so he'd never last in the church. But Myles is different. Certain men are chosen by God to do His work and Myles is one of them. He's not for you, Nora.'

'Is it that obvious, Eileen?' Nora was amazed her friend had such knowledge of how she felt. 'Does everyone know?'

'No, only me. I have sat with you for weeks now and I know you better than anyone else in this town. Myles will be at the wedding and so will his family. His mother is the proudest woman in Ireland. She always said her baby was going to join the clergy and make bishop some day.'

Nora was about to say something else when the door of the shed opened. Thomas entered.

'Dawdling again, eh, ladies? It is past two o clock so I really must ask you both to move along. Eileen, I hope you were happy enough with your little gratuity?'

'Very happy, sir, and I was hoping that you and Nora might be able to drop by next Saturday to bid us good health.'

'Well, yes, of course, that would be nice, but, as I am sure you understand, it would prove difficult, that is if we were to do so. Nora is still learning the way of things and well, as for myself, my best wishes will of course be, as it were with you and your young man. Now, if you young ladies would get to it, it is getting near the end of the month and there are bills to be sent out. I dare say I might have to come looking to you Eileen for a loan if I don't get the pounds shillings and pence in.'

Nora and Eileen followed him out. He turned towards the yard and they returned to their office. Sure enough, a stack of bills and invoices was waiting for them on the table.

'Invoices or bills?' Nora asked.

'Invoices. All those bills remind me of what I am letting myself in for by getting married.'

As they set to work, Nora spoke again.

'About what you were saying in the shed, Eileen..'

Before she could finish, her friend interrupted.

'Shush, now. We'll finish this and we'll talk after. I don't want Uncle Tom coming in vexing me again. He's off to Galway he said so I'll bring you to my house after work and we'll have a right chat.'

'That's perfect,' Nora beamed. 'Mrs Browne is going out for the evening so I have plenty of time. Come on then slow coach. These pounds shillings and pence will not do themselves.'

Giggling like schoolgirls, they set to work, balancing the books.

A light mist was falling as they left the shop that evening, even though the sun was also shining through the drops.

'I hope the weather picks up for the wedding,' Eileen grumbled.

Walking briskly, they soon reached the street where Eileen lived. Unlike Mrs

Browne's house, which stood alone with a large garden, Eileen's house was part of a terrace of small houses, each with a small garden in front. Most of the dwellings were neat and well kept but a few looked run down, with badly kept gardens.

'Don't take too much notice of my family,' Eileen warned Nora. 'It can get a bit noisy inside.'

Nora could actually hear voices as they went in the garden. The door flew open when they were about half way up the path and three children, aged about ten or eleven, raced out.

'Eileen's home, Eileen's home,' they screamed as they hugged her.

'Get inside you pack, or I'll skin you all alive,' Eileen yelled at them.

A tall, thin woman appeared at the door.

'Hello, Mam,' Eileen said , 'this is Nora from work that I told you about.'

'Lovely to meet you, Mrs Tracey,' Nora said, extending her hand, ' I can't tell you how helpful Eileen has been to me.'

Mrs Tracey wiped her hands on her apron and took the young woman's hand.

'Eileen is an awful woman, bringing the likes of yourself here, and not saying a word to her poor mother about it. The place is like a kip and I'm like something dragged through a ditch. Surely, Eileen, you are not going to bring a lady like this into this house?'

'Don't be so fussy, Mam, Nora is not like that, sure you're not, Nora, you don't mind what the place is like?'

'Not at all, Mrs Tracey, don't go making a fuss over me.'

'In you come so,' Mrs Tracey sighed, shaking her head.

Inside was like nothing Nora had ever seen before. She had known that Eileen had seven brothers and sisters but this was the first time she had seen so many people in such a small space. In fact, everything about the house was small. The hall way was barely wide enough for two people to pass. The stairway, which seemed to have a child on every step, was equally narrow. At the end of the hall way she could see a kitchen. This seemed to be the central focus of the house. A table stood in the middle. It was piled high with thickly cut bread. There were pots of jam and a big slab of butter as well. A jolly looking man was sitting at the table, oblivious to the chaos, with a chunk of bread in one hand and a copy of the local paper in the other. A mug of tea steamed in front of him and he was chewing thoughtfully. He spoke without looking up.

'There's a good one now. They found an American plane crashed on an island in

Clew Bay. It crashed in a fog, it says here, and no one knew a thing about it. Two skeletons, fully dressed, it says, looking towards Croagh Patrick. Well, that beats all.'

'Dad, this is Nora from work.'

The man swallowed, put down his paper and stood up. He wiped his hands on his shirt and took Nora's hand.

'Nora, well this is a pleasure indeed. Nora was the name of James Joyce's' wife, did you know that? One of the great geniuses of the world but the clergy and the government of this country treat him like a devil out of hell. Anyway, you are welcome to this house.'

He took a bundle of dirty clothes of a kitchen chair and invited her to sit down.

'Where are your manners, Joe,' his wife called from the hall. 'Send that girl into the parlour.'

'Parlour, bedad! I thought that was for the priest when he came for his Christmas visit and to drink my whiskey.'

Eileen took Nora's arm and brought her back into the hall. The parlour was an oasis of peace, though the voices of the family could be heard clearly.

'Don't mind them,' Eileen said. 'I'll be glad to get out of this madhouse. Though there's never a dull moment at the same time. Sit and I'll get a cup of tea.'

Even though the parlour was tiny like every other room, it was spotless. A large picture of Jesus, pointing to His exposed heart, hung from one wall. A glass case held some fine china. It was obvious from the musty smell that the room was not used very often.

Eileen came back with two mugs of tea and chunks of bread and jam.

'This was all I could grab from the crowd. My Mam wanted to go to the shop for some ham and tomatoes but I told her not to be daft. Dad said he'd go but he might have got lost, if you know what I mean.'

Nora regarded her friend fondly.

'I don't know if I would last in a house like this. I'm used to a bit more peace and quiet.'

'You should visit some of the other houses around here. There's ten of us here but one place has fourteen children and the father is an alcoholic. I often hear them crying with the hunger when I go for a walk at night. Another man, his wife died in childbirth three years ago, leaving him with five kids to rear.'

'How do people like that manage?'

'Well that man was like the rest of them, work to the pub, pub to the bed.

When the wife died, he joined the Pioneers and hasn't touched a drop since. I do hear his children laughing every time I pass the house. Times are hard for a lot of people, Nora'

'So how can you afford to get married and have a wedding?'

'That man in the kitchen, my Dad, comes from a well off family. Farming people. He did well at school and there was talk of him joining the priests. He met my mother during the Civil War. She was on the run with her brother from the Free Staters. They were hiding out in a barn in my Dad's farm, unbeknownst to my Dad's people, who were all Staters. Two soldiers were shot one night in town. The Staters found out about Mam and her brother and went to arrest them. The brother, Johnny, a lunatic by all accounts, opened fire and the soldiers fired back and he was killed. My Dad came running out of the house roaring and waving a sheet. The soldiers would have shot him too but the officer was local and knew him. Anyway, my Dad swore that he was with my Mam the night before and she had nothing to do with her brother. Some of the Staters wanted to shoot my Mam anyway but Dad piped up that they were going to get married.

'Of course, the family disowned him straight away. So, he had no choice really. Either he married and was disowned or stayed single and got shot. He's such a loveable rogue, though, that his mother never saw him short. She tied up bit of money and land in his name and that's what is paying for the wedding.'

'I thought this was a simple little place when I arrived,' Nora said. 'Now I wonder will I ever understand the place.'

'Don't bother trying to work it out, Nora, you'll go daft like the rest of them.'

'Now, Eileen, tell me about the wedding.'

'Well, of course, I'll be beautiful and Seamus will be handsome. I have a suit I bought in Galway and a hat of my mother's that she got from England. Seamus has a blue suit as well so we'll be the most handsome couple that ever got married in this parish. The Mass is at eleven. Then we'll go to the Royal hotel for the wedding breakfast. Then there will be a bit of a hooley. Some of Seamus's friends play music so there should be a bit of a dance. After a while, I'll throw my flowers for all the single women to try and catch them and see who will be married next. Then, me and my man will go and do what Seamus has been panting for for the last twelve months.'

As always, Nora was amused, though mildly shocked, by her friend's candour.

'Will there be many people there?' she asked.

'I hope just myself and Seamus.'

'No, at the wedding, at the what did you call it, the hooley?'

'You never know how many turn up for a do like this. Usually there's a good crowd. I think we should be honest with each other, Nora. I know what it is you are trying to say.'

Nora had to avoid her eyes. She waited for her friend to continue.

'Myles will be there, Nora. Unlike most people around here, we were brought up without having to think the clergy were so wonderful. My Dad does all his duties and Mam takes it fairly seriously but we've always been allowed think for ourselves. I don't think it's right that fine men like Myles should be locked away from women, With them brown eyes and fine broad chest, he'd be good company for any woman. I have to tell you though, Nora, brave and all as I am, I wouldn't talk like this to too many people. Myles is his Mammy's pride and joy. He's supposed to be fierce bright as well and the talk is he has the makings of a bishop. I see the way he looks at you as well as the way you talk about him. If the world was any ways right, the pair of you would be churched, wedded and bedded a long time ago. But you, Nora, are a beautiful, charming young Protestant. Myles is a handsome, charming young Catholic, who will soon be ordained a priest. Put those things together, especially in this country, and you have a recipe for disaster and heart break.'

Eileen was heartbroken by the expression on her friend's face. Nora looked absolutely devastated and on the verge of tears. She went to her and put her arms around her shoulders.

'Nora, I am only telling you the truth, you know that.'

'I know,' Nora said, fighting back tears, 'but I am so confused. Every time I see Myles on the street or in the park, I get this felling, these feelings, that I've never known before. Maybe it would be best if I went away, went back home, or maybe go to England. At least then I'd be out of harm's way.'

Eileen shook her head.

'You bring something to this town. You have a light about you that cheers people up and makes them feel good. Stay here, Nora. Maybe it's God's will that you arrived for Myles before he makes his final vows. There's enough oddities in the religious life as it is. You should hear Seamus and the boys talking about the brothers and the beatings they give.'

'But what can I do, Eileen? If I stay and tempt Myles away from his priesthood, I'll be ostracised. If I stay and ignore him, I know I can never be happy. If I go, I'll be forever wondering and never be happy either. What can I do, Eileen?'

Before Eileen could answer, there was a knock on the parlour door. Eileen's mother leaned in and told her that Seamus had arrived. The door open fully and Seamus came into the room.

'Well, look who it is. Our own little Unionist, Miss Fortune. How are things in the Empire today? Are there any rebellions you need to put down?'

'Talk is one thing, Seamus, we've had plenty of that' The strength in the voice of Mrs Tracey surprised Nora. 'And often talk can cause a lot of problems. We won't have any of that in this house.'

Seamus looked embarrassed. 'Sure it's all a bit of craic, that's all, isn't it, Nora?'

'Of course, it is Seamus. You know I don't take you seriously.'

Seamus's eyes flared but he thought better of replying.

'So what brings you here, Seamus? I thought you were going to call later,' Eileen asked.

'It's a poor do if a man can't call into the house of his intended and be questioned. And my mother in law to be won't ask me if I have a mouth on me itself.'

'If it's tae you want you know where the kettle is,' Mrs Tracey said. 'If it's anything stronger, you won't get it in this house.' With that, she left the room.

'I hope I won't have to put up with that abuse after we're married, Eileen,' Seamus said.

Eileen threw her arms around him and kissed him full on the lips.

'Seamus,' she said with a grin, 'you'll never want in our house. Whatever your mother can't give you, I'll look after.'

'I'd better be off,' Nora said.

'I'll walk down the street with you,' Eileen suggested. 'What was it you wanted, anyway, Seamus?'

'There's going to be a few extra people there for the do, that's all. There's a few musicians coming down from the North and they're bringing a few friends. Just so you'll know, that's all I wanted to tell you.'

'Well, there might be a few surprise guests on my side too. Come on, Seamus, walk down the street with me and Nora.'

I won't. I have to go back to the factory .There's a problem with one of the trucks and I said I'd help out. I have no intention of labouring all my life, Nora. I'll be moving up in the job before long.'

A few minutes later, Nora and Eileen were strolling down the street. When they reached the corner, Eileen spoke.

'I was going to say something to you, Nora, before we were interrupted back there. I think you and Myles need to get together for a while. I've seen enough sadness so maybe it's for the best. Leave it to me to organise something. I'll see you before the wedding.'

Nora walked on, lost in thought. She appreciated all the difficulties her friend had outlined about Myles. In her time in Castlecarraig, she had come to realise how central the Catholic Church was to the lives of the people. At times, she was amused, and sometimes horrified, by the power the clergy seemed to wield. She had reached the Park and decided to continue her stroll for a while. She also secretly admitted that she hoped she might catch a glimpse of Myles as he often seemed to visit the park at this time of the day.

She was right. He was sitting on a bench, reading what seemed to be a small prayer book. Again, the strange feelings welled up inside her. She decided to take the opportunity to spend time with him.

As she approached him, her shadow crossed his book. He looked up. She was pleased to see that he smiled. They stood like that for several moments.

'May I join you?' she asked

'I would be delighted,' Myles answered.

'What are you reading?'

'It's called the office. I read it several times a day.'

'Is it any good?'

Myles laughed.

'It certainly doesn't fall into that category, Miss Fortune.'

'Please cal me Nora. I have been looking forward to talking to you for weeks. The first time I met you here, you said you'd like to talk to me. How soon will you be a priest?'

'I'm kind of a priest now, actually. I take my final vows in a few months and then I'll be a real priest. How do you like Castlecarraig?'

'I think I could be happy here. I have met some lovely people and my uncle and Mrs Browne have been so good.'

'Do you miss your family?'

'Terribly, but Thomas says we will visit after Christmas, when the shop is quiet. Will you miss your family, when you are a priest and go away?'

'The life of a priest is such a busy one I doubt I'll have time to be lonely. I have an uncle who is a priest in Africa, in a place called Northern Rhodesia. He writes sometimes about the life. He is very fulfilled and seems to be working twenty four hours a day, seven days a week. In the seminary they keep telling us that the harvest is great but the labourers are few.'

Nora could have sat listening to him for hours. His voice was so gentle, with a distinct West of Ireland accent, but with a cultured edge.

'Is life very difficult in the Seminary?' she asked.

'Difficult enough, yes. There is always study to be done. Lots of Latin, of course, and I also found that I have quite an ear for Greek as well so I'm learning that. Since this is my final year, we are learning a lot about the celebration of the sacraments and the life of a priest generally. Also, since I'll be going to America, I have to learn something of the way of life there.'

'I must admit, ' Nora said, ' I've often wondered what it is that makes one decide to live a life such as the one you have chosen.'

Myles thought for a moment. The dark eyes seemed to be looking far away. For the first time in their conversation, he looked straight at Nora.

'There are many reasons why a man chooses priesthood. I have always felt called in a special way to serve. A neighbour of ours joined a few years ago, to serve in China. He left just last year. I believe that is a heroic sacrifice, to go like that, into a strange land and risk persecution and even death. I don't suppose the New York Diocese is that dangerous but I've been to the pictures a few times and seen James Cagney and Mr Bogart so maybe it's dangerous enough. For me, the decision to join was not that difficult. The Brothers at school were a great encouragement. My parents are very pleased and the people of the town are happy to have another priest to their credit.'

'But what about your choice, Myles? The Brothers, your parents, the people of the town, your friend in China, surely they can't make the decision for you? How do you feel?'

This time Myles did not look at her. Instead, he looked to where the red sun of evening was setting, behind two large chestnut trees.

'What I think or feel is not really important. Many men before me have made greater sacrifices than I am making. It is probably difficult for you, as a member of a different church, to realise how important this is, not just for me but for others as well.'

''I know it's important, Myles, and I want to understand. Can you help me understand?'

Myles shook his head, again without looking at Nora.

'I have spent more time with you in the past little while than I have with any woman, apart from my mother. The people in the seminary tell us regularly that Satan sets traps for the unwary seminarian. Maybe I should be a bit more wary, Nora. What do you think?'

'I think Satan might choose someone a bit more skilled than I if he wanted to trap you. Don't change the subject. Can you help me understand more about your religion?'

'I think I could introduce you to one of the local priests and he could help you.'

'I'll be here at this time tomorrow, Myles, and I do not want any local priest to instruct me. You be here or you will have it on your conscience that I will burn forever in a Protestant hell.'

'You seem to know plenty already about us Catholics.'

'This time tomorrow, Myles, or I burn for eternity.'

She left Myles shaking his head and grinning broadly.

'Seven o clock so, by the clock on the Protestant church behind you.'

As she walked away, Nora was also smiling.

CHAPTER 14

They were approaching Galway. Much of the journey had passed in silence, except for the radio, which Nora insisted on keeping tuned to a pop station. Malachy tried several times to change the station but had his wrist slapped each time he attempted to do so. When they reached the sprawl of Galway city, the traffic thickened.

'God,' Malachy remarked, ' I remember coming here twenty odd years ago and it was a lovely place. Now there's houses every place. How in the name of God was this allowed to happen?'

'The price of progress, Malachy, my dear,' Nora answered. 'We can't very well have a Celtic Tiger if we don't feed it well on pollution and cultural destruction, now can we? I was in Galway many years before you, and you're right, of course, it's not what it was. But would you rather it was still like our friends that threw us out of the pub tonight? Small minded and petty, stuck in the past.'

'There has to be some sort of a happy medium all the same.'

'The only happy medium I ever heard of was at a séance when they called up the ghost of Groucho Marx. Seriously, Malachy, do you honestly believe the Paddies give a damn about happy mediums or aesthetics. Look around you, for God's sake. It amuses me when I hear people on about the destruction caused by centuries of British imperialism. Poor old Paddy has done more damage in seventy five years than my lot did in seven centuries.'

'I can' disagree with you there, Nora. Still, where there's life there's hope.'

'That's what I love about you people,' Nora laughed. 'No problem is so big that it can't be avoided by a cliché.'

As they drove around Eyre Square, it was getting dark, marking about the mid point of a Summer's evening drinking. Bands of inebriated and loud young drinkers roamed around the square, some singing, some laughing, all swearing.

'At least we only threw up inside the Skeff,' Malachy grumbled.

As the smells of puke and urine receded, Malachy vaguely got the scent of sea air and fish and chips.

'We must be near Salthill.'

'Almost there so, Malachy, I'll stand you a pint in about ten minutes.'

'I'll expect a lot more than a pint, and you after dragging me away from my hectic nights activities that I had planned.'

'And what activities might these be?' Nora enquired.

'I was going to rent a video, possibly, and get a pizza delivered. And watch the late news on Sky before a hectic night's sleep.'

'But you sacrificed all that for the sake of an old woman's fantasy. You are a good man, Malachy. Here we are.'

They had arrived at a hotel that Malachy had never noticed before. It was more of a very large house, covered thickly in ivy, and surrounded by tall, mature trees. A discrete brass name plate, almost obscured by the ivy, identified the building as the 'Regal Hotel.' Malachy was glad to note that it also stated the hotel was fully licensed.

Once they stepped inside the door, Malachy was surprised at the size of the place. The reception area was very spacious. To the left, was the bar and that too was bigger than he had anticipated, and doing a very brisk trade. There was a satisfying hum of conversation.

A tall, elegantly dressed woman approached them.

'Nora,' she greeted them, 'you look wonderful. How lovely to see you. And this is the toy boy you told me about.'

'I'm more of a toy man really,' Malachy said, ' because I'm over twenty five.'

'Don't pay any attention to him, Michelle. He is a wonderful and kind young man. He is also desperate for a drink and I am desperate for a room, a bath and a sleeping pill. So, if we could be checked in, we can both do our thing, as the young people say.'

'Don't worry about checking in. I'll give you your keys and we can do the paper work in the morning. It's so lovely to see you! After breakfast tomorrow, have them page me from reception and we'll have a good old gossip. Now, if you will just pop over here to the desk, we'll get you on your way.'

She handed them each a key.

'Nora, I've put you in the west wing, away from all the noise in the bar. Malachy, I've put you in the east wing so you'll be close to all the noise in the bar. Have an enjoyable night both of you and I'll see you both after breakfast.'

Nora picked up her overnight bag.

'Goodnight, Malachy.' She said when Michelle had left. 'I actually picked this hotel for a couple of reasons. I'll talk to you tomorrow and you can tell me what you think.'

Nora kissed him on the cheek and headed off to her room with easy familiarity. Malachy had to look around to find the directions to his room. He was, it turned out, not far from the bar, and quite close to reception.

The room was luxurious. He had over the years stayed in the best of hotels. The Hilton in Brisbane was a favourite from his few visits there. He enjoyed going up in the glass lift, watching the crowds shrink as he zoomed upwards. When he went to Dublin, he often stayed in the Clarence and did some celebrity spotting. He'd spotted a few and once said hello to Mick Jagger, who had asked him if was having a good time. He'd also been ignored in the lift by Naomi Campbell.

The room in the Regal was a much more sedate and old-fashioned affair than those, though. There were oil portraits of long dead soldiers looking sternly from the walls. Antique armchairs sat each side of a cast iron fire- place. Heavy velvet curtains added to the sense of opulence.

Malachy decided his thirst was more urgent than hygiene so he settled for a quick wash and change of shirt. Thus prepared, he headed for the bar.

The bar was still crowded but he was able to find an empty bar stool. He glanced along the counter to see if many people were drinking stout. He had learned a long time ago that there was often a negative correlation between the quality of a premises and the quality of the pint. He was gratified to see that many of the drinkers were enjoying his favourite tipple so he ordered one for himself.

While waiting for his pint, he looked around. There was a lot of brass and dark wood. Two barmen were kept busy. They were smartly dressed, black slacks and white shirts. They were obviously full time staff, not students working part time.

When his pint arrived, Malachy placed a five pound note on the counter.

The bar man pushed it back towards him. 'Compliments of the hotel, sir.'

Things are looking up, Malachy thought.

Supping his porter, Malachy checked out the clientele. The customers seemed to be his own age, or maybe a little younger. There seemed to be a balance of males and females .Everybody was well dressed and had that look that Malachy had often heard described as 'Paddy no more.' It was as if they were trying to distance themselves from the hungry generations that had gone before, dressing in the best labels and displaying the flashiest jewellery.

Malachy got comfortable. The piped music was barely audible, a Christy Moore CD. As was his wont, he ordered a refill before his first drink was quite finished.

Once again he offered his fiver, but once again the bar man shook his head.

'Is this on the house as well?' Malachy asked him.

The bar man just smiled and left him.

'Even better,' Malachy thought.

His reflections were interrupted by a woman's voice.

'Enjoying your pint?'

He turned to see an attractive woman in her mid to late thirties standing behind him.

'Very much,' he said. 'To what do I owe the pleasure, or to whom?'

'The whom is Vera and the what is that it's not often we get good looking single men in here, stranger men especially.'

Malachy shifted on the stool so Vera could squeeze in beside him. He was delighted to see she was wearing a silk blouse that was open enough to allow him a good view of a pale freckled and very attractive cleavage.. Her eyes were amused, but there was a touch of hardness about them. In one hand she held what Malachy recognised as a gin and tonic. A cigarette burned in the other hand.

'Malachy is my name, Vera. I must say it's a while since an attractive young lady bought me a drink. I hope you don't think I can be bought so cheaply.'

'We all have a price Malachy. What's yours?'

'Two pints should do it.'

'Sold so. I'll buy you another one.'

Climbing off the stool, Malachy offered it to Vera. She accepted gratefully.

'You're not from around here, then Malachy?'

'No, I'm living in the States, just over here for a few days, doing a bit of work.' Malachy was pleased to find he had not lost his knack for deception. In fact, he was enjoying himself immensely. A good hotel, a good pint, a fair chance of a shift.

'And the old lady who came in with you, is that your mother?'

So, Vera was as cute as himself.

'Not at all. That's the bosses wife.' That at least was the truth. 'I'm helping her trace her roots while I'm here.'

'So you have a room then? Just curious.'

'I have a room surely, Vera. And yourself?'

'Not at all. I'll be straight with you, Malachy. Most of us in this bar are separated or divorced. I don't know how long you've been away but most of the marriages in the country seem to be on the rocks or heading for them at least. I was married for fifteen years, two kids, then himself announces he's leaving and setting up shop with a floozie he met in Dublin. He was going up and down for months to meetings, he said, now I know what kind of meetings. Next thing, he's gone, moved in with the floozie. I cleaned him out, I tell you. Got the house, car, the kids, the lot.'

They had replenished their drinks at this stage and their thighs were pushed together in a body language that both understood to well.

'It's like the old song,' Malachy suggested, ' "You got the goldmine, he got the shaft." Did he get ere a thing at all?'

'I let him keep the apartment in Spain, except for the months of June, July and August.'

'You're a softie at heart, Vera. So where are the kids now?'

'Don't fret, Malachy, they're not going to appear looking for lollipops or money. Molly is fifteen and Robert is thirteen, so they're both probably off doing drugs.'

Malachy must have looked shocked because Vera laughed and punched him on the arm.

'Only messing. God, you're an innocent auld Yank, all the same. The kids are with my sister and her two. She threw her husband out as well when she found out where he was putting his putter at the golf club. I'll baby sit next week and she'll have a night out. Not a bad system, eh?'

Malachy had to admit it was efficient.

More drinks followed. Malachy changed to gin and tonic in the long held, and long disproved theory that he would not have such a bad hangover the following day.

And disproved it was, not too many hours later. Malachy was wakened by the ringing of his phone. Even though he had woken up in many strange rooms in many strange places, it still took him a moment to remember where he was. When it registered where he was, he realised that the sun was shining outside and he was alone in his bed.

He grabbed the phone, more to stop the dreadfully grating ring than to find out who was calling him.

'Good morning, lover boy.' He was relieved to hear Nora's voice. 'I told you there was more than one reason for picking this hotel. Say thank you to your Auntie Nora.'

'Thank you, Auntie Nora.'

'Don't mention it, now come on down for breakfast. See you in half an hour.'

Malachy hung up the phone, closed his eyes and tried to put together the sequence of events of the previous night.

Vera had become more and more physical with each drink. Her hand was in his crotch by drink four and they were kissing passionately by number six. Seven, eight and nine were a blur but he remembered finishing ten, or maybe eleven, in his room while Vera got undressed. The drink had heightened his desire but, as usual, severely impaired his performance. Vera didn't seem to notice. She spent her time astride him, riding him as if he was the favourite in the Galway plate, urging him home to the shouts and cheers of the crowds at Ballybrit.

As he stumbled towards the shower, Malachy promised himself that next time, he would definitely insist on using a condom. Two if he met Vera, and if his memory served him right.

CHAPTER 15

The weeks approaching the Leaving Cert took even John out of circulation. Malachy knew that he himself had a natural ability with mathematical type subjects but needed to study the more creative stuff. He read and reread Macbeth. He learned tracts of poetry. He drew and redrew maps of Ireland, by rainfall averages, by industry, by population, by vegetation. He studied each night until midnight and often everything became a blur. His mother generally kept out of his way and his father made clumsy attempts to support him. Now and then, he would arrive at Malachy's bedroom door with a glass of milk and a few Ginger Nut biscuits. Malachy appreciated the gesture but got fed up of the same type of biscuit. His father even tried to engage him in conversation one night, an occasion of great discomfort for both of them.

'So, Malachy, you'll be doing th'auld Leaving Cert. Ha?'

'I will. Th'auld Leaving Cert is right.'

'I never got that far, of course, but, sure, says you, that's the way.'

'That's the way, indeed.'

'As the fellah says, things is different now, so they are. Isn't that right?'

'Oh, begod, that's right. Things change.'

'I heard a song on the radio lately about times changing, Bob somebody, the times are changing, he says, the times are changing.'

'That'd be a fellah called Bob Dylan. He's good alright, so he is.'

'The times are changing. No doubt about that, so there isn't. What'll you do after th'auld exams, at all?'

'If I do middlin' and get the grant, I'll go to Uni. To study.'

'That'd be great. Study is the way, there's no doubt about that. Don't go breaking your back like I did. The times are changing as Bob yer man says.'

There was a long pause.

'So, Malachy, if you go to th'auld Uni, herself and meself were wondering. How are you fixed for th'auld facts of life and that?'

Malachy and his father sat in mortal discomfort. Malachy eventually broke the silence.

'I'd say I'm sound enough, like we did th'auld biology at school so we did, so the basics are there.'

His father got up and seemed as if a great weight had been lifted from his shoulders. He smiled and patted Malachy on the back,

'You were always a good lad Malachy. So the job is sound as far as th'auld sex department goes, then?'

'Sound as bell iron, Dad.'

'Like the man says, when I was a gasur, we didn't have much of a clue about that department. We didn't talk about it, like, but sure I suppose you see it all on the telly. And there's the books for th'auld biology at school.'

'The books are fierce handy.'

'So if herself asks if we had a chat, says you, we did.'

Now that the awkward lesson on sex was over, his Dad seemed more relaxed.

'I envy you young people, so I do. I left school at fourteen. The teachers them times were tough men. In a country school, if you got a wallop, you said nothing at home for fear you'd get the same again from your parents. Our teacher, Mr Horan was his name. He was the contrariest man and he'd lace you with a sally rod if he was in bad form. Drink, of course, had a lot to do with that. If he was in the rats from the night before, he'd kill all around him. Used to put children standing on the window sills and wallop their legs. Tough man.

' I was the only boy in sixth class with a pair of shoes on my feet would you believe that? We worked hard them times but we learned the value of a pound too. My first job was in the stables for the Brownes. I looked after their horses and they were often better fed than meself. Lord Browne was an arrogant bastard. Some said he was grand til he lost a son in the great war. Sure if you go to war you have a great chance of getting killed anyway, hah?'

Malachy was restless. He'd heard snatches of this story before, especially on Friday nights when his father usually had a few pints after work.

'That reminds me Dad,' he said, ' we have th'auld History first on Tuesday so I'd better make a shape to doing a bit of work.'

'I loved th'auld History meself, indeed. Sure there's no history now, says you, it's all in the past, says you. I'll go and tell herself so that we had a chat about your future and the rest of the stuff and you work away.'

When his father left the room, Malachy nibbled at the Ginger Nuts. The chat about the sex had reminded him of Breege. As his father had spoken, he kept seeing images of her in his mind. He saw her against the advertising boards of the soccer pitch, but it was his arms, not John's that held her. He saw her by the lake, but it was his trousers, not John's, she was poking inside of. He saw himself and Breege walking hand in hand by the leafy avenues of the University, humming tunes together. He saw everything but the average rainfall of temperate regions and that question was bound to come up in Geography.

And so the days slipped away, sometimes with glacial slowness, other times like lightening. He did not meet John until the morning of the first exam.

'I suppose you have it all done, Malachy, y'auld swot?'

'It was hard to do in a week what we were supposed to be doing for the last two years. If the right questions don't come up, I'm bollocksed.'

'Bollocksed is right. After this morning, if anybody ever asks me about the average rainfall of anywhere in Ireland, I'll tell them to shag off.'

Together, they traipsed into the hall of the local primary school. Rows of desks filled every available bit of floor space. The two lads were at opposite ends of the hall. At nine o clock precisely, seventy three boys, of varying degrees of intelligence, commitment and ability, made the first pen strokes to decide their futures.

The next two weeks were spent by Malachy and John trying desperately to atone for five years of neglect. Each spent night after night in a lather of worry and speculation, trying to second guess the examiners. In the examination hall, the students dredged their memories to regurgitate as many facts as they could relevant to the subject in hand.

Time passed uneventfully for Malachy until the morning of the final exam. The subject was Latin. The custom was that each subject teacher would be at the hall as the boys went in and out. The teachers tried to give encouraging nods and looks to each of them, while trying not to betray their despair as troop after troop of disorientated academically unfit students filed in and out.

True to form, the Latin teacher was there at the door. As Malachy approached, he heard his name called out.

'Malachyeah!'

The Lizard.

'Malachyeah! A quick word with 'oo, by!'

Malachy reluctantly went over to him.

'Oorself and Johnnyeah finish today, don't oo?'

'Yes, Brother.'

'And oorself and Johnnyeah used to serve Moss wan time, didn't oo?'

'We served Mass, yes, brother.'

'We are hoving Moss said in the Monasteryeah tonight, to pray for all the bys who hov finished their studyeah. I want oorself and Johnnyeah to serve and the pair of oo con hov oor supper ofterwords with ourselves and the priesht. Can oo be there ot sevin, like a good lod.?' He walked away without waiting for an answer, secure in the knowledge that refusal was not an option. Malachy was furious. All the Leaving crowd was going to the lake to celebrate with a few bottle of beer and the hope of a court. Mass and supper would drag on until God knew what time. Before he could talk to John, the bell sounded for the start of Latin.

Whatever else about the Lizard, he had drilled the class well. Malachy flew through the declensions, the unseens, the texts. Caesar venied, vidied and vicied and before he knew it, the invigilator called time up and Malachy was officially finished school. He looked about to see if he could spot John to tell him the Lizard's plans but there was no sign of him. When he left the hall, however, there was John nodding away and smiling as the Lizard spoke to him.

'Malachyeah! Johnnyeah will call for oo tonight ot hof past six. I want oo boat in the Monasteryeah by tin to sevin so thot oo con set up the altar for the priesht. I'll tock to oo boat about oor exom thin os well.'

When he had left, Malachy exploded.

'The bloody cheek! Serving Moss on the last night of the Exoms! What are you looking so happy about?'

John was shaking his head and smiling.

'What were you going to tell your old lady and old fellah tonight? "Mammy, I'm going up the lake to get a shift and drink cider." And they'll say," Good boy, Malachy, give her a length for me and don't vomit on your clothes, like a good boy." Would you cop onto yourself, Malachy. We're the golden haired boys. Out at half six, rapid Mass, a bit of grub with the Brothers and off we go for sport. On me solemn oath, even thinking about it, I have a leadog on me that I could bate an ass out of a sand pit.'

Malachy regarded his friend with a mixture of distaste and respect. That he could be still thinking of deflowering the beautiful Breege upset him but he also admired the fact that John was able to rescue an advantage from having to serve Mass on one of the biggest nights of the year. John clapped him on the shoulder.

'Malachy, auld stock, it's like a game of tennis. You play to advantage. I'll see you tonight outside the monastryeah at a quarter to seven.'

'And what colour balloon are you using this time?' Malachy wanted to now.

'No balloons, Malachy, everything is planned so it is. I'll talk to you later.'

John disappeared into the throng of delighted and relieved students. Malachy chatted half heartedly to a few of them and headed home.

He was depressed so he decided to take a wander through the park. As he strolled up the central path, he was surprised to see Breege seated alone on one of the benches. She did not see him until he was in front of her. It hurt Malachy to see that she looked as if she had been crying. He sat beside her. As always, he felt a surge of emotion as he shared her space. He dearly wanted to tell her how he felt and ask her out.

'How did you find the Latin?' was all he said.

'Fuck the Latin and everything else,' she replied.

The language, he felt, was another example of John's bad influence. He tried again to muster up the courage to speak honestly and with feeling.

'It didn't go well so?' He cursed himself for his cowardice.

'Malachy, nothing went well. Every paper was wrong, I made a mess of the whole bloody exam. My parents will kill me when the results come out. They'll say it was because of John but it's not. I did the work and sure I haven't seen John for more than a couple of minutes for weeks. I'll never get the marks for Uni, I know it.'

Malachy wished he could leap in with the right words, mature and comforting.

'So it didn't go well at all, you reckon.'

Breege just closed her eyes and seemed close to tears.

'I wouldn't mind,' she said, 'but Marian flew through everything. She seemed to have all the answers while I sat there like a dodo. The nuns will kill me as well. They kept saying all along that I was going to do great things and I did rubbish.'

Malachy wanted to take her hand and comfort her, to allow his words to be balm to her troubled spirits.

'Sure that's the way.'

Breege got up to leave.

'I suppose you'll be going up the lake later to celebrate?'

Malachy told her about the Mass in the Monastery.

'I'll see you both so,' Breege said. 'By the way, Malachy, I don't know what you said to Marian but she's fierce annoyed with you. It'd be a favour to me if you were nice to her tonight.'

Now it was Malachy's turn to sit with his eyes closed, close to tears. He had had a glorious chance. He had met Breege alone, vulnerable and needy. He could have moved in and stated his case and set himself up. Instead, he had landed himself with the titless wonder of a friend.

His mother was delighted when he told her about serving Mass that evening.

'You won't want a tea so.'

When his father arrived from work, he was pleased as well.

'Serving Mass for the Brothers, bedad! Stay in with them lads. They're the boys with the connections.'

He then slipped Malachy a ten shilling note.

'Say nothing to herself,' he said with a wink. 'You're a big lad now. I know the story. Just behave. And, remember our little chat. I know there'll be a bit of a do now th'auld exams are finished. This family was always respectable, as the fellah says, so don't piss on your own doorstep. Sound man, the job is oxo now, so we'll say no more.'

And so, Malachy the man left his house to put on a white lacy dress - like garment and serve Mass.

John was waiting for him as planned.

'Tonight's the night, pal. School finished and shift waiting. Eyes down for a full house, what do you reckon?'

'I reckon you've begun to speak in a strange, foreign language lately. Where did you pick it up?'

'O Murchu is home from Uni and he has all the chat now. The birds in Uni love the chat, he reckons. Some of his buddies went to California lately and there's hippy women at it like rabbits from one end of the day to the other. Non stop, the boys reckon.'

'We might talk about this after Mass,' Malachy suggested

'Any time, Malachy, any time. O Murchu reckons there's women in Uni take a tablet to stop themselves getting snigged. Bates balloons,'

'That's the tackle they call the Pill. It's supposed to make women's backsides awful big, they reckon'

'O Murchu said nothing about that, mind you, but it'd be a small price to pay to be able to go bareback. This auld boil in the bag job is a fierce lot of trouble. I tried different types of balloons since but there's not a bit of comfort. O Murchu reckons the boys in Uni bring back the real thing from England. The girls from the North can buy them in Protestant chemists as well. He reckons if you can peep into a girl's handbag and see a box of johnnies, the job is oxo straight away.'

They had reached the ornate door of the Monastery. Malachy lifted the enormous brass knocker and banged it twice.

'Do you like playing with knockers, Malachy?' John asked.

'For Jaysus sake, Joyce, will you take you mind out of your groin for an hour at least? We have to make a good job of this because we'll be looking for references from these lads. Now stop.'

There was the sound of whistling inside the building and the door was opened by the Brother known as Birdy.

'We're here to serve Mass, Brother.' John said solemnly.

Whistling under his breath, Birdy nodded and led them upstairs.

At the end of a long landing, he opened a door to a small oratory. The altar was covered in a heavy tapestry and stood in the coloured light of the sun beaming through a stained glass window. There were six rows of pews, smoothed and shined by generations of Brotherly backsides. Birdy left without a word and the Lizard breezed in.

'Malachyeah! And Johnnyeah as well! Oo are mighty min, there's no doubt in the world about that, ha? Fader Tommyeah will be wit' oo in a minit. Ooo know Fader Tommyeah? He is a past poopil of this school. He is on the Missions in China. Imagine thot, can oo? Over there wit' Commoonists and Atheists and the divil knows fot. No doubt but it's a great ting to do in the eyes of the Lord. He'll tell oo himself, it is a hard road to trovel but tis a poth to Heaven. It brings great blessings on the fomilyeah that gives a prieesht for the gloryeah of God. And here's Fr. Tommyeah!'

A handsome man in his early forties entered the room.. Malachy recognised him. On a previous visit from the Missions, Fr. Tommy had visited the school, telling tales of Chairman Mao, the oppression of the Faith and the rape of the women. The boys of the school had their nocturnal fantasies fuelled for months after that.

'I know these two lads, I think, no?' the priest said. He spoke with a strange accent, half Mayo and half Chinese. 'This one is Joyce, no? Your sister is Helen, no? And the other one, your father, he fixed my car, I think, no?'

Malachy and John looked at each other and were unsure exactly how to answer, yes or no.

'So, you boys will serve Mass for me, no? This is good. How long since you boys did this thing?'

'Well,' John said reluctantly, 'it's been a whileen to be honest.'

'A whileen,' Father Tommy said with a grin. 'That is a long time maybe?' Turning to the Lizard, he asked him: 'Brother, I will need some water. Can you get this thing?'

The Lizard beamed and went for water with the air of one who has been given the most important chore he has ever been asked to perform.

Fr. Tommy smiled again at the two boys.

'Listen, lads, I know the score.'

'What happened to your accent?' John asked him.

'I put on that for the religious. But seriously, I was brought up here twenty two years ago to serve Mass because everybody said I had a vocation. And I had, as it turned out. But in the last few years, hundreds of the lads have left the priesthood. So, the story is, if you want to be a priest, you will not find a more challenging and rewarding job, but, for God's sake do it because you want to, not because your mother or the Lizard or anybody else wants to, OK?'

Before the boys could reply, the oratory door opened and the congregation of Brothers filed in. John and Malachy watched in wonder as they arrived. All the familiar figures were there – Monkey Man, the Hopper, Snakey and of course, the Lizard. There were also a few ancient figures, whose wispy grey haired heads sat like little wizened spuds above their cassocks.

Fr. Tommy beckoned the boys and led them behind a screen. His vestments hung there and two sets of surplices and soutanes for the servers.

'Tog out lads,' he said, 'you're picked. By the way, have you any idea how to serve Mass?'

'Not as such, Father.'

'Just follow my lead. I'll be saying the Mass in Latin and the responses might come back to you. If not, hum along. The main things are to change the book from one side to the other and to put plenty of wine in the chalice. Are we right, so? Now, we do this thing for the Lizard, no?'

They filed out and took their places at the altar.

Fr Tommy began the Mass without any preamble. He rattled off the Latin. The two servers hummed as instructed. During one particularly long oration by the priest, John whispered to Malachy.

'I reckon I'll just put it in and out tonight, Malachy. That's supposed to be safe, what do you reckon?'

Malachy closed hid eyes and hummed fervently.

'Do you reckon, Malachy? Is the auld cuir isteach and amach safe?'

A cough from the priest saved Malachy from having to make a reply. Fr Tommy was nodding at the cruets that held the wine and water.

The Mass passed without any further discussions on contraception. Before the final blessing, Fr Tommy addressed the congregation.

'Reverend Brothers and my young friends. That was very nice, no? We come here to praise God and this is a good thing. I served this Mass over twenty years ago and it's good to see old faces, no? But so many old faces! I ask this thing. Where are the young faces, yes? I see changes happening. Young people today, they have good times, no? Maybe more money, more pretty girls too maybe, I think. The Church, our mother needs labourers for the harvest is great. Many priests and Brothers, they now question this life, no? That is why we make the decision to follow Christ only after we think hard. In China, there is no God they say, but the people are not happy. In Ireland, there is maybe too much God and the people are not happy. Maybe God is in the middle somewhere, no?'

With that, he raised his hand and blessed everybody.

As they were divesting behind the screen, Snakey appeared. He was breathing deeply through his nose, and as usual, smelled strongly of tobacco.

'Supper will be served in the refectory downstairs in a few minutes.' He spoke in a slow, monotonous drawl. 'You know where it is, Father, I'm sure.'

The refectory, when they arrived, was quiet. The Brothers sat in the allocated places. The Lizard sat alone at a small table which had three unoccupied chairs.

'Fr Tommyeah, Johnnyeah, Malachyeah! Over here beside meah.'

Plates had already been placed on each table. Each plate was piled high with chicken, ham and all kinds of salad. Baskets of bread were there as well.

'We're waiting for Fr Tommyeah to say grace.'

'Heavenly Father, we ask your blessings on this beautiful food, and we thank the Brothers in this place. They pass on the Faith and we pray you will bless them more and more. Amen.'

Malachy had never seen so much food. In his house, spuds, cheap meat and boiled vegetables were the standard fare. He ate with relish, barely listening to the Lizard's constant prattle.

'I grew up in Kerryah, a smawl village called Ra'more. People from outside call it Rathmore but to us from the place, 'tis Ra'more and notting else. My father, may God rest him, was jailed by the British, he wos shot at by the Tans and jailed agin' by the Free Shtaters. He served Ireland well but God better. Every night, when he wos home, we knelt and sed the Rosaryeah as a familyeah. I remember the turf fire burning and the pot of spuds biling on it and my father would say, "Meehall, love God and love your countryeah and oo'll hov lived well." Times were hard in them days, thot's for sure. We hod to walk two miles to school and not a shoe on our feet. The Master would bate oo as soon as look at oo. But it made min out of us! Min of fait' and patriots. I was teaching in Watherford during the Emergencyeah and we used to watch the German and the English planes hoving fwat they called dog fights out over the seayeah. Fwen an English plane wint down, we'd cheer and clop. But fwen a German plane was shot at, and we'd see a parachutist, we'd lep into the nearest boat and row out after him. Fait' and patriotism, are oo listening to me, byes?'

Malachy was disturbed to see that the Lizard's face had grown red and flushed as he spoke. Bits of lettuce and chicken skin hung from the corners of his mouth and breadcrumbs flew from his lips as he spoke.

'God wants min to serve Him, min like Fr Tommyeah. Min who are min of fait' and patriotism. If oo are lukewarm, He'll spit oo out. Chastityeah, charityeah and obedience. Thot's fwat will get oo into Heaven. Some byes think they con fornicate and drink and indulge in the pleasures of the flesh.' He paused to tear off a lump of chicken leg. As he chewed, he fumbled beneath is cassock. He grunted with pleasure as he extracted a packet of cigarettes. Still chewing, he managed to light a Sweet Afton.

He gazed across the table at the two boys. With cigarette, chicken skin and lettuce clinging to his lower lip, he smiled.

'So, Malachyeah and Johnnyeah. Oo hov finished oor studyeah and done oor exom. Tis time to decide fwat to do with oor life. Are oo going too waste it like so many other of the dallamoos or are oo going to do something marvellous like young Tommyeah?'

John spoke up.

'Well, Brother, it's like this so it is. Me and Malachy reckon we'll take a few weeks and think long and hard about the future. We're going to talk to Father Tommy as well and sure, as the fellah says, that's all we can do.'

'Well, byes, the Brothers hov to say their final prayers before they finish their supper. I'll show ye out.'

There was a marked chill in the Lizard's manner as he led them through the Monastery and to the front gate. He lit another cigarette and placed his elbows on one of the gate pillars.

'Byes, I hov been in the religious life, bye and mon, for nearlyeah sixtyeah years. I hov directed many byes on the right poth. In thot time, I've also known many dissappintments. I'll say no more.'

With that, he turned and re-entered the Monastery without a backward glance

'Time for waskey so, Malachy, what do you reckon?'.

CHAPTER 16

The following day being Saturday, Nora had a busy day in the shop. Thomas called her from her office to oversee the unloading of a delivery of bags of flour at the back of the shop.

'It's very dusty work for the men, Nora, so be sure to stand to one side,' he told her.

Nora stood as far as she could from the truck as it reversed to the loading bay at the back of the shop. The driver and his helper untied the green tarpaulin that covered the back of the truck and removed the tail board. Both men were dressed completely in white and placed empty flour sacks across their shoulders. The driver climbed onto the truck and hefted the large sacks one by one onto the other man's shoulders. Nora made a tick on a sheet of paper for each sack unloaded. The day was overcast and Nora did not have to concentrate very hard so her attention kept wandering. A river ran by the end of the extensive yard. On the other side, the local Catholic church stood in all it splendour. Nora assumed the church must have been built in the previous century and wondered how the poverty stricken population of the time could have afforded to build and maintain such a grand church.

As she watched, she saw two men come out the back door. Both were dressed in black. She recognised one immediately as Myles. She could see his broad shoulders and dark hair. His usual erect posture was nowhere to be seen, however. The other man, smaller and stockier, seemed to be in a very agitated state. He was pointing his finger at Myles and pacing up and down. Myles looked abjectly at the ground. Nora knew instinctively that she was the cause of his dilemma and felt a surge of anger towards the older priest. She wished she could hear what was being said and would have liked to leap to Myles' defence. Instead, she sat back further in the shadows.

Soon, the truck she was supervising was empty. The driver came to her with a docket which she signed, everything being in order. Glancing back towards the church, she saw the two priests had left.

She returned to her office and once more attacked the piles of bills, invoices and dockets that never seemed to get any smaller.

Later, that afternoon, she looked out her window that looked onto the shop floor. Her heart missed a beat as she saw a stocky figure, dressed in black, striding purposefully through the shop. She recognised him as the priest who had been talking to Myles. Thomas approached him and after a few moments whispered conversation, lead him towards his office.

Nora was not surprised when there was a soft knock on her door five minutes later and Thomas entered.

'I wonder if you would be so kind as to come to my office for a moment, Nora.' Thomas said in a voice that meant he did not expect no for an answer.

As they walked through the shop, Nora was sure people were watching her. Nobody looked in her direction as she passed and a couple of old women covered their mouths with their shawls as they spoke.

Inside the office, the priest stood beside the filing cabinet.

'Father Reilly, this is Miss Nora Fortune, Nora, this is Father Reilly,' Thomas said.

'Miss Fortune,' Fr Reilly said in a stern voice, 'it is a pity we could not have met in more favourable circumstances.'

He was, as she had noticed, a stockily built man. Beneath his black beret style hat, he had thick, silver hair. A pair of gold rimmed glasses perched on a small nose. The mouth too was small, and pursed in disapproval.

Nora remained silent. Fr Reilly began to pace the small floor space that was available.

'I am proud to call Thomas a friend, ' Fr Reilly continued. 'In this town, we have always enjoyed excellent relations with our Protestant neighbours. Indeed, Thomas and I have worked together, discretely, on several projects. Thomas understands better than most just how important it is that we work together, not against each other. I would never dream of interfering with any member of his faith who has chosen a career or vocation. I think you know what I am referring to.'

'I do not know of any interference that I have been party to, Father.' Nora decided she would not be intimidated.

'Oh, don't you now?' Fr Reilly said, raising his eyebrows sarcastically. 'Don't you indeed? You are, are you not, familiar with a young man from this parish, called Myles Walsh?'

'I have indeed met him.'

'Met him?' Once again the eyebrows shot up. 'Met him, you say. And when you met him, where did these meetings take place?'

'As you know, Father, I am not of your flock. I am, therefore, not quite sure what it is you wish me to say.'

'What I wish you to say, young lady, is that you will stop seeing young Walsh,' said Fr Reilly, glaring at her over the rim of his glasses.

'I am hardly "seeing" him, Father. That seems to imply that we are pursuing some sort of relationship and that is nonsense.'

'Thomas,' Fr Reilly said in a voice that was low and threatening, 'I realise I am in your shop, and as such I am your guest. Perhaps you could explain to this young lady that she too is a guest in this town and should behave accordingly.'

Nora refused to be browbeaten.

'I am no more a guest in this town than you are. I am a citizen of this State and very proud of it. I have done nothing to be ashamed of and certainly nothing to apologise for.'

'You behaviour has scandalous implications for young Myles.' The priests voice had not risen but he was no less angry. 'Not just for him but for his family. A young priest cannot, cannot, be seen in the company of a young woman, be she of the true faith or otherwise. Have you any idea of the vows he will soon be making? He will take a vow of chastity, pledging himself to a life of celibacy and service to the Church.. I will not allow his future to be threatened by a thoughtless girl like you.'

'Now, Father Reilly,' Thomas said softly. 'I am sure we can settle this without rancour. I believe Nora is prepared to listen to reason.'

'Reason, Uncle Thomas?' Nora could not believe Thomas was taking the side of the parish priest. 'What do you mean reason?' She was close to tears but determined not to cry.

Thomas then surprised her by taking her hand in his and speaking gently.

'Nora, I am more than your employer, I am your family. As your family, I have an obligation to protect you from any harm or hurt that endangers you. I have known Father Reilly a long time. We have seen so many people damaged by ignorance and misguided hopes. Please, Nora, I want you to promise me that you will at least listen to what Fr Reilly is saying, listen and take heed.'

Nora felt torn between responding to the gentleness of Thomas and challenging attitude of the priest. She took a deep breath and spoke to the two men.

'I do not understand what the fuss is about. I talked to Myles on only a few occasions. We spoke about religion, about yours, Father and mine. So much hatred and pain could be avoided if people spoke more, don't you think, and listened? But I have no wish to make trouble for Myles. He will make such a fine priest, he is warm and intelligent. I do not wish to cause any embarrassment for Thomas either, or indeed myself. So, I will undertake not to initiate, under any circumstances, any contact with Myles.'

'Well done, Nora,' Thomas beamed. 'I believe that settles it then. Father Reilly?'

Fr Reilly regarded Nora coldly.

'They say that society is changing,' he said quietly. 'They say the war has changed the world. I have been a priest in this Diocese thirty years and I've heard all this before, that things will change. Maybe some things will but once a man has been anointed to serve the Church, he is committed for life. If you wish to talk about religion, young lady, your own Parson Potter is an experienced and educated man. I too would be happy to provide you with any information you may require regarding the tenets of our faith. I shall expect you to keep your promise.

'Thomas, I am pleased this unpleasant business is dealt with. I am sure we shall not have to speak of it again.'

'I certainly hope so, Father. Now, just before you go, I picked up a couple of bottles of exceptional claret during my visit to Galway yesterday. Wait one moment and I'll get a paper bag.'

Nora and Fr Reilly stood facing different walls in the small office.

'You probably think me cruel,' he said.

Nora made no reply. The priest laughed gently.

'Do not underestimate me, child. I have the power not only to crush you but also to make life extremely uncomfortable for your uncle. People listen to me, you would be well advised to do so as well. Thomas!' He took the bag from Thomas who had re-entered the room. 'You are too kind! '

He peered into the bag.

'Excellent year. This will certainly be appreciated and bring back some memories. Good day to you both.' Without so much as a glance at Nora, he left.

'What did he mean, bring back memories?' she asked when he had gone.

'He served in the Great War, in France. He was one of the men saved by Monty Brown.'

Nora smiled at Thomas.

'When Eileen Tracey got confused doing her work, she'd often say: "Sweet Jesus, this is complicated". I know now how she felt.'

'True, Nora,' Thomas replied, laughing, ' and as I've heard some of the men hear say on many occasions, "Sweet Jesus, this calls for a drink!" Come, let us take an early evening and find Mrs Brown. She will want to hear all about this.'

'Early evening, indeed, Thomas,' Nora teased, pointing at the clock that hung on the wall, ' it's ten minutes before my usual finishing time.'

'You can make them up next week, Nora' Thomas said, taking his hat from a stand beside the door.

'It's good to hear you laugh, Thomas, you can be very serious, you know.'

'Until we leave the premises, Miss Fortune, I am still your employer and you will treat me with the respect I deserve.'

'Certainly, Mr Williams, sur,' she said affecting a local accent. 'I musht thry to be betther.'

As they walked along the Main Street, Thomas was pleasantly surprised when Nora linked his arm with her own.

'Thomas,' she asked, ' I wonder sometimes why you never married.'

'I wonder sometimes where you learned such appalling manners. Certainly not from my side of the family. You ask the most impertinent questions. Father Reilly has sense to separate you and that playboy priest.'

'Playboy priest! Really, Thomas. But you did not answer my question. You are such a fine, handsome gentleman, well off no doubt.'

'Please, Nora, I barely keep the wolf from the door.'

'With the wages you pay me, the wolf is well away from your door, Thomas. But as a young man, you must have broken many hearts.'

'I am still a young man, I'll have you know. Seriously, Nora, I have devoted my life to my business. In some respects I resemble the unfortunate young Myles and Father Reilly in that I have chosen career over family but they had to make the choice whereas mine was made for me.'

'In what way?'

Thomas did not answer immediately.

'You have a way of making people feel comfortable about you, Nora. Maybe that's what worried Father Reilly. You bring out the honesty in people. My choice was in part made by my upbringing. Boarding school and all that. I have never felt entirely comfortable with the opposite sex, women, that is.'

'I know who the opposite sex are, Thomas,' Nora said kindly.'

'You see, that's exactly what I mean. I should be terribly embarrassed using phrases like that with a young woman but you really do make one feel at ease. So, boarding school, then straight to the shop. Being a member of the merchant class, as it were, meant there were only certain females one could associate with. And, of course, being a Protestant narrowed the already minuscule opportunities even more.'

They were approaching Mrs Brown's house. Suddenly, Thomas seemed no longer quite at ease.

'In fact, Nora, it had crossed my mind, that is I was going to perhaps..'

Before he could finish, Mrs Browne appeared at her front door and waved to them.

'Thomas,' she called. 'Nora. What a lovely surprise. Come in, come in. It is such a lovely evening, I've set up a table and chairs outside in the back garden. Thomas, you will join us for tea, I'm sure.'

'I would be delighted, and I have a present for you.' he said, waving the bulky leather case he was carrying.

Mrs Brown had indeed set chairs and tables outside but she had also set the table with a lovely china setting. She quickly set another place and produced three crystal goblets for the wine Thomas produced from his case. He also produced a brass cork screw and expertly pulled the cork from the bottle.

'Now, Nora,' Mrs Brown said, 'while we allow the wine to breathe, tell me all about your day. I hope it was interesting.'

Nora and Thomas looked at each other and laughed out loud.

'Oh, it was interesting, Mrs Browne.'

Between them Nora and Thomas told of the encounter with Fr Reilly. Nora decided not to mention what he had said while they were alone. When they had finished, Mrs Brown shook her head.

'What a pompous little man he can be at times. I could be cruel and suggest Monty might have left him and saved a German but I won't. Still, Nora, I don't wish to sound too serious but he does have a lot of power. You will have to tread carefully. What do you intend to do?'

' "Intend"?' Thomas asked. 'There is only one thing she can do. She must honour her promise, her promise to Father Reilly.'

'And indeed she shall, Thomas. I will ensure that she does not break her word.'

Nora looked at her and wondered what exactly she was saying. Mrs Brown's face, however, revealed nothing. Thomas too was regarding her with a slightly puzzled look.

'Well,' he remarked, pulling a watch from his waist coat pocket, 'I must be getting along. Shall I call on my way to Service in the morning?'

'That would be lovely, Thomas. Nora and I will be ready.'

'And afterwards,' Thomas continued, 'perhaps we might go for a drive, perhaps to the sea side.'

When he had left, Nora helped to tidy up.

'I could not help feeling, Mrs Brown, that you were not being entirely frank with Thomas.'

'Tell me again what you promised exactly to Corporal Reilly?'

' I said that I would not initiate any contact with Myles,' Nora replied blushing slightly.

'And I shall ensure that you will not. However, if your path and his should cross, then, why, there will be little I can do.'

Nora threw her arms around the older woman.

'Sweet Jesus,' she cried, 'this calls for a drink. Is there any wine left?'

As Mrs Brown poured the last of the wine, she smiled broadly at Nora.

'I must advise you, Nora. Should you decide to mix more extensively with our Roman Catholic brethren, you will be well advised to decrease your use of the sacred name and increase your tolerance of hard liquor.'

CHAPTER 17

'Do you reckon there'll be many up the lake?' Malachy asked as they walked away from the Monastery.

'So long as Breege is there, warm and willing, I'm away for slates. You owe me six shillings for the drink, by the way.'

'Six shillings! Did you buy the shagging brewery?'

'O Murchu bought it for me and he took a cut for himself. Shag it Malachy, in a few weeks, we'll be officially and legally men. We can go into any pub we want and order a pint of Phoenix and smoke a cigarette and go to the dance half shot and pick up any bit of skirt that takes our fancy. What do you reckon?"

'I reckon we might as well because when we join the priesthood, we'll only be able to smoke and drink'

'Poor auld Lizard! We disapinted him, Malachyeah! Did you see the face of him when he was telling us to feic off at the gate?'

'What did you reckon of that Father Tommy lad?' Malachy asked.

'He was a queer auld fish. What was the story there, talking one way to us and then putting on the act for the Brothers?'

'I reckon he was sound. He was telling us we'd be total disasters as priests.'

'How do you reckon he made that out, Malachy?'

'It's a mystery, John, it's a mystery.'

'Anyway, we have to meet O Murchu in the park to collect our booze. I told him half nine so we have a few minutes.'

As it happened, when they reached the park, O Murchu was already sitting on a bench just inside the gate.

'Well, if it isn't Father John and Father Malachy. I need to have Confession. I sinned against the body.'

'Whose body, my son?' John asked him.

'I can't remember her name but she was a red head.'

'What did I tell, you, Malachy? Uni is the place for it. Give us the drink O Murchu. I have a hot date waiting and I have a leadhog on me that could bate an ass out of a sand pit.'

O Murchu handed him a large brown bag that rattled as he passed it over.

'What about you, Malachy, have you a hot date as well or are you practising for the celibate life already?'

'A gentleman never tells, O Murchu.'

'In other words, you're getting nothing. By the way, John, did I tell you about the girl

I met lately on the train going to Belfast?'

John shook his head and Malachy could see the admiration in his eyes.

'You never mentioned that. What happened?'

'Now, I don't want to be getting poor Malachy all excited and him without a boiler to take the bone out of his trousers but this lady was something else, lads. She said she was a student in Queens so I reckon she was a Prod and you know what they're like, no qualms at all when it comes to the queer thing. Anyway, we started chattin' and I put the soft talk on, the good line in soft shite, and next thing she gives me the glad eye. Off we went into the jacks, up against the sink, in and out, end of story. Back to the seat then and she left the train at Portadown, so she must have been a Prod. Enjoy your night, lads'

John watched him leave with awe, his mouth open.

'In and out, end of story. Jaysus, I hope I get enough marks to get to Uni. Come on Malachy, I need to get me end away before me balleens burst.'

When they reached the lake, the party had begun. There were about twenty people there, most of whom Malachy knew. Everybody had a drink of some sort in their hand and a number were smoking. Breege was sitting on the grass with Marian. As soon as she saw the lads, she got up and ran to John.

'What kept you, lads, we were getting worried.'

John hugged her and she closed her eyes in surrender and ecstasy.

'I'll leave ye to it so,' Malachy said. 'How's Marian?'

'I'm grand, Malachy. There's who I've been waiting for. See you later.'

A small group of people had just arrived. Malachy knew them all, except for one girl. Marian took the hand of a boy Malachy knew as Donal, who lived a mile or so from town. She pulled him towards her and glued her face to his.

'Point taken,' Malachy thought. He took his few bottles of beer and found a dry rock beside the water to sit on. He sat at an angle that allowed him to keep a discrete eye on the party. He could see John and Breege, wrapped around each other. John broke off the embrace regularly to swig from a bottle of beer or a baby Powers.

The night grew cooler and the sky filled with millions of stars. In the far West, he could see the conical shape of Croagh Patrick, in a vague silhouette against the sky.

He became aware of someone sitting beside him. It was the girl who had arrived with Marian's date, Donal.

'You seem to be having as much fun as I am,' she said in a refined English accent.

'It's funny, I suppose, you look forward to something all year, the biggest night out, and you end up with a cold arse from sitting on a damp rock.'

'I must say it's not my idea of a fun night either.'

'You're a stranger,' Malachy said.

'Rose. My name is Rose. I'm a cousin of Donal's, here on holiday, from England.'

'Malachy. My name is Malachy. Donal stole my date and I'm stuck here.'

'Oh dear, did he do that?'

'Yerrah, not really. I'm just pissed off generally. Marian wanted me to bring her tonight but I hummed and hawed and she gave me the bum's rush.'

'I'm rather pleased she did, Malachy, otherwise I'd be left on my own. Do you really fancy her then?'

Malachy got up from the rock He saw John and Breege leave the party and disappear into the trees.

'Would you like to go for a stroll along the shore, Rose? My backside is getting mouldy and mossy.'

'How could any girl resist an invitation like that? Come on then.'

Together, they strolled along the pebbles that lined the shore.

As they walked, they saw a falling star.

'Make a wish,' Malachy said.

'So,' Rose asked again, when they had gone a little further, ' do you really fancy her?'

Malachy felt like crying, he was so frustrated.

'It's not her at all I fancy,' he blurted out. He regretted it immediately.

'Oh, I see,' Rose said slowly. 'You know Malachy, sometimes, it helps to talk about it to a stranger.'

And so he told her. He told her of how much he fancied Breege and how she had asked him to fix her up with John, how he had hoped it wouldn't last and how John was using her.

'And that, Rose, is how we treat people we like in Ireland,' he finished.

'And this, Malachy, is how we treat people we like in England.'

She leaned in and kissed him gently on the lips. Malachy was stunned.

'I..I..' he stammered.

'Shh, just enjoy,' Rose whispered.

Malachy was lost in the feelings he was experiencing. Her lips were red and soft as fuchsia petals. She smelt faintly of suntan lotion and soap. When he placed his hands behind her neck, her hair was like a silk scarf and her skin soft as down to the touch.

Her hands were around his neck also, gently caressing the skin beneath his ears.

For the first time in his limited experience with girls, Malachy was utterly at a loss as to how to proceed. He stood there, eyes closed and suddenly realised he was not thinking of Breege. He smiled.

Rose broke away and asked him what he was smiling about.

'I made a wish on the falling star that you'd like me,' he said.

In reply, she drew his head towards her and kissed him again. Soon, he felt the tip of her tongue against his lips. He opened his mouth wide and stuck the full length of his tongue into her mouth.

Rose stepped back, laughing.

'Take it easy, Irish boy, I can see I have a lot to teach you, and I've only got four weeks. Lesson one, kissing.'

The lesson lasted for God knew how long because Malachy lost all track of time. They were interrupted by a voice calling for Rose.

'That's Donal, ' she said. 'Over here, Donal.'

Donal and Marian arrived, hand in hand.

'We have to go now, Rose,' Donal said. 'It's after midnight and Mammy'll kill me if I don't get you home.'

'How's Malachy treating you, Rose' Marian asked slyly.

'He's a wonderful, gentle lover,' Rose replied sweetly.

'I'm going to walk Marian home now so can you meet me with Rose in the park in twenty minutes, Malachy?' Donal asked.

'Of course he will,' Rose answered.

When her cousin had left, Rose smiled at Malachy.

'There are benches in the park, I presume?'

Malachy could only smile back. He felt like he used to feel when he thought he had a chance with Breege. He couldn't wait to tell John. An English shift! He'd have to find out if she was a Protestant. If she was black, it would have been perfect.

John and Breege emerged from the trees in front of them. John looked shocked and dazed while Breege looked flushed and very, very angry.

'Fuck you, John Joyce,' she hissed. Then she saw Malachy.

'Malachy,' she said, 'have you seen Marian?'

'She left with Donal not two minutes ago, he was walking her home.'

Breege rushed off. John winked at Malachy.

'A quick word, auld stock?' he asked.

'A very quick word, pal, I'm busy,' Malachy answered and followed him over to the trees.

'Who's yer wan?' John asked.

'Just an English bird I picked up. What's the story with Breege?'

John looked uncomfortable.

'Bit of an auld disaster, I'm afraid. I tried the put in on the QT but, as the fellah says, I got a bit too excited too quick so I sort of shot before I wanted to.'

'Oh my God, John, you didn't. Christ Almighty, the purple balloon trick was daft enough but this tears the arse out of it altogether. What did Breege say?'

'She gave me a clout and said nothing. Do you reckon a girl could get snigged if only a little bit got in?'

'I'd have to look that up, John. I'm heading off for a shift with my bird now. I'll give you a shout tomorrow.'

'Sound man, Malachy. And if you bump into Breege, see if she's up to another rattle because I'm staying here to finish off my beer.'

Shaking his head, Malachy returned to Rose. She took him by the hand and kissed him again. Malachy forgot all about John and Breege as he and Rose headed for the park, eager to continue the course in kissing.

They sat on a park bench waiting for Donal. Malachy could not get enough of Rose, sipping at her delightful lips. She guided him in the art of French kissing, telling him it was a matter of gently knocking at the door rather than going at it like a bull at a gate. She nibbled his ear lobe, a thing he had never heard of and that sent shivers down his spine. She moved his shirt collar to one side and gave him love bites that had him gasping in pleasure. His ecstasy seemed to last forever, until Donal arrived to collect Rose.

Malachy was in such a state of arousal that he knew he would not be able to stand for a minute or two, much less walk without an obvious and embarrassing limp. He invited Donal to sit with them.

'I suppose I could sit for five minutes before we head home,' he replied.

'How was Breege when you left her?' Malachy asked.

'She went into Marian's house with her. She seemed in a bit of a state. Herself and Joyce must have had a row, I suppose.'

The thought of Breege being unhappy took Malachy's mind of his courting.

'I might take a stroll and see if I can talk to her. Will you be in town tomorrow?'

'Try and keep me away,' Rose said with a smile.

'This very spot so,' Malachy said. 'Seven by the clock on the Protestant church behind us.'

He walked through the town to Marians house. It was the last in a row of terraced houses so he was able to get around the back easily. The light was on in the kitchen and he could see the two girls at the table. He tapped gently on the window.

Marian came to the back door.

'Malachy!' she said when she saw who it was. 'Do you know the time? What are you doing here?'

Breege joined them at the door. Her eyes were red and puffed looking. Malachy reached and touched her cheek. She flinched slightly but did not draw away. She moved gently against his fingers. Her eyes closed and tears fell slowly down her cheeks.

'I'm fine Malachy. You are so good. Thank you,' she said after a few moments.

'How did you get on with your English bit, Malachy?' Marian enquired.

'A gentleman never tells,' he said.

'Gentleman me arse,' Marian said, but she was smiling. 'Now, feic off home before me Dad comes down and murders me. I'll look after Breege.'

As Malachy walked away, Marian followed him.

'I suppose you know what happened. Not a word to anybody. And tell Joyce that goes for him too. You're twice the man he is, Malachy.'

Malachy leaned forward and kissed Marian on the cheek.

'I'll talk to you tomorrow.'

As he walked home alone, Malachy wondered it he was getting maturity overnight.

CHAPTER 18

The shower did little to ease the throb in Malachy's head but did aggravate a slight tingling in his groin. Thinking again of his failure to use protection, he hoped it was friction burn.

He was about to leave the room when his mobile phone rang. Picking it up, he was surprised to hear Felicity's voice.

'Malachy, I got your number from himself. Hope you don't mind.'

'Not at all. Is there anything wrong?'

'I hope not. I'm just worried about Mum. How is she?'

'Having a ball, I think. Chasing dreams and youth, sure how else would she be?'

'I know Mum has really taken to you, Malachy. For all her show, she's fragile enough so, take care of her OK?'

'I think I need more taking care of than she does, Felicity, but there's nothing to worry about, she's grand.'

'Thanks Malachy. Don't mention that I called. And, Malachy, when you get back, we want to hear a blow by blow account. Bye.'

Her last comment reminded Malachy of one episode during the night which probably explained the tingling in his groin.

Feeling much better suddenly, he went for breakfast.

The dining room was as ornate as the rest of the hotel. Oil paintings on the walls, fine china on the table. Nora was seated at a window, sipping a coffee and smoking a cigarette. She regarded Malachy through the smoke.

'Sit.' She smiled as she spoke. 'Tell me all.'

'A gentleman never tells,' Malachy sniffed.

'That's why I asked you, as you are not a gentleman.'

The arrival of a waitress saved Malachy from having to respond. He ordered the full Irish breakfast.

'No wonder you have a weight problem,' Nora observed.

'Still a babe magnet, Nora. I was fighting them off last night. You would have been proud of me.'

They were joined at the table by Michelle. She too seemed to be smirking at Malachy.

'Did you both have a pleasant evening?' she enquired.

'We both went to bed, anyway' Nora said, smirking again.

Malachy refused to respond, instead checking out his full breakfast, which had just arrived.

'You can tell this is a classy place, Michelle. Anywhere you get a slice of cucumber and a bit of parsley with the fry has definitely got class.'

'So what exactly are you both up to, Nora? I gather you are heading home.'

Malachy's ears pricked up at the word home.

'Are you from Castlecarraig too, Michelle?' he asked

'Did I not mention it, Malachy?' Nora said. ' Michelle is a sister of my dear old friend Eileen, Lord rest her soul.'

'Do you remember the first time you came to our house, Nora?'

'I do indeed, Michelle. It was chaos remember? I'd never seen anything like it. It was just before the wedding. She was cool as a cucumber, though probably not as cool as the one under Malachy's scrambled eggs.'

'Didn't she marry O Murchu?' Malachy asked.

Nora and Michelle exchanged glances.

'That was part of the trouble,' Nora said disapprovingly.

'I knew one of the lads, he went to Uni a few years ahead of me. What's the story? What happened?'

'The story is, Malachy, that Eileen's husband, my dear brother in law Seamus, got deeper and deeper into politics. A few years after they

married and the kids started arriving, Seamus got involved in what they called the border campaign. He was jailed in England for years and when he came out, he got stuck in it again. This time, he was jailed in Ireland. When he came out of there, he was one of their back room generals. Eileen was left to rear a family all on her own. Oh, we all helped out but she was very proud, wasn't she, Nora?'

'She was the proudest person I ever met,' Nora agreed. 'I remember vividly the first time I was introduced to her. Dear old Uncle Tom, as we called him. He was horrified at a member of his staff marrying a well known republican.'

There was silence as both women gazed out the window, seemingly lost in thought.

Malachy wanted to hear the rest of the story.

'Well?' he prompted.

Michelle took up the story.

'Eileen did her level best to keep the children away from politics. She'd seen what it had done to Seamus's family and wanted nothing to do with it. The boy who was at college with you. Kieran was it?'

'That was him, Kieran. He used to drive myself and my mate daft telling us stories about the women and the sex at Uni.'

'Pity he didn't stick to the women and the sex. He followed in his father's republican footsteps. I remember how proud Eileen was when he graduated. She thought he'd get a job at home and forget all the nonsense. He didn't, of course. He went teaching in Dublin but was up to his neck in the struggle, as he liked to call it.'

'Poor Eileen. She was worn out trying to get him out of it.'

'By the way, Malachy' Nora asked, 'since you spent most of the last twenty odd years out of the country, did you ever hear what happened to young O Murchu?'

Malachy thought for a moment.

'I seem to remember that he was jailed.'

'Jailed, released, jailed, released,' Michele said. 'Married during one of his stints out of prison. Managed to father a beautiful little girl. Eileen stormed Heaven, hoping this would be the end of it. Then there was a bank robbery that went horribly wrong. Two of the robbers were killed, one of them was Kieran. He was two days short of his fortieth birthday, the other lad was a nineteen year old from Derry.'

'Eileen died that day too, didn't she Michelle?'

'She never got over it. Seamus was proud, a martyr for Ireland. Eileen said Ireland had enough martyrs. She never spoke to him again, rarely spoke to anyone in fact. Except old Mrs Brown. She was very good to her all along. Eileen used to be a great one for the funerals. After Kieran, Mrs Browns was the only one she went to. That and her own, of course. She literally died of a broken heart.'

'Poor auld O Murchu,' Malachy mused. 'He often tried to recruit some of us into the movement. But I'm afraid, we were more interested in liberating bra straps than the North.'

'Do you have time for a walk, Michelle?' Nora asked. 'I'm sure Malachy can amuse himself for an hour.'

'A walk sounds lovely. Malachy, all the papers are in the lobby. Help yourself. Order all the coffee you want on the house. Order something stronger if you feel like it.'

When the two ladies left, Malachy settled in the lobby to read the papers. He found it impossible to concentrate. He was saddened immensely by what he had heard. O Murchu had been regarded as a bit of a bullshit artist but obviously he had been more active than Malachy had imagined. He smiled when he thought of John Joyce's eyes wide open as O Murchu told them of his sexual encounter on the Belfast train.

He also felt a strange twinge of guilt. Maybe if he and the others had joined up the whole thing might have been settled. He dismissed this thought immediately. He knew from his travels around the world that there were always fanatics who kept the trouble going, no matter what. O Murchu got what he deserved, he supposed, he who lives by the sword and all that. Still, it was hard not to experience a sense of waste. Malachy had been away from Ireland for most of the Troubles. He had joined in sing songs in New York with Provost and worked with an ex SAS man for a while in South Africa. Live and let live had always been his motto. That and there's always time for one more had gotten him thus far.

Malachy was dozing in the oversized armchair in the lobby when the women returned from their walk.

'The sleeping beauty,' Nora said. 'God, anyone would think you were the pensioner in the company, doddering away there. All you want now is a pair of slippers and a rug over you.'

'Nora tells me you met a nice lady last night,' Michelle said.

'A nice lady, indeed she was,' Malachy agreed. 'We had a pleasant evening discussing the finer things in life. We discussed literature, art, cinema. As Nora well knows, I am a master of social intercourse.'

'You were right, Nora,' Michele said. 'He is an incredible bullshitter.'

'Creative is the word, Michelle, creative,' Malachy corrected her. 'I suppose I'd better pay my bill and bring this old one on the road before she croaks on me.'

'Don't worry about the bill, Malachy. I think it's a lovely idea for you and Nora to do what you're doing and I'll sponsor the hotel.'

'And, Malachy,' Nora said with a glint in her eye, 'if what Michelle tells me about the medical condition of your companion of last night is right, you'll be paying for it for a long time.'

Trying not to scratch his crotch, Malachy went to get his bag.

CHAPTER 19

When she and Mrs Brown finished the last of the wine, Nora rose unsteadily to her feet.

'Goodness, I will have to increase my tolerance,' she said. 'I do believe I am a little tipsy.'

'I think you had better go to bed, Nora. We don't want you rambling around in that state. Come, I'll escort you up the stairs.'

Nora slept soundly that night. When she awoke, she had a throbbing headache. She knew immediately that this was because of the wine. Rising slowly, she made her way to the bathroom and splashed water on her face. As she returned to her room, she realised that she had arranged to meet Myles the previous night. She felt guilty but then reflected that following his exchange with Fr Reilly, Myles would probably not have turned up anyway.

When she came downstairs, Mrs Brown was sipping tea in the kitchen.

'You poor dear,' she said when she saw her. 'You look tired. Have some tea. Would you like some breakfast?'

Nora shook her head, and immediately regretted it.

'I didn't realise you had never drunk wine before, Nora. Perhaps we should have taken it more slowly.'

'I'm not as bad as I look. I think I'll have that cup of tea and have a walk around the garden.'

'Excellent idea. Thomas will be here in an hour or so to go to Sunday service.'

Nora stood at the end of Mrs Brown's garden, in the shade of the apple trees. The fresh air soon cleared her head and she felt much better. She noticed a figure walking along the lake shore. As it got closer, she saw that it was Eileen.

Eileen waved and approached the garden wall.

'This is a surprise,' Nora said.

'I've actually been watching the house for a while, hoping to see you.'

'Is there something wrong?'

'Very. Fr Reilly came to my house last night, asking about you. He told my mother you were a bad influence, a troublemaker. Somebody must have told him we are friends, probably someone in the shop. My mother was mortified, the priest coming to complain. My father got a great laugh out of it. '

'I'm so sorry. What did Fr Reilly say to you?'

'He said that I had a duty to talk to you about Myles. I told him I did not think I had any duty at all. He said I would be looking for a church in a few days for my wedding and bringing my children for Baptism and if I did not do my duty now, he would remember it in future. So I agreed to speak to you.'

'But all I ever did was talk to a young man. That's all. Why is everybody getting so upset?'

'Come around here and walk with me, Nora.'

Nora went around to the garden gate and joined Eileen outside. The walked along the lakeshore, linking arms.

'I did tell you, Nora, that there would be trouble,' Eileen said.

'I never dreamed it would come to this. What can I do?'

'The choices are still the same, Nora. See Myles again and risk great unhappiness. Never see again and be unhappy for a while.'

Nora looked miserably at her fried.

'Last night, I drank alcohol for the first time. Even though I paid dearly for it this morning, I still think it was important to try it. I need to talk to Myles again. I need to look him in the eye and to hear him tell me that this is what he wants. I don't know how I'll arrange to meet him though.'

She looked at Eileen as she spoke the last words.

'Oh my,' Eileen laughed, ' you really have learned a lot since you came here. You can be an evil woman, Nora, and I think Fr Reilly is absolutely right to keep you from the young and innocent. You obviously want me to get involved, don't you? You want me to risk my wedding and my children's immortal souls so you can have a chat with your priesthteen, don't you?'

Nora just looked demure and proper, pouting her lower lip.

'May God and Fr Reilly forgive me. Right, listen. Come along to the Royal next Saturday after work. At about seven o clock, I'll be dancing the wedding waltz with my handsome new husband. I'll tell Myles to slip out as I'm dancing. There's a tiny garden behind the hotel. You can meet him there and nobody need know anything about it.'

Nora smiled at her friend

'And I didn't even have to ask,' she said.

When Nora got back to the house, Mrs Brown had another pot of tea ready.

'Thomas does like his tea,' she said. 'He is the most punctual man I know.'

As she spoke, there was a knock at the front door. Nora opened it and Thomas stood there in his Sunday finery. Nora had to admit he was an attractive figure of a man. His pin stripe suit was well cut and black leather shoes had been polished to a bright shine. His hair was sleeked and smelt pleasantly of scented oil.

Stepping into the hall, he beamed at Nora.

'I have a treat in store today,' he announced. Nora followed him to the sitting room, where Mrs Brown had cups of tea waiting.

'Mrs Brown, Nora. It is such a lovely day, I have taken the liberty of packing a picnic lunch. After Service, I propose we drive to the sea side. What do you say?'

Mrs Browne looked at Nora.

'Are you up to it, my dear?' she enquired.

'It would be nice to see some of the country side. Thank you, Thomas.'

They sat together in the small congregation. Nora loved the atmosphere in the church. The regimental flags that lined the walls linked her with the imperial past and glories of her people. The rector had served as chaplain to a parachute regiment in the war just finished and always prefaced his homilies with a description of some scene of destruction and death that he had witnessed. His voice echoed his Home Counties upbringing. Like the flags, this served to remind Nora of her heritage and culture. Today, however, a different voice, a different accent , a different clergyman intruded on her thoughts.

She thought back on her conversation with Eileen. No doubt her warnings were true enough. Myles was almost untouchable. Being a Catholic excluded him from her society almost completely. Being a student priest removed the almost from the sentence.

Filing from the church, they were greeted by the Canon.

'Mrs Brown, Thomas, Miss Fortune. Bless you all on this wonderful Summer's day. How are you enjoying our little community, Miss Fortune?'

'It is lovely, Canon. Everybody has been so friendly.'

'Friendly, yes, everybody is. That is the most important thing of all, that and love. Must keep that to the fore. No doubt. Well, see you all.'

As the Canon went off to greet another group of parishioners, Mrs Brown smiled and shook her head.'

'Poor old dear,' she said. 'They say he saw too much in the war. Still, at least he doesn't go on for ever like his predecessor. Now, Thomas, lead us to your trusty chariot and whisk us away.'

Thomas's chariot was a shiny new Ford Prefect. Inside, the smell of leather welcomed the passengers. Mrs Browne insisted on sitting in the back. She said she still did not feel too comfortable travelling at such high speeds.

As they drove towards the coast, Thomas gave a running commentary on the scenery and landscape.

'That ugly building is the local mental institution. I imagine many of the poor souls are there because of loneliness. And some because of the local propensity for alcohol.'

A cough from the back seat caused Nora to smile. Thomas was too distracted to notice.

'That, of course,' he continued, 'is the upper end of the lake you can see from your garden. My father used to fish for pike there, a pastime for which I myself have little inclination. All these little hills, I read somewhere, were formed during the ice age millions of years ago. I mentioned this to Canon Warren a little while ago and he referred me to the Bible for the story of creation.

'The place names are all taken from the Irish language, so beloved of our Mr O Murchu and his compatriots. This town land is called Ballygowna, which means town of the goats. Apparently there was a goat fair here years ago.'

As Nora listened, she was impressed by his love of the area. Even though she had heard him speak often of his detachment from the community, he had an obvious affection for the place and it's people. She wondered if she would ever have the chance to become so close to the area.

'And now, ladies, we are entering the lovely village of Westport. Notice the lovely layout as we descend the hill. That mountain looming a little to the west is called after St Patrick. Legend has it that he spent forty days and nights there. Our Catholic brethren climb it in their thousands every year, many in their bare feet.'

'Why ever do they do that?' Nora asked.

'To atone for past sins, my dear,' he answered.

'And think up future ones, no doubt,' Mrs Brown sniffed from the back seat.

'Quite,' Thomas smiled. 'The parson says that such short bursts of piety are the work of the devil.' He laughed heartily at this. Nora noticed how relaxed he was and how he had an attractive face when he was not frowning or worried looking.

'And that island has quite a history to. Perhaps I'll take you there some day, Nora. In fact, I'll definitely take you there. It was home to pirates for centuries, including one lady pirate who had something of a fearsome reputation at the time.'

The town was quiet as they passed through, with just a few men standing at the doors of the public houses, waiting, no doubt thought Nora, for them to open.

They travelled along the coast for another few miles, Thomas driving quietly, as if allowing the breath taking scenery to speak for itself. They passed by the very base of the holy mountain and gazing upward, Nora could clearly see the small church on the peak against the blue sky. A few minutes later and she was standing on the most beautiful beach she had ever seen. Golden sand stretched for miles while the sea had the deepest imaginable shade of blue. The pirate island dominated the horizon.

'Let us have cup of tea,' Thomas suggested.

The boot of the car seemed huge to Nora. Thomas removed from it a small table, three folding chairs, several baskets and an enormous vacuum flask. Soon, they were seated, enjoying strong, sweet tea. A few other small groups of people had set up along the beach. The sun was warm and a gentle breeze, smelling of sea weed, added to their comfort. Mrs Brown's head began to nod and soon, she was asleep.

'I wished to have a talk with you, Nora, if I may be so bold,' Thomas said.

Nora noticed he was his nervous self again. She felt apprehensive, wondering what it was he was about to say.

Thomas stood up and stood facing the sea, hands clasped behind his back.

'I know, Nora, from what Fr Reilly says, and indeed from the evidence of my own eyes, that you have formed, shall we say, an affection, that is possibly an attraction, to young Myles. A handsome man, no doubt, but also, no doubt, a state of affairs that can only lead to terrible conclusions. He, dear Nora, is not, and indeed, never can be a match for you.' Here he cleared his throat and stared even more intently at the ocean.

'I, on the other hand, am a, shall we say, bachelor, a man that is, of an unmarried status. Please, allow me to continue,' he said as Nora began to speak. 'I will never speak of this again if that is your wish but for now, indulge me, please, dear Nora. I have not had the pleasure of female company for many years. I have, never, in fact, been fortunate enough to get to know any woman. Having spent these last few months watching you in my shop and elsewhere, indeed, I have formed what I would call a deep fondness for you. I realise I am much older and not perhaps as dashing as the soon to be Father Myles, but I do possess certain advantages as an eligible suitor.'

Here he paused and looked at Nora. She was regarding him with such a mixture of affection and sadness that he could not go on. Neither of them spoke. Then Thomas turned away and walked down the beach.

Nora closed her eyes. She had never really regarded Thomas as a man, much less a suitor. She had to admit, however, that lately she had noticed certain changes, like that morning as they travelled together and he spoke with such warmth and feeling.

She wished Eileen was there to talk to, to try to work out the emotions going through her. A few short months previously, she had not even considered a relationship with a man, now she was facing a dilemma.

She considered following Thomas and trying to speak to him. Before she could do so, there was a stir to her left and Mrs Brown woke up.

'Goodness, I must be getting old. I don't usually doze in the middle of the day. You are a bad influence on me, Nora, drinking and staying up late. Where's Thomas?'

'He went for a stroll.'

'That's unlike him. He is, you know, a lonely man. He seems to be so absorbed in his business and the shop that he doesn't have time for any other life. But, he is a man, after all. Did he say anything to you?'

'Were you really asleep, you old fox?' Nora asked smiling.

'Oh, I was asleep, alright. Still, I have a woman's intuition and a country woman's eye for what's going on. We really will have to decide what we are going to do about poor Thomas. He is getting more infatuated by the day.'

Nora glanced around her, at the blue sea, golden sand, the stark mountain.

'It really is such a beautiful world. Why do we have to complicate it with infatuations and affections and men?' she asked.

Mrs Brown laughed.

'Thomas and I often drive over here when the pilgrimage is on. It really is amazing. Literally thousands of people climbing, many of them barefoot. Pilgrims cycle here from all over the county. Their bicycles line the ditches on both sides of the road for miles. There are little huts selling beads and statues. The little pub supplies tea and sandwiches, as well as oceans of alcohol. The point is Nora, it looks like chaos. But, once the people reach the top, they tell me, there is a great sense of peace and calm. Life is like that too.

'I knew Monty for years. I never saw him as more than a neighbour. Then, out of the blue, he asked my parents if he could take me out. My feelings were a bit like the scene at the foot of the mountain, rather chaotic. Then, as time went on, we settled into a comfortable journey with each other. I thought we had reached the peak but, as you well know, life did not quite follow the pilgrim's path for us. For another while, my life was chaos. It took a lot more to get back on even keel the second time. I was on my own, everything had been stolen from me. I experienced such dreadful loneliness. I still do and there really is not a lot I can do. Thomas, though. He sees a chance now, an opportunity to fill a huge emptiness in his life.'

'Tell me what to do, please,' Nora pleaded.

'I will not tell you what to do,' Mrs Browne said, shaking her head, ' but I will tell you what I would do. You need to meet both men and spend some time with them. Be true to yourself but be honest. Ask yourself which man will be best for you, not just today or next week but for the rest of your life. When you are my age, and I am fifty seven, and if you ever tell anyone that, I will drown you, you will have to look back at the choices you made. You will have to decide not only if you are happy, but how many others you have made happy as well.'

'Maybe if I could become a nun,' Nora said miserably, 'then all my troubles would be over.'

'Oh dear, now that would be a bit drastic. I don't think the good nuns have as simple a life as all that. My good friend, Mrs Hoban, who brings me the eggs and milk, saw two of her lovely daughters leave last month for a life of the cloth. It takes great courage, Nora, and while I do not doubt your courage, I don't think a convent is really the answer to you problems.'

Nora nodded, smiling ruefully.

'I will be seeing Myles next week,' she admitted. 'At Eileen Tracey's wedding.'

'And Thomas invited you to Clare Island. Why not take up his generous offer? There is no place more romantic to encourage him or reject him. Look at him, Nora,' she said, indicating with her eyes.

Thomas was indeed walking towards them. Hands behind his back and head bowed, it was difficult for Nora not to feel sorry for him.

'Thank you, Mrs Brown,' she said. 'Let's get his lunch ready and show him he still matters to us.'

When Thomas arrived at the table, the two women had the lunch laid out.

'You went to so much trouble, Thomas,' Mrs Brown said. 'We are so fortunate here in the West to have such lovely country side and beaches. You should show Nora more of it really.'

'I would love to visit the island over there. I've actually never been on an island,' Nora remarked casually, gazing towards the sea.

Thomas looked to Mrs Brown but she had closed her eyes again and was sitting back in her chair. He knew there was something going on which he could not grasp. He was terrified to say anything in case it was the wrong thing. He sat in silence, a chicken leg in one hand, a cup of lemonade in the other. It was Mrs Brown who broke the silence.

'For God's sake, Thomas. Invite her to the bloody island!'

CHAPTER 20

Malachy and Rose spent as many hours as they could together in the days that followed. Malachy had a job in the local bacon factory and each day he rushed home, had his tea and doused himself in Cossack hair spray and Old Spice to cover the lingering smell of dead pigs.

He and Rose spent their evenings walking by the lake or sitting in the park. On wet nights, they went to the pictures. No matter where they went, they kissed and kissed and kissed. Malachy now considered himself an accomplished kisser. He was now trying to get his hand into her blouse. Rose had her own ideas about this also. She gently stopped his roving hands but each night, teasingly, she allowed him an extra centimetre or so of flesh.

Malachy was content enough to allow this to continue. Going out with an English girl had given him huge status. He allowed the lads of the town to believe he was on the pig's back in the courting stakes. If any of them asked how he was getting on, he smiled at them in a patronising way and told them a gentleman never told.

The only thing that really worried Malachy was what was happening between John Joyce and Breege. John was working with a local painter for the Summer. Since he had passed his eighteenth birthday, he was prone to go to the pub most nights. Rose had no interest in pub life, she had informed Malachy. Growing up in the Irish community in London, she told him, she had seen enough of the damage done by alcohol. Her own father, she told him, was an alcoholic, although he had not touched a drop for years. Now, he was fiercely anti drink and threatened dire retribution on any of his family that ever came home with even a whiff of drink. Malachy had seen her father when he dropped or collected her in town. Though he was not a tall man, he was broad and tough looking. He had gone to England as a sixteen year old. Once he gave up the booze, he had set up his own plant hire business and had become very wealthy. Malachy understood when he looked at him just why the family respected his wishes.

It suited Malachy not to go to the pub. His few forays into boozing sessions ended with him being very, very sick the following morning. Instead, each day as he wheeled barrows of pigs innards around the factory, he looked forward to Rose and kisses.

After two days in the factory, Malachy had decided a labouring life was not for him. Like all young lads, he had to work in what was called the gut room. As the animals were slaughtered, their innards were collected in large barrels. Malachy collected these barrels and wheeled them to the gut room. Here, he had to separate the intestines and he and the other lads had to squeeze all the shite out of the intestines. The empty tube was then thrown into a vat of boiling water for future use as casing for sausages and puddings.

The work was filthy and mind numbingly boring. He started at eight, had a ten minute tea break at eleven, lunch from one to two and finished at five. The lads from the gut room had the indignity of having a table of the canteen to themselves.

One morning, as Malachy was crossing the road from the gut room to the canteen, he was surprised to see Marian waiting outside.

'I always fancied a man in uniform,' she greeted him, wrinkling her nose in disgust at the sight of his blood and gut stained clothes.

'Tends to drive women daft, alright, Marian,' he replied. 'Is that why you came up, to have a quick thrill?'

'Yeah, that bit of grey stuff hanging out of the pocket of your apron will keep we awake at nights, alright. Seriously, have you seen John Joyce lately?'

'I've bumped into him around the place but I've been busy.'

'I know, between the guts and the roses, right?'

'Listen, Marian, I have a ten minute break and I need to get the taste of the innards of two hundred pigs out of my throat. What's bothering you?'

'I'm worried about Breege. She's in a bad way.'

At the mention of Breege's name, Malachy mellowed.

'Tell you what, Marian, I'll meet you in the park at seven. How's that?'

The whistle sounded, signalling the end of tea break.

'Thanks, Malachy. Make sure you brush your teeth before you meet herself tonight. English girls prefer tooth paste to pigs guts any day. See you at seven.'

Malachy found it hard to concentrate on his work for the rest of the day. Fortunately for him, wheeling and cleaning guts did not take a lot of concentration. He thought about what Marian had said. 'In a bad way' sounded ominous. He realised the worst possible scenario would be that she was pregnant. On the other hand, it could be simply a case of her missing John and wanting Malachy to arrange a get together. As he squeezed the shite out of a particularly lengthy intestine, Malachy allowed himself to fantasise that Breege had suddenly realised it was him all along that she really loved and wanted to declare her undying devotion to him.

His pleasant imaginings were interrupted by the voice of one of his workmates.

''Tis only a piece of inteshtine, Malachy, shtop shmiling at it and get another barrel load of it.'

That evening, Malachy arrived at the park ten minutes before seven. He usually met Rose there between eight and half past. She still had two weeks of her holiday left and Malachy often wondered if he was in love. As he sat waiting for Breege, he compared how he felt about Rose with his feelings for Breege. Rose certainly made him feel comfortable and relaxed and she was a fantastic kisser. Breege made him feel like jelly all over and made him want to shower her with kisses and walk along beaches at sunset, holding hands and laughing. He was sure she was a fantastic kisser as well. The most important difference between the two, he had to concede, was that his relationship with Rose was real, while his relationship with Breege was in his head only. Rose, on the other hand, would be gone soon and Breege would still be around. Having said that, Rose actually held and kissed him while Breege had never indicated the least bit of physical interest in him. As he ruminated on these things, sitting alone on a park bench, Malachy scratched his crotch and thought life was indeed complicated.

Marian eventually arrived at quarter past.

'You don't look as dashing as you did earlier, Malachy,' she greeted him. 'Still, a few of the girls have remarked that you have smartened up since you started courting the Brit.'

Malachy was chuffed at the compliment. Rose, in fact, had taken him on a tour of a couple of men's shops and pointed out a few combinations of shirts and trousers that would suit him. Tonight, he was wearing one of those combos, jeans and denim shirt.

'So, what's the problem, Marian? You didn't call today so we could talk about my clothes.'

'John will be fierce keen to borrow your trousers now, I suppose. Speaking of whom,' Marian paused and surprised Malachy by taking a packet of Silk Cut from her cardigan pocket. A box of matches came from the other pocket. She offered Malachy the packet.

'When did you start?' he asked her shaking his head.

'Oh, I've always wanted to smoke. I think it looks elegant and mature, don't you?'

'Not really. Foul breath and smoky clothes don't really do anything for me.'

'That coming from a lad I saw today with bits of pig gut hanging from him really worries me. So, have you seen Joyce lately?'

'Only in passing. Why do you ask?'

'You remember what happened the night we finished the exams, up the lake? He hasn't spoken to Breege since. She's heart broken over the miserable bastard.'

'What do you want me to do about it? You know how I felt about Breege and she chose John. Why should I give a toss about the pair of them?'

Marian squinted at him through a cloud of cigarette smoke. Malachy did not think she looked elegant or mature, just cross eyed.

'You don't fool me, Malachy. You're the nice one, all the girls still say that. And, I know you still fancy her, in spite of your little bit of English fluff.'

She was right, of course, but Malachy remained silent.

'Malachy,' Marian leaned closer to him, 'I'm afraid Breege might be in trouble'

Malachy still did not speak.

'I don't mean she was caught smoking, Malachy or that she stayed out late. She could be pregnant.'

'What's it to do with me?' Malachy blurted. 'Did I throw me leg over her, did I? Did I poke her, did I? What has any of this got to do with me?'

'She needs all the friends she can get, Malachy. I know she treated you badly and everyone knew you were crazy about her. But she needs you now, Malachy.'

'What can I do? If she's snigged, she's snigged. If she's not, she can go back and try again.'

'No, no, Malachy, I know you better than that. You're only saying those horrible things because she hurt you. You know you wouldn't let anything happen to Breege.'

'OK, Marian,' he said. 'But really, what can I do?'

'It's not you as such, Malachy, but your English friend I want to talk to.'

'Rose? Why?'

''Because me and Breege have not a clue how to find out if she's expecting or not and what to do if she is. I think Rosey might be able to help. This kind of thing goes on in England all the time.'

'Her name is Rose, but why should she help?'

'Because she's a woman. Because she's crazy about you and if you ask her, she'll help.'

Malachy thought about this for a while. He was terrified to think that Breege might be pregnant. He only knew of one case in town of a girl that had been rumoured to have gotten pregnant outside of marriage. He remembered vaguely that she had gone away for a while and the man involved had gone to New Zealand.

'You're right about one thing, anyway, Marian. I'll do whatever I can to help out. Does John have any idea of what the crack is?'

'Not a clue that he'll admit to,' she answered. 'I tried to talk to him a few times but he ignores me. You'll have to talk to him, Malachy, get him to contact Breege. She really is in an awful way.'

Marian lit another cigarette.

'Remember the day we went to his sister's house and we met in the snack bar afterwards?' she asked.

'Vaguely,' Malachy said.

'Liar. I told you your face was like a book. I can tell you're worried about Breege. I know well you still fancy her, even if your bit of London fluff is giving you a good time. I know you'll help, Malachy, won't you?'

'I said I would. I'll be meeting Rose here in a whileen. I'll see if I can find John later. Today is Thursday. He usually goes to the Frenchman's Inn for the music on Thursday nights. I'll see if I can spot him. What will I say if he's there?'

'Tell him to stop being such a bollocks and do the decent thing and contact Breege. Tell him if you want that she might be in trouble and that might put a fire under him. Maybe I should go myself, I'd soon sort him out.'

'No, no, I'll talk to him. Can you get Breege here maybe tomorrow evening and we'll take it from there?'

Marian smiled at him.

'Rosey is a very lucky English girl, Malachy. I hope she looks after you and if she doesn't, I'll sort her out as well. Tomorrow night it is then.'

Malachy sat alone in the park. It was over a month since the party by the lake. He'd been so occupied with pigs insides, and indeed Roses outsides, that he had not really felt the time pass. He and John had talked vaguely earlier in the year about climbing Croagh Patrick at the end of the month and he had hoped that that would have got them going as friends again. That pilgrimage was only two days away now. He decided he'd ask John if he saw him if he was still interested in the climb. If he was, he wouldn't mention Breege until then. If they were on top of a mountain, he reckoned, John Joyce would have nowhere to run.

CHAPTER 21

It did not take Malachy long to pack. A tooth brush, a razor and change of shirt and drawers all fitted neatly and quickly into his overnight bag. His years of living out of suitcases had taught him a lot about travelling light. His head was still throbbing slightly so he reached for the one other item he always packed, a packet of Panadol, and swallowed two of them.

Nora was not at reception when he came back down. Michelle was behind the desk. She came around to him.

'She's a great old trooper, isn't she,' she asked.

'Oh, she's that alright. She seems to have been very fond of your sister.'

'Eileen worshipped her. I was a teenager at the time this whole business happened so I remember it all very well.'

Malachy did not ask her what she meant by the "whole business". He felt it was important that he allow Nora to tell him whatever was left to be told.

'What was Nora like those days?' he asked instead.

'She was so elegant and sophisticated. The day she came to our house it was like pearls before swine. She was so beautiful. But you felt she did not know just how beautiful she was. All my brothers were drooling after her. Even my father, God rest him, was struck by her. No wonder she had her pick of the men.'

Michelle took Malachy's elbow and led him outside. The sky had become overcast and a slight mist was falling.

'Nora only spent a Summer in Castlecarraig. She touched so many lives in that short time you would not believe. There are a lot of memories there, Malachy. I'm sure you have a few ghosts there yourself. Take care of her and take care of yourself as well. If things get too serious, come back here straight away. I'll keep a couple of rooms free to be on the safe side. Nora deserves every happiness, Malachy, and we'll do our bit.'

Michelle went back inside. A few moments later, the hotel door opened again and Michelle came out again, accompanied by Nora.

Michelle walked to the Merc with them.

'Are you insured to drive my car, Malachy, do you think,' Nora asked.

'Insured to drive and licensed to thrill,' Malachy answered.

'God,' Nora said, 'he's off. Michelle, thank you for your kind and wonderful hospitality. We may see you on the way back, if we are still on speaking terms. Home Malachy, and don't spare the horses.'

'Certainly, madam, home it is.'

The Merc was a joy to drive. Malachy had driven all kinds of cars over the years, from battered old Land Rovers in Africa to top of the range Fords in the USA but he had never driven a Mercedes. It took a few minutes to get used to the vagaries of the car but he knew that by the time he got to the open road, he would be rearing to go.

Galway looked the worst for wear this damp Sunday. Fast food wrappers and cider cans littered the streets. Broken glass lay on the footpath outside several pubs. He had spent four years here at Uni and couldn't remember it being this grotty. He took a detour around Wood Quay to see his old digs but the building was gone, replaced by an apartment complex. He mentioned this to Nora.

'I don't expect to recapture my past entirely on this trip Malachy. Some of the past connections are well and truly buried. But you have your memory of those digs, you know what they were like and what they meant for you. Isn't that something?'

'It's something alright, Nora, but fuck me if I have any idea what that thing is.'

The cloud was beginning to clear as they drove through the sprawl of housing estates that clung to the side of the city.

'Scenic route or good road?' Malachy asked.

'Your scenic enough for me, Malachy, take the good road.'

Malachy followed the series of roundabouts that brought him to the Tuam Road. Even though it was Sunday morning, the traffic was heavy, mostly new cars, with a lot of four wheel drive vehicles that would never see rough terrain.

'You should get one of those yokes, Nora,' Malachy said. 'A big four wheel drive, make a statement about what you are.'

'If I want to make a statement that I am a pretentious wanker, I'll take out an ad in the paper. I've seen some of Felicity's friends with those monsters, all noise and power.'

'And that's just the husbands,' Malachy quipped.

'Quite, Malachy. But I really get annoyed when I see one of these jeep things being used as a family bus. It's like having a prime greyhound as a house pet.'

'You can be such an old hypocrite, Nora. Here you are giving out about Felicity's friends and their cars and at the same time, you are driving round in a top of the range luxury car, when a Morris Minor is what a pensioner like you should be driving.'

Nora laughed at this.

'Malachy, do you remember what Margaret Thatcher said about being a lady.? "Being powerful is like being a lady, if you have to be told you are, then you are not". Or something like that.'

Malachy drove in silence. Nora regarded him with curiosity.

'There's something on your mind, Malachy. You know, your face is like a book. I can read it very easily.'

This time it was Malachy's turn to laugh.

'The legibility of my face has been my downfall for years, with women and poker players. There is one thing though, that I have been trying to figure out.'

'And what might that be?'

'You told me you had to go to Castlecarraig in the first place because your family was going through bad times. You worked as a clerk in a huckster's shop in a small town. And now you're talking about people as if they are somehow your social inferiors.'

'That's because they are my social inferiors, Malachy. Have you not being paying attention?'

'And am I included as a social inferior?'

'Of course! Oh, I know you've been educated and got your degrees in Galway and America, and you've travelled and stayed in the best hotels. You know how to act and speak socially. But, Malachy there is a natural order of things.'

Malachy said nothing.

'Now you're sulking,' Nora said.

Malachy said nothing.

'Oh dear, you don't see it, do you, Malachy? Yes my family fell on hard times and I had to go out to work with the great unwashed. But I never have forgotten where I came from. And that's the difference between me and the four wheel drivers. I know and I am comfortable with where I came from. I am so proud of my Protestant, old establishment background. I am fiercely protective of my vicars and country houses and rose gardens. But what do these jumped up peasants stand for? What do you stand for, Malachy? What do you connect with? Are you so removed that you are past connecting?"

'Right, you've made your point.' Malachy conceded.

They had arrived at the outskirts of a small town in south Galway.

'There now Malachy, is a classic example of what I'm talking about,' Nora said as they were passing by a hotel. 'Stop here. Come inside and we'll have a coffee and I'll explain.'

When he had parked the car they went into the hotel. To Malachy, it was a well built and tasteful building. He pointed this out to Nora.

'Of course it is,' she replied.

The staff were young, attractive and friendly. Their order was taken by a cheerful teenaged girl who flirted with Malachy. Malachy preened under her attention.

'So, what is wrong with this lovely place?' he demanded.

'Do you remember what was here before the hotel was built here?' Nora asked.

Malachy thought for a moment. He had passed through the place hundreds of times years before. Then he realised.

'It was a convent,' he said.

'Exactly,' Nora said with a satisfied grin. 'A convent. It stood for something, didn't it?'

'The past pupils might say it stood for thumps and sticks.'

'They might Malachy, as they drop off their spoilt kids in their four wheel drives. But be honest, what did a convent stand for?'

'Commitment,' Malachy said reluctantly.

'And?' she prompted.

'Faith, community. Serenity.'

'Very good, Malachy. And a hotel stands for what?'

'Progress,' Malachy said with an air of triumph. 'Progress, employment. And craic.'

'And so,' Nora said with surprising gentleness, ' progress and craic are a fair trade for serenity and commitment. Is that what you believe?'

'O Murchu and his buddies were right,' Malachy replied frowning, ' your lot should have been driven back into the sea and left us poor unfortunates alone. We were doing nicely.'

'I rest my case, Malachy. Finish up that vile coffee and make that young girl's day by leaving her a decent tip and then leaving her life. Come on then.'

Back in the car, Malachy looked at Nora as they put on their seat belts.

'You know, Nora, you can be a right bitch.'

'Malachy, you ain't heard nothin' yet.'

CHAPTER 22

The open air and late night took their toll on the two women. The journey back from the beach passed in silence. Thomas made no observations on the passing scenery and Nora looked glumly at the passing landscape. Mrs Brown sat in regal seclusion in the back seat.

Arriving back at Mrs Brown's house, Thomas opened the doors for them and escorted them to the front door.

Mrs Brown went inside with a wave at him but Nora paused on the door step.

'Thank you for a lovely drive and the beautiful lunch, Thomas.'

Thomas smiled shyly. Once again, Nora was struck the fact that he was a handsome man.

'I trust, Nora, that I have not done irreparable damage to our friendship. However, I make no apology for what I said. I will trouble you no more about it but if you should ever wish to speak of it, I will be waiting. In the meantime, I shall see you in the shop tomorrow and I shall make arrangements for us to visit the island as soon as I can. Good evening to you.'

As he raised his cap, Nora leaned forward and kissed him on the cheek before stepping inside and closing the door.

After a light supper Mrs Brown announced that she was retiring early. She had , she said, a good book and a lot to think about. She suggested that Nora also had a good deal of thinking to do and suggested that she too should sleep on her problems. A good nights sleep usually cleared the mind she always found.

Nora agreed and they bade each other good night.

Sleep, however, proved elusive. Nora lay in her bed, gazing at the darkening sky through her window. There was silence apart from the occasional passer-by.

She closed her eyes and considered her options. There was no doubt that any relationship with Myles was fraught with problems. The parish priest was a powerful man. Myles' family would do every thing in their power to make sure their son finished his priestly training and brought whatever status that conveyed to them. Then there were all his neighbours and the people of the town. To offend them would have possible ramifications for Thomas.

Thomas. He had never entered Nora's mind as a possible suitor. She had, until today, regarded him as the kindly uncle he was. He had treated her with nothing but respect and kindness. He was, however, at least by Nora's reckoning, twice her age. On the other hand, she reluctantly conceded to herself, he was a wealthy and successful man while Myles himself was essentially a penniless seminarian. Nora had watched as her own family slid from well to do comfort to discrete poverty as her father's health and business failed. Her early years were spent with servants and in comfort that the local population certainly regarded as luxury.

Mrs Brown's stories of the grandeur of the cricket ground echoed her own parents' tales of colonial pomp. Her father used to bring her to Dublin on occasion and walk her through the still elegant parts of the city. He often stood with her outside Trinity College and showed her the old Parliament buildings. They would go to the General Post Office and he would point out the bullet marks on the walls.

'We are like those walls,' he remarked once. ' We used to be proud, in control. Now, if we do not stand together, we too will be destroyed.'

When she was no more than five or six, he brought her and her brothers and sister to Dublin once to see people gather for what was called a Eucharistic Congress. They stood outside the GPO that day too, watching people pass in their tens of thousands. Nora could still remember the lines upon lines of priests and nuns as they marched in full regalia. The crowds were singing strange songs that thrilled her and confused her. As they returned home on the train, her father spoke very little. As they were having tea later, she remembered telling her mother all about the parade, the music and the colours.

When she was putting the children to bed that night, her mother told them: 'Remember, that was once our city.'

These were the thoughts and memories that meandered through her mind as she tried to sleep years later in Castlecarraig.

Eventually, sleep did come and she awoke the next morning feeling at least a little rested.

In the shop, she noticed that Thomas seemed a little distant. She asked him at lunch time if he was alright.

'Still a little embarrassed, actually, Nora, about my little indiscretion if you like.,' he told her.

'There is no need, Thomas,' Nora assured him. 'I actually spent a lot of time thinking last night about what you said. I really want to finish that conversation with you. You have been absolutely generous and kind to me since I arrived and you deserve my respect and gratitude, and my time. So, when do we go to the island.'

Thomas smiled and Nora smiled with him.

'Next Sunday, weather permitting,' he answered.

As Nora sat poring over her work later, she realised she was going to have a busy and fateful weekend. Saturday, she was going to meet Myles at a Roman Catholic wedding and Sunday she was being taken to an isolated island by a handsome, single man.

'My oh my,' she thought happily, ' haven't I grown up?'

The weather for the rest of the week was cold and showery so she spent most of her free time at home with Mrs Brown.

She met Eileen as she was going to work one morning.

'I hope the weather will be better on Saturday,' Nora said to her.

'I have no doubt about that at all,' her friend replied.

'You sound very optimistic,' Nora said.

'Optimism has nothing to so with it, Nora, it's all faith. That's one huge advantage we ignorant peasants have over you. All we have to do is put a statue of the Infant of Prague in the garden for seven weeks and we are guaranteed fine weather.'

'Does it work, though?'

'Not only does it work but when we're married, I'll stick a shilling to the base and we'll never know a poor day.'

'I can't see Thomas putting such faith in statues, somehow.'

'That skinflint must have forty pounds under forty statues he has so much of it. Are you set for Saturday?'

'Seven in the Royal? I'll be there.'

Thomas's new found capacity to surprise was demonstrated again Saturday morning. He came into Nora's cubicle and handed her an envelope.

'I have a favour to ask of you, Nora, if you are not too busy.'

'Not at all, Thomas, what can I do for you?'

'I have a docket I wish to have delivered to the Religious Brothers' monastery. I realise it is unusual to ask but I would be obliged. Do you know where the monastery is?'

'Of course, Thomas, it's next to the Catholic Chu…' Suddenly it dawned on Nora what he had in mind. ' Why yes, Thomas, I'd be delighted. I should get there before eleven, shouldn't I?'

'That would be perfect,' Thomas said, smiling.

Walking to the Monastery, Nora realised the sun was shining. 'I'll have to get one of those infant statues myself,' she thought

Climbing the steps to the Monastery door, she saw the first guests arriving at the Catholic church. The door was answered by a fresh faced countryman, with a long black robe like garment and two white shiny rectangular pieces of material beneath his throat.

'And who have weah here, at awl, at awl?' he greeted her.

'My name is Nora Fortune, sir, and I work for Williams and Sons.'

'Do oo indeed,' he boomed. ' and to fwhat do I owe th'honour of oor wisit, Miss Forten? Tis not offen weah get cawled on by gir'ills as prettyeah as oo, unfortunatelyeah.'

Nora found she had to concentrate to interpret what he was saying.

'I have a docket for you,' she said handing him the envelope.

Another figure came to the door and Nora found herself face to face with Myles. There was an awkward silence.

The Brother looked form one to the other. Then his eyes narrowed.

'I hov oo now, young ladyeah. Ou work for oor uncle Tomas. I work for the Lawrd. I teach the bys Lawtin but I awlso encourage vocations in the bys. Tis a great ting to recognise a by called by the Lawrd and see him go on to follow his holy vocation. Tis a terrible ting to turn a by from thot. Off oo go, now, Miss Forten. Myles, I hov wan or two more tings for oo inside.'

'I'll call for them later, Brother. I must go the church to assist at a wedding' Myles said. 'The happy couple will be arriving any moment. Excuse me.'

He walked towards the gate with Nora. They were interrupted by a call from the door.

'Miss Forten, can oo come back a minute?'

Myles shrugged and Nora went back to the door.

'Miss Forten,' the Brother, eyes narrowed and tongue licking his lips in a way that reminded her of a lizard. ' Oor uncle Tomas makes his living in dis town. People would take a dim view if ony of his fomily was to spile a priesht. I'll be honest with oo, Miss Forten, I gave Myles a word of warning. In Ra'more in Countyeah Kerryeah, I towld him, we do say dat dere are tree tings in life to beware of. De horn of a bull, de hoof of a horsh and de smile of de Saxon. Oo smile a lot, don't oo?'

'I have absolutely no idea what you are talking about,' Nora said.

'Hoven't oo, now?' he said, tongue licking rapidly. ' De brudders will be in dis town long after oo and all belonging to oo are forgotten. Good day to oo.'

When Nora reached the gate, Myles was outside.

'I do apologise,' he began. 'I know our innocent chats have been misconstrued into something terrible. I am sorry if it caused any difficulty.'

'I have been educated about life in rural Ireland in the past few weeks, I must admit.,' Nora answered.

Before they could continue, a shiny black car parked outside the church. Seamus O Murchu stepped out, dressed immaculately in the new suit. His hair was sleeked back and even at the distance of several yards, Nora could smell the sweet scent of the oil.

'I'd better rush,' Myles said. ' I hope we get a chance to talk again.'

'Perhaps we shall, Myles,' Nora said as he left.

Nora would have loved to enter the church but she knew, without looking, that she was being watched from the monastery. She crossed the road and stood in the shade of a cherry blossom tree.

Another car arrived. Eileen's father emerged through the back door and offered his hand to Eileen, who followed him out. She looked radiant. Her suit fitted her beautifully and she wore a small, pink hat that had a net that covered her face. In her hands, she held a beautiful bouquet of wild flowers. As her father turned to close the door of the car, Eileen glanced in Nora's direction. She recognised her friend immediately. Running awkwardly in the tight skirt of her suit, she came over to her and hugged her.

'This makes my day. Will you make it later?' she asked.

'I'll be there. I have so much to tell you. Go on or you'll be late for your own wedding.'

'Lady's privilege, Nora. What do you say to my Infant of Prague now, you pagan you?'

'Go away and get married, you superstitious Fenian.'

Eileen's father came over to them.

'Now, girls, it doesn't bother me a bit but your mother will be having palpitations inside,' he said mildly.

Nora watched the two of them enter the church. Eileen turned and waved as the door closed. Nora saw several curtains in the Monastery flutter as she turned to go back to the shop.

Strolling home that evening, she debated whether or not she should tell Mrs Brown about her plan to visit the wedding celebration and her clandestine meeting with

Myles. Her encounters with the priest and the Brother bothered her more than she cared to admit. She felt that she was strong enough in herself to stand up to them but the implied threats to Thomas' business were causing her a great deal of unease. She had no doubt that she would meet Myles, that she had already decided. After tonight's meeting, though, she would have to make some difficult choices.

Mrs Brown was in the back garden when Nora got home. She was strolling among the apple tree, examining the fruit. The cooking apples were bright green while the eating apples were vivid red.

'It's a dangerous time of year, Nora. The trees are full of apples but they need another month or so before they are just right. The local boys are not prepared to wait that long so I have to act like a human scare crow to keep them away. I must admit, though, that sometimes I pretend to be asleep and watch discretely while the bravest and boldest creep over the wall to rob my orchard, then chase them like a fury.'

'I think I know how those boys might feel. Sometimes, it seems like everybody in the town is watching me and waiting for me to commit some dreadful offence so that they can chase me to perdition.'

'Poor Nora. Welcome again to small town, rural, Ireland. In so many ways, it's an absolutely idyllic place to live, isn't it? People are easy going and nothing moves too quickly. The sunsets are ravishing, we have our gardens, our trees. When I was a girl, I thought I lived in paradise, with servants and parades and military bands, like your parents growing up. Then everything changed, Suddenly, the great houses were being burnt , officers and soldiers we knew were being murdered. People we knew well appeared armed and in the uniform of the rebels. But those days too passed.

'Now, everything's different but life in Castlecarraig goes on. We may not rule the roost but I still have my garden and my apple trees and the young boys are trying to rob me. There are those who would like to rob us of more than a few apples. Some still regard us as intruders. But, you know, that too will change. Look how our Northern brethren have carved out a peaceful and prosperous state.'

She joined Nora sitting on the small patio outside the back door.

'You are still young, Nora. I was born while Victoria was on the throne, you were born under an Irish flag. Next year, we will be half way through this century. Picture life in another fifty years after that. This State will be in an even greater shambles than it is now, bankrupt most likely and all the youth still leaving as soon as they can. The O Murchus of this world will still be dancing up and down about their Republic but Ulster will have had a hundred years of peace and harmony.'

'That's all very good and interesting,' Nora said, 'but I am more concerned with the next two hours than the next fifty years.'

Mrs Brown said nothing and waited for her to continue.

'How I envy you,' the younger woman said eventually. 'You have had such a difficult life. You lost the man you loved and everything that meant anything to you and yet you talk as if you have found total contentment and happiness with a few trees and spectacular sunsets. I wish I could find some of your wisdom and insights.'

'The reason maybe that I have any wisdom and insight is because I lost so much. But you are wrong in one thing. I did not lose everything. I kept my pride, in myself and in what I am. I kept my love for my man and my country. I kept my friends and my love for this corner of the world, with all it's faults and all it's beauty.'

Again, both women lapsed into silence. This time it was Mrs Brown who spoke first.

'Think seriously about this, Nora. What does Thomas stand for and what does Myles stand for?'

Nora covered her face with her hands.

'Different things, different times,' she answered.

'What things, what times?' Mrs Brown persisted.

Nora got up from her chair and pace around the patio.

'Myles is the new Ireland, really, isn't he?' she said. 'He's young, he's visionary, he's committed to his Catholic Faith, a bit smothered by his mother and his priests. Thomas is old values, hard work, loyalty, reliability. A bit dull.'

'My goodness, you can be harsh,' Mrs Brown laughed. 'So, where does that leave us?'

'That leaves you here minding your bloody apples and me sneaking off to meet a priest in half an hour and heading off to an island tomorrow with a man twice my age who wants to bloody marry me!'

'And you thought Castlecarraig was a dull place!'

CHAPTER 23

Rose arrived in the park just after eight. Straight away, she embraced Malachy and kissed him passionately. By now they had a scale of kissing. The first one was passionate but brief. As the evening progressed, she opened her lips a little further each time, until by the time she was about to leave, they were, as Joyce once put it, "ate' in" each other.

'By the time I get back to London, I will be so fit. Walking in and out that mile and a half so many times, I will be ready for the bleeding Olympics in a couple of years.'

I'll be in the pole vault meself, Malachy thought, trying not to limp.

'So, Malachy,' Rose asked, beaming at him in a way that made him go all watery inside when they were alone but mortified the hell out of him when there were other people around.

'I know you don't like pubs, Rose but I have to talk to my friend John Joyce,' Malachy said.

'I don't like him either so why should we waste a night in a place I don't like meeting someone I don't like? Especially when I could be with someone I like, doing something I do like.' As she said this, Rose squeezed Malachy's left buttock and licked his right ear. Walking became very difficult.

'Sit down here now, Rose,' he managed to whisper hoarsely.

He told her about his chat with Marian and the possibility that Breege might be in trouble. He did not mention that she had specifically asked for Rose's help, as he guiltily thought Breege might be impressed if any good ideas seemed to come from him.

'God, I don't envy poor Breege,' Rose said when he had explained. 'I know some of my friends in England had buns in the oven and that was disaster but being up the spout here, wow, that is just hell, really.'

Malachy was not sure what she was talking about but did not want to display his ignorance. He wanted to be seen as a man of the world.

'So,' he said, 'these friend of yours, did any of them ever get pregnant?'

He felt very grown up being able to use a word like that to a girl but Rose regarded him with a strangely.

'Did Marian say if Breege had missed?'

Now Malachy was completely puzzled.

'I think the problem was that John didn't miss,' he said.

'No, Malachy, did Breege miss? Her period?'

Malachy looked around to make sure nobody was nearby. Suddenly, he did not feel so secure or grown up. He rubbed his hair, folded his arms, pulled his ear lobes.

'I don't believe it Malachy! That's the first thing you ask to find out if someone might be in the family way. We'd better find that out first up. Where will we find Breege or Marian?'

Malachy did not reply.

'Are you sulking, Malachy?' Rose asked. 'Come on, mate, cheer up. When you come to visit me in London, I'll get some condoms and we won't need to worry. How does that sound?'

Malachy knew walking was now out of the question for several minutes at least.

'Let's just sit for a while,' he whispered, more hoarsely than before.

'Oh, Malachy,' Rose whispered as she snuggled against him, 'you are such an innocent sometimes.'

The familiar figure of old Mrs Brown approached along the path.

'Ah,' she said pausing beside them. 'Young love, how romantic.'

'Hello, Mrs Brown,' Malachy said, 'this girl's from England.'

'England! Well, what part of England do you hail from?'

'London,' Rose replied.

'I used to visit London as a young girl, hundreds of years ago,' Mrs Brown said, smiling. 'I was actually there before the First World War and shortly after the second one as well.'

'My grandfather fought in the First World War,' Rose said proudly. 'He was wounded at Mons.'

'Really,' Mrs Brown said. 'He must have been a very brave man. Enjoy your evening, lovely talking to you. I must stand guard over my apple trees. The young scallywags will have them stripped bare before they are ready if I don't.'

'Dodderin' auld bitch,' Malachy muttered when she had left.

'She's a very nice old lady,' Rose chided, 'don't you be so nasty and horrible. Come on then, let's sort out your friends.'

The Frenchman's Bar and Lounge was an apostrophe free watering hole which was cashing in on the new surge of interest in traditional Irish music. The Bar was the stretch of the premises that was inside the front door. The Lounge was at the end, separated from the Bar by an arch. The distinguishing feature of the Lounge was a large television set that sat on a high shelf in the corner. There was also a table soccer machine but it was strongly rumoured that this was soon to be replaced by a pool table.

Malachy and Rose arrived at the Bar at the same time as a bunch of local musicians. They carried battered instrument case, covered in stickers from various continental cities, to which the musicians had never been. The banjo player was attempting to cover his case entirely with Guinness stickers.

John sat in a corner of the bar immediately inside the door. He was still in his painting overalls and drinking in the company of another painter and a mechanic, both of whom were considerably older than he. An ashtray was overflowing onto a counter that was sloppy with spilled drink.. A young barman slouched over the counter, reading the Irish Press racing section.

He looked surprised and pleased to see Malachy.

'Bravo, Malachy, auld stock. And herself. Rosie O Grady, Are ye having one?'

'Just the one, John. And the name is Rose, so it is. I'll have a pint of beer and Rose will have an orange.'

'An orange? Will you not have something a biteen stronger, now, Rosey?'

'If I wanted something a biteen stronger, I'd have asked for it now, wouldn't I, Johnny?' Rose told him.

'Ho, ho, Johnny boy,' the mechanic shouted, 'that girleen will soften your cough for you. Fair play to you, girleen.'

Malachy could see that Rose was getting annoyed.

'C'mere,' he said to John, 'is there ere a chance I can have a quiet word?'

'Off you go, John,' the mechanic said, 'that auld music'll be starting shortly so meself and Pete'll motor on to Paddy's for a bit of peace and quiet. We'll see you some other time.'

Malachy and Rose took the stools vacated by the two men.

'These are the best seats in the house,' John told them. 'Nuts' Corner they cal this spot. Drink up now, let ye.'

Malachy sipped his pint while Rose examined her glass.

'There's lipstick on my glass,' she said with a frown. 'Hello, barman, can you change this glass.'

The barman had returned to his racing page and did not seem to happy to be disturbed. He poured the drink into a fresh glass.

'You should be thankful lipstick is all that's on it,' he muttered as he replaced it on the counter and returning to his paper.

Before Rose could make a scene, Malachy spoke to John.

'I reckon you're spending an awful rake of time in here, John.'

'But the craic is ninety, Malachy, wait'll the lads start playing a few tunes and the crowd comes in. The craic will be ninety.'

'But are you not saving a few bob for Uni? We'll have to have the craic there as well, you know.'

'All sorted, Malachy' John replied, shaking his head. 'I'm making enough bobs to keep meself over the Summer. The grant will pay for the craic in Uni. Are you goin' to Uni, Rosie?'

Rose ignored him.

'Oops,' John said, 'not very popular in that quarter, am I , Malachy?'

'No,' Malachy agreed, 'and you are not very popular in other quarters either.'

John looked at him innocently.

'What are you on about?'

'You know shaggin' well what I'm talking about. Breege, that's who.'

'Sure I haven't seen her for weeks.'

'Exactly,' Malachy said, ' you dumped her and she deserves better than that.'

'If you're so worried about her, Malachy, why don't you call on her yourself. Rosie, you wouldn't mind if Malachy called on another girl, would you?'

'Right,' Rose said, getting off the stool and standing between the two lads. 'Listen to me, you ignorant pig. I know Malachy is your friend but I think you are a selfish and ignorant, good for nothing user. You talk like you are a big man and sit here drinking like a fool and all you are is a little boy whose afraid to take responsibility for his life. You are a prick.'

With that, she stormed out, just as the musicians began to belt out a tune Malachy recognised as "the Rakes of Castlebar".

'Fair play, Malachy,' John grinned, 'I'd say she's a thunderin' shag. Did you doodle her yet?'

Malachy was torn between hitting his friend, helping Breege and rushing after Rose to protect his courting interests. He went to the door but there was no sign of Rose on the street. He took his seat beside John at the bar again.

'Are you climbing the Reek on Saturday?' he asked him.

'Jaysus, Malachy, I don't know if I'll bother. I'm working all day and there's supposed to be a mighty session here Saturday night'

'Ah, but we've been talking about it for months, John, feic you.'

'Can't you bring Rosie with you? She'd be better company for you that I would. She'd be a better hault, anyways.'

Malachy knew there was no point in talking to him when he was in this state. He'd obviously had a few drinks, and while by no means drunk, he intended to be.

'I'll see you Sunday so, probably. Will you be around?'

'They reckon there'll be a mighty session here after the climb so I'll be here early.'

As Malachy got ready to leave, John grasped his hand and looked him in the eye.

'Two things, Malachy, auld stock,' he said with a slight slur. 'Say a prayer for me on the summit.'

'I will of course,' Malachy said, moved by the intensity of his friend's words.

'And give Rosie a length for me.'

Malachy just sighed and left the pub, closing the door on the strains of an American style country song about a Vietnam veteran having a hole in his arm where all the money goes.

'If he was a Paddy,' he thought, 'the hole would be in his feicin' head.'

He wandered around the town, hoping to find Rose. He wasn't too worried about her as she had relations in the town and it was still bright enough for her to walk home if she decided to do so. He was trying to figure out how he was going to talk to Joyce when he heard his name. Turning, he saw Fr Tommy.

'You must have been a million miles away, Malachy, I've called you three times,' the priest said in a friendly voice.

Malachy was pleased that he remembered his name.

'Maybe not a million miles, Father, more like one or two.'

'That's very profound for a young lad just finished school and heading off into the world.'

Malachy just smiled.

'I wouldn't worry too much about the Lizard, Malachy, he'll get over his disappointment at not having two more vocations. It's not his first disappointment and they way things are going, I don't think it will be his last. Where are you going now?'

'Short term or long term, Father?'

'I mean right now, are you going anywhere in particular or are you just rambling?'

'More or less rambling, Father.'

'Would you like to stroll with me? I'm going back to China in a few days and I wanted to have a last stroll around the lake. I'd love a bit of company.'

'Can't send a man back to China without a bit of company. I'd be delighted Father.'

They walked through the grave yard and onto the lake shore.

'I suppose you had a party here after the exams?' Fr Tommy asked.

Malachy laughed.

'Actually, Father, it was the night we served Mass for you in the Monastery.'

'Some things never change. The only change is that in my day we had the party the far side of the lake, near the castle. Good night, was it?'

'Royal, Father. I met a lovely English girl and we are more or less going out since.'

'And what about your comrade, John, did he do anything for his country?'

Malachy was not at all used to speaking so openly to a priest.

'You know the seal of Confession, Father, that you can't tell what's said?'

'I'm familiar with it, Malachy. Is there something bothering you that you want to talk about?'

'There is Father, but it's not me directly.'

'Apart from the Seal, Malachy, in a few days I'll be in China, well, Taiwan, technically, so anything you tell me will be confidential. Unless Chairman Mao's Red Guards capture me and torture me and one of them is from Castlecarraig. Then we'd all be in trouble.'

'It's funny you should use that expression, Father.'

'Oh, I see.'

They walked along the shore in silence. Fr Tommy looked thoughtful, Malachy could think of nothing to say.

'Over the years, Malachy, I have met many young girls in this dilemma. Funny, it always seems the girls dilemma even though, as the Yanks say, it takes two to tango. One time, not too long ago, such poor souls were put into mental hospitals, just like that big building behind the trees there. Others were taken care of by the Sisters but having met some of them in later years around the world, I am not sure if care is the word they would use.'

Fr Tommy paused to watch the sunset. He picked up some flat stones and skimmed them across the surface of the water.

'Funny,' he remarked, ' all the stones seem to get the same chance. Still, some of them don't make it, others glide off into the sunset.'

He resumed walking.

'Remember, Malachy, the night I read the Mass? Can you remember what I spoke about at all?'

Malachy tried to recall but could only shake his head.

'Nobody listens,' Fr Tommy said with a rueful smile. 'I spoke about how Ireland is changing. There is some wealth here, people are getting optimistic. The Church is losing it's grip. And that can only be good, Malachy. People like you will have to think for yourselves, not be told what to do and what to think by celibates like me and Fr Reilly and the Lizard. But that freedom will have a price. And your unfortunate friend is now discovering that. Ireland is changing, yes, but how quickly?

'I see a day when girls will no longer be seen as in trouble when they are pregnant and not married. That will be good but there will be a price for that too. But, this philosophising is not helping you, is it?'

'It's very interesting, Father.'

'What a polite young man and what a shame you have not a vocation. The Church needs more young men like you. You say you have an English girlfriend. Where is she from?'

'London.'

'A big place. No matter. I have a friend, a lad from here who helps Irish girls. He does not judge them. He can fix them up with families until their time comes and get good homes for the babies. He detests abortion but will turn no one away.'

He took out a wallet. From this, he took a letter and ripped the address from the top. Taking a pen from his pocket, he wrote a phone number under the address.

'I write to him regularly, even wealthy Chinese girls sometimes need the sort of help only a poor Irish priest like myself can offer. If you want to bring your friend anywhere, this is the best place.'

Malachy took the piece of paper and put it in his shirt pocket.

'Thank you, Father. Maybe if me and John had met more priests like you, the Lizard might indeed have two more vocations to his credit.'

'If there were more priests like me, Malachy, the poor Pope would have a lot of sleepless nights. The Lizard and the rest do the best they can and often enough, that's good enough.. So many things change but one thing never changes.'

'What's that?' Malachy asked.

'These bloody midges! They are eating me alive. They're worse than the mosquitoes in Hong Kong harbour. Come on, let's walk back.'

Malachy walked with him as far as the Presbytery. At the gate, Fr Tommy shook his hand.

'People often ask me if I envy the young people of today,' he said. 'Sometimes I do. I was in California a few years ago and the hippies were dressed in a way that took the eye out my head near enough. But each generation has it's own challenges. I was born the same year as the Civil War ended and I saw plenty of hard times but I've an awful feeling you'll have it as tough in your own ways. God bless you, Malachy. You're a good lad. Take care of your friends, they're all that matter when all is said and done. Now, I must go and talk to my friends, no? When all else is past, we look to our friends, no?'

Malachy left him feeling good about himself. It was nice to be complimented, especially by a priest. He'd have to tell his mother he went for a walk with a missionary. She'd be chuffed. He took the note from his shirt pocket. London. He remembered what Rose had said about condoms and began to feel very randy. He thought he'd better find her for a quick court before she went home.

Instead, he met Marian as she left the shop near the Presbytery.

'Well,' she asked, 'have you spoken to Romeo yet?'

'I tried to but he was half drunk so I'll try again.'

'And what about Rosie?'

'It's Rose, for Jaysus' sake, and yes, I discussed it with her.'

'And?'

Malachy felt this was an opportunity to make himself feel mature again.

'The main thing we need to know, Marian,' he said gravely, 'is if she's missing.'

'Missing? Missing what?' Marian demanded.

Malachy began to feel flustered.

'Missing her , you know, her , you know.'

'I have not got a clue what you are talking about. If your old flower is going to help, then she'll have to do better than send you looking for something that's missing.'

Malachy tried to regain lost ground.

'I did speak to another friend who has a contact in London, who looks after girls who might be in trouble.'

'What part of London?' Marian asked him.

Again, Malachy looked blank.

'For Christ's sake, Malachy, Breege is in serious bother. Are you going to help or not?'

'Right, right, leave it with me.'

Marian left without another word.

As Malachy passed by the Frenchmans, the music was blaring into the street. The pub was crowded, cigarette smoke, beer fumes and people overflowing through the door.

He pushed his way through the crowd. John was still sitting in Nuts Corner. The counter in front of him was full of empty glasses and butts of cigarettes. He was talking to a dark haired woman a few years older than himself..

'C'mere Malachy,' he said when he noticed him. 'Say hello to Frieda, she's from Holland, so she is.'

'Actually, I am from the Nederlands but it is too difficult to explain to your friend. Now, I must go, John, I may see you later.' She rushed away as quickly as the throng would allow her.

'What do you reckon, Malachy?' John asked through a haze of smoke. 'Them Dutch girls are supposed to be flyers altogether. There's a red light district in Amsterdam, O Murchu told me one time. I was wondering after you left the last time why Rosie was so annoyed with me. What's the story, pal?'

'The story,' Malachy said patiently, 'is , first of all, her name is Rose, and second of all, you have not gone next, nigh, nor near Breege for weeks. Marian gave me a lash about it and Rose heard so she thinks you are a bollocks. So does Marian and I would imagine, Breege, and for that matter, so do I.'

'Ho, ho, Malachy, ya boy ya! What do ya reckon?'

Malachy looked at his friend. He saw a boy, trying to be a man. He saw someone who was drunk, reeking of tobacco and terrified of what the future held.

'Sunday,' he said eventually, ' remember? Here, around five, right?'

Malachy left the Bar and Lounge. He walked the streets for a while hoping to find Rose but gave up at midnight. Walking through the park, he passed by where the hanging tree had stood.

'By Jaysus,' he said out loud, 'if you were standing today, I know one drunken gobshite that'd be swinging from your highest branch.'

CHAPTER 24

'**W**e'll be there shortly, Nora,' Malachy said. 'How are you feeling?'

'I'm actually a little bit excited. Or maybe it's nerves, I don't know,' she answered.

The conical tip of Croagh Patrick appeared on the western horizon.

'Did you ever climb it, Nora, when you were in the area?' he asked her.

'No,' she replied, with a faint smile, 'but I've seen it from a few angles. Actually, what we'll do when we get to the town is, we'll skirt around it to the Newtown side. I want to see if I can find a particular place.'

'No problem, Mrs,' Malachy said. 'I feel a bit excited myself.'

They passed through small villages, as sleepy today in the Summery Sunday sun as they had been twenty years ago for Malachy and fifty years ago for Nora.

The village of Ballatha boasted a very wide street and Malachy remembered the flowers from previous visits, particularly one night coming back from Galway when Joyce had thrown up in several of the flower beds. On the way back to Galway, he had piddled on the same beds.

'I remember Thomas bringing me here once. There was a large shop somewhere on the left that he did business with. He stayed in the shop and I went for a walk through the village. I remember the flowers then, it's good to see they're still here.'

The terrain was becoming more hilly and pasture was giving way to bog. In spite of himself, Malachy began to feel a surge of belonging.

'Do you feel any sense of place at all, Nora, coming back here? Does the place have any sort of a grip on whatever it is you call a soul?'

'Not in the least, Malachy. These bogs and hills are as far removed from my consciousness and nature as class and manners are removed from yours. Don't mistake my memories for affection, young man. I spent some important times here, for sure, but time passes.'

'Well, maybe I'm a peasant at heart because I feel at home here,' Malachy said.

'And what about all you wandering, did you not feel at home there? Outside the Opera House? On Fisherman's Wharf? Looking up at Table Mountain? What about all those places?'

'It's hard to explain to a placeless Protestant like yourself, Nora. Ireland holds you by the balls if you let it. If you're a man, of course, though in your case, I suppose the analogy holds. It's like James Joyce leaving but not leaving, if you see what I mean.'

'My old friend, Senator David Norris, could not have put it more succinctly, I'm sure. God, how did people scratch a living from these little fields? What possessed them to breed like rabbits when there was nothing for them? Well, Malachy, you, by your own admission are a peasant. What possessed them?'

'Stall the digger now, Nora and shut up. We're coming into town. Where do you want to go?'

Like most Irish towns, Castlecarraig was surrounded by roundabouts. Sign posts seemed to be chosen for their ability to confuse.

'There,' Nora shouted, ' follow the Achill signs.'

Malachy turned left at the roundabout. If, he mused, all records of public life were suddenly to disappear in some natural disaster, historians would at least be able to identify the constituencies which had been represented in Government by elected representatives who had become Ministers for the Environment. Ireland was honeycombed by random stretches of super highways which bore testament to the cabinet office of their elected deputies. The road they were now on was continental quality, smooth. It was also Irish decorated, strewn with plastic bags and burger wrappers.

Nora was looking around, trying to orientate herself to the new maze of infrastructure. After some toing and froing, they found themselves on the Newtown road.

'Go out about two miles,' Nora instructed.

Malachy did as he was told. Nora was looking intently ahead.

'There, on the right, that's it, there should be a small church down here.' she said.

The road they turned onto was narrow and pot holed. They passed the church

'Slowly, Malachy, we'll have to turn again soon. There, there, left.'

Nora was becoming excited. Malachy was intrigued to find out where they were going.

'Slowly, Malachy. It's somewhere on the right.'

They were climbing a steep hill. The sides of the road were overgrown with brambles and fuchsia. A fallen down house stood on a bend.

'Park outside that shack, Malachy,' Nora said, very quietly.

The shack was similar to ones seen all over Ireland. The roof had long caved in and the windows stared blankly at a spectacular landscape.

Nora walked around the side of the house. Malachy followed.

'Look, Malachy,' Nora whispered, pointing forwards.

The panorama before him took his breath away. He was looking at a valley that stretched for miles. The blue shine of the Atlantic lay like a pencil line on the horizon. The house backed onto a bog that fell steeply to a small lake. Whin bushes, fuchsia, dog daisies and all sorts of wild flowers lent an endless array of colour to the landscape. Inevitably, Croagh Patrick brooded in the distance.

'Oh, Malachy, it hasn't changed a bit. I don't believe it,' Nora said.

Malachy noticed that her eyes were glistening, surprising him because of her usual hard attitude.

'Why is this spot special, Nora?' he asked her.

Nora just shook her head and moved further into the bog. The heather was damp but she did not appear to notice. She sat on a small mound, lost in thought. Malachy, despite his banter and her snobbishness, was genuinely fond of her. He sat beside her.

'Do you know what that lake is called, Malachy?' she asked after a while.

'I remember it's called after some animal or something.'

'It's called the Leg of Mutton, Malachy. After the shape, obviously. This hump of a bog we are sitting on is called a peacawn. I'll bet you didn't know that either.'

Malachy just laughed briefly.

Nora closed her eyes and breathed so deeply she seemed to be asleep.

CHAPTER 25

As Nora approached the Royal, the clock on the church struck seven. From an upper window in the hotel, she heard the strains of a waltz, played on accordion and piano. She crossed the road to enter the hotel. Before she reached the door, she heard her name. Looking around, she saw Myles sitting in a car. He beckoned her.

'Would you like to come for a drive, Nora?' he asked her through the window.

She did not hesitate and soon they were driving away from Castlecarraig, towards the west, but on a different road than the one she had travelled with Thomas and Mrs Brown.

'What happened our rendezvous in the garden, Myles? I was quite looking forward to that,' Nora teased.

'I will show you a far more magical garden. Besides, Fr Reilly and half the clergy of the dioceses are in the hotel, watching me like hawks. I decided to borrow my father's car for a few hours so we could really be alone.'

Nora felt a thrill of excitement.

'Wouldn't it be lovely if we could just keep driving, Myles, driving forever?'

'I don't have that much petrol,' Myles laughed, ' and I only need to go about two miles to get where I want to.'

He turned onto a side road and the car climbed a steep hill. There was a deserted house on a bend of the road. He parked outside it.

'This was my mother's people's home,' Myles explained. 'All her family has moved on, and both her parents have gone to their reward. But what I really want you to see is around the back.'

Behind the house, Nora felt her breath taken away by the view. Thousands of years ago, a glacier had obviously created a valley that ran all the way to the ocean. Trees, flowers and shrubs of every shade and colour carpeted the landscape.

'Isn't it beautiful, Nora?' Myles asked.

'How can you leave all this, Myles? So much beauty.'

Myles was gazing into her eyes.

'You are beautiful, Nora.'

They looked at each other in silence. Myles took her hand. Nora closed her eyes and soon she felt his lips on hers. When they broke apart, Nora smiled.

'Everybody tells me this is wrong, Myles'

'They tell me the same thing,' Myles answered. He leaned forward and kissed her again. They became more passionate and soon were lying together on the grass. Myles paused to remove his coat and lay it on the ground. In her heart, Nora knew that he could never be hers forever. Feeling his hands gently tease her blouse from her skirt, she knew one night, one evening was all they would have. Breaking away from his embrace for a moment, she looked intently into his face.

'Will you remember me?' she whispered.

'Forever,' he said.

She closed her eyes and let the feelings take her over. She heard the evening song of the birds and Myles breathing. She smelt the damp of the heather and the musk of his body. She tasted the sweet air of the evening and the salt of his sweat as she kissed him passionately. When she did open her eyes and turned her head, she saw the red sun setting behind the mountains etched against the darkening sky. Then, she was swept away in an ecstasy that swept everything else from her consciousness.

Later, they sat, wrapped in his coat, leaning against a mound of earth.

'This mound is called a peacawn. Did you know that, Nora?'

'Does it matter?'

Myles laughed again.

'Nothing matters except me and you at the moment. I am now damned, I've committed mortal sin.'

'Two minutes in Confessions will sort you out, Myles,' Nora said, smiling.

'You must be genuinely sorry to get forgiveness.'

'And you're not sorry, are you, Myles?'

'Not sorry for what I've done, no. But I am sorry for the choices I have to make.'

Nora remained silent. She looked at the beauty of the countryside, at two swans on a small lake.

'Tell me your choices, Myles,' she said eventually, when he did not continue.

'This,' he said, indicating the countryside, 'and this,' he said, kissing her on the lips. 'All this, and banishment by family, friends, clergy. Or I leave you and my country and do what my vocation tells me to do.'

'Could you do it, Myles? Just me and you. Do up this old house, grow our own food, live off my pay from the shop.' Even as she spoke, Nora was aware of the not too subtle threats from the clergy which she had received. She knew Myles' family would shun her, let alone allow them live in this idyllic spot. She kissed him fiercely on the lips, then gathered up her clothes. She moved behind the peacawn and dressed quickly. She walked back to the road and stood by the car. Myles arrived and stood with her.

'I am sorry, Nora. I'm not strong enough to do what's right,' he said.

She smiled at him kindly.

'I don't even know what's right anymore, Myles. Let's get back to the wedding.' She laid her hand on his cheek. 'I think I may have loved you.'

Myles dropped her across the park from the hotel. She saw a crowd at the door of the Royal. Crossing the park, she saw Eileen and Seamus were leaving the building, about to get into a waiting car. Guests crowded around them, cheering and clapping. Eileen looked radiant and Nora felt happy for her. The female guests gathered on the road and Eileen prepared throw her bouquet. The women and girls giggled and jostled for position. As Eileen raised the flowers, she glanced towards Nora. Grinning broadly, she threw the bouquet in her direction. It sailed across the road and Nora reached out and grabbed it. The women groaned good-naturedly and some cheered. Nora held the flowers high in triumph and she and Eileen grinned at each other. Then, Eileen drove off with her new husband while Nora strode homewards.

Mrs Brown was sitting reading when she came in.

'And how did your evening with your Papist go?' she enquired, as Nora took a chair opposite her.

'Do you know what a peacawn is?' Nora asked.

'Is it some kind of bird, or sweet cake?' the older woman replied.

'It's actually a mound, or small hill in a bog. It can, I discovered, bring people together or keep them apart. This evening, Myles and I sat together on a peacawn but by the end of the evening, we were on opposite sides. And that's where we are meant to be, I suppose.'

Mrs Brown rose from her seat and sat on the arm of Nora's chair. She handed her a handkerchief and put her arm around her shoulder. Nora burst into tears.

'How did you know?' she sobbed.

'Hush, child. Remember, I once lost the man I loved too.'

CHAPTER 26

Romance was far from Malachy's mind next day in the gut room, wheeling barrows of intestines around the factory. The foreman was in foul form as well. He was a prominent member of Fine Gael and the last Thursday of the month was the night they held their branch meetings. As the party spent their time in permanent opposition, the branch meetings themselves were short but the drinking sessions afterwards lasted most of the night. The over indulgence in alcohol, combined with a realisation that he had backed the wrong political horse all his life, and the inability to pronounce the word "sausages" in a bacon factory, made the foreman a very bitter man.

'Get a feicin' move on, for feic's sake. We need rakes of casin' for the hausages. Malachy, you lazy article, fill them barrels with more guts. The vans need to be full of hausages for Westport and Achill. The pilgrims on the Reek love their hausages so get more feicin casin!'

There was no banter in the gut room when the foreman was in this humour. Even tea breaks and dinner breaks were kept short as intestines flew in one door and casing came out the other.

It was well after seven when Malachy got home. He stank of pig shite. He was mortified when he saw Rose sitting with his father on the window sill of his house.

'What about the workin' man?' his father greeted him. 'You never told us about your lovely girl friend, son, you're some detail, alright.'

Rose came up to him and seemed about to throw her arms around her but the combination of Malachy's scowl and the stink of shite put her off.

'I hope you don't mind,' she said, 'but Uncle Ger gave me a lift into town early so I popped up.'

'No harm done,' his Dad said. 'Always good to meet the young crowd. I knew your father well, and all belonging to him. Your mother wants to know if you want any tae, Malachy.'

'No, we ate above.' One of the customs in the factory was that those on overtime were allowed to help themselves to the freshly prepared meats. Malachy did not want to explain to Rose that this meant holding a couple of slices of bread under the machine that spewed out black pudding, and making a steaming sandwich of a warm mixture of boiled pigs' blood and spices. Or taking a pig's foot from a vat of scummy hot water and eating the flesh while tipping out a barrel of intestines onto the floor. 'I'm grand.'

'I reckon you need to have an auld bath son. This lovely girl isn't going to want to hang around with a gasur that smells like a tin of corned beef. I'll keep her company while you scrub up.'

Malachy knew there was nothing he could say that would not cause him to be even more embarrassed so he smiled weakly at Rose.

'See you in twenty minutes,' he said.

It took half an hour but he felt it was worth it. He had Old Spice on his chin, Cossack on his hair, Pond's talcum powder on his willy and in his shoes, and Lux soap scented his underarms.

Rose and his father applauded when he came back out.

'Look at that now,' his dad said, 'shiny as a hound's balls.'

He was still laughing as the young couple walked away, Malachy making a point of holding Rose's hand.

'Where to?' he asked.

'I'd like to talk to your friends, Marian and Breege.'

They were saved the walk to the girls' houses as they were both in the park. Malachy was shocked when he saw Breege. Her hair did not have it's lovely sheen and she looked tired. Her eyes did not have the sparkle that had set her out from many drab crowds. She managed a small smile for Malachy.

'We've been waiting for you, Malachy,' she said.

He felt a tremendous erection coming on so he sat quickly on the bench beside them.

'This is Rose, Breege. Marian reckoned she might be able to chat with you.'

Rose squeezed onto the bench between Malachy and Breege.

'What makes you think you might be in a spot of bother, Breege?' Rose asked her in the gentlest voice Malachy had ever heard.

'Everything,' Breege replied, rubbing her already reddened eyes. 'Mornings are dreadful, I'm sick all the time. I haven't had an ounce of energy for weeks.' She rubbed her stomach. 'I feel this is getting bigger and everyone is looking at me.'

Rose took Breege's hand in hers.

'Most importantly,' she said in that gentle voice, 'have you had a period since the night?'

Breege's shoulders shook and she shook her head vigorously.

'No,' she whispered, 'no, no, no.'

The four of them sat in silence, the only sound being Breege's heartbreaking sobs. When she was eventually able to speak, she looked imploringly at Rose.

'What can I do?' she pleaded.

'This happened to a girl in my class last year.' Rose said. 'I used to travel on the same bus as her. I asked her what she planned to do. She told me she had three choices. Abortion, adoption or keeping the baby. That's about it really.'

'Did you talk to John, Malachy?' Breege asked him.

'It's impossible to talk to that fellah now. It's all drink and soft talk. I think you'll have to do whatever it is you want to do without that useless yoke,' Malachy told her.

Breege stood up and faced the other three.

'No matter what I do, I'll regret it,' she said. 'I can't keep the baby, lads. I'll be disgraced. I can still go to England before anybody knows the story. I've never even been to Dublin, let alone England. Can you help me Rose?'

'It depends on what you want to do when you get there, Breege. If you're going for adoption that means staying over there for the next seven or eight months.'

Breege did not reply.

'I spoke to someone,' Malachy said. 'He gave the address of an Irish priest who helps girls in bother. I've his number as well.'

'Whatever you plan to do, you'd better make up your mind,' Marian said. 'Your parents are a bit suspicious as it is. If your belly grows, the whole town will know..'

'Why don't we ring Malachy's friend right now?' Rose suggested. 'Tell him the story and see what he says.'

Breege began to cry again.

'I can't have a baby!' she whispered. 'I can't tell my parents. I can't throw away my life. I can't. I'm sorry, but I want to get rid of the baby.'

Malachy felt his heart break. He still loved Breege with a teen age passion but pregnancy was never part of his fantasy. His fantasies had always ended after they had made love in an endless variety of positions, physical and geographical.

'If that's what you want,' he said , 'I'm ready to do anything Rose suggests.'

'Hold on,' Rose said, 'I'll help too but the decision is Breege's and hers alone.'

'You know I'm here too, Rose,' Marian said.

'How do you get to London?' Breege asked Rose, with an innocence and hope that brought a lump to Malachy's throat.

'Whenever you decide to go, we can be there the next day,' Rose told her.

'Can we go next week?'

'No problem for me. Malachy?' Rose said.

'I can take a few days off from hauling guts to help out a friend, I suppose,' he said with a smile towards Breege. She leaned down and hugged him. 'I made the wrong choice when I picked John,' she whispered in his ear. 'Maybe after we can talk.'

Malachy could not answer.

'Time to start making arrangements then,' Rose said, bringing them all back to the problem. 'Train and boat tickets, for a start. Then where to stay in London. Can you organise that with your friend, Malachy? Good. Now, what are you going to tell your parents, Breege?'

'I've had a pen pal in England for years,' she said. 'I've already mentioned a few times that I might visit this Summer.'

'What about you, Malachy? What will you tell your parents?' Rose asked him.

'Dad will be delighted I'm off to th'auld smoke with a grand girleen from beyont, as long as I remember our little chat about the quare thing, as the fellah says. Me mum will be happy if he's happy.'

Breege smiled for the first time.

'I honestly think I might actually get a night's sleep tonight for the first time in weeks. Can we get together here tomorrow and see what's happening?'

They all agreed and the two friends went away, leaving Malachy on the bench with Rose.

'And you thought Castlecarraig was a dull place,' Malachy said.

'Lets' take a stroll by the lake,' she suggested.

Grey clouds were gathering to the west as they walked by the lake shore. Croagh Patrick could not be seen beneath the mist. Malachy thought of Breege. He thought of her as the young girl he had known just a few months ago, asking him to fix her up with his friend. He thought of her as the beautiful, attractive teenager who had lit up so many of his days and sweetened so many of his thoughts. He thought of her then as the troubled young woman he had just left.

'You're quiet, Malachy,' Rose said.

'I'm thinking about another woman,' he said, squeezing her waist.

'Rotter,' she laughed. 'What will happen if her parents find out?'

'Her father is a rough man, came up the hard way, like mine and yours and the rest of them. Not that he has come up far. He works for the Council. The mother lives for the Church. She puts flowers on the altar and helps to keep the place clean. She'll be shattered. She'll feel she'll never be able to hold her head up in town again. The father might throw her out. I don't know.'

'And what about that bloke, Joyce?'

'What about him?'

'What will happen him?'

'Nothing, sure he's not in trouble.'

'Are you serious, Malachy? He's the one who got her in trouble, remember?'

Malachy thought about this.

'I suppose. His mother will be embarrassed and the auld fellah will give him a hard time. Overall, he'll go on about his business. Breege is the one with the problem, Rose, that's the way it is.'

Rose moved away from him and stood gazing at the lake.

'Do you think that's fair, Malachy? She takes all the blame and he goes about his business?'

'Sure what does it matter what I think? I'll help Breege out and do what I can.'

Rain began to sprinkle lightly. The surface of the lake was soon covered by tiny circles where the drops landed. Malachy and Rose began their walk back towards the town. The rain got heavier. Neither was wearing a coat, though he had a corduroy jacket that had arrived in a parcel from America about four years previously. He placed it over both their heads but the shower became a down pour. They sheltered under an old chestnut tree. By snuggling against it's trunk, they stayed dry. Soon, they were atein each other. Rose took his hand and placed it on her breast outside her tee shirt. Then, she moved his hand so that it was touching the bare skin between her jeans and shirt. His hand crept under the material and rested on the stiff material of her bra. Both were breathing heavily. Malachy was conscious of a drizzle of snot between their noses. Whose it was he was not sure but he was not prepared to break any contact to wipe it. He snuck his roving hand under the strap of the bra, moving it off her shoulder. Rose groaned and moved and suddenly, he found he was holding her entire breast in his hand. He was not sure what to do next, waiting for her to take the initiative and make a move. It crossed his mind that it was somewhere around this spot John and Breege's trouble had begun. Before he could dwell too much on this, he felt a cold stream of water on his back The rain had made its way through the leaves and a channel had formed directly over him. The shock made him shudder and let out a groan.

Rose said, 'That's OK, Malachy, I don't mind,' and pushed her bra back into place, 'next time we'll go a little slower.'

'It wasn't that,' Malachy hastened to correct her. 'The rain is piddling on top of me.' Rose laughed. Malachy had learned one thing in his courting career. When a woman laughs early, it was a good sign. When she laughed after she had adjusted her clothes, then it was time to call it a day.

They stood by the tree until the rain eased. They talked about Breege and the journey they were going to make. Rose had a return ticket on the ferry and she agreed to organise the tickets for Malachy and Breege. He was concerned that his savings for Uni were dwindling but decided to say nothing, in case Rose thought less of him. He was torn still between the reality of Rose, a mature woman who had allowed him to fondle her boobs and had promised to get condoms in England, and the ideal of Breege, a beautiful girl he had idolised for years but had never seemed interested in him. Though now, when she was pregnant and facing social and domestic ruin, suddenly found him to be Mr Wonderful.

When the rain had evened off to a soft drizzle, they made their way homewards. Traffic westwards was heavy as pilgrims for the holy mountain, and drinkers for the all night bars, made their ways to their individual ideas of salvation. The pubs Rose and Malachy passed were crowded, with traditional music emanating from several of them.. Malachy asked if Rose wanted to go into one to dry off and warm up.

'Nah,' she said. 'It's clearing up. Will you walk me to my uncle's?'

Malachy was tired, wet, cold, sexually frustrated and entertaining grave worries about his future, short and long term. A three mile round trip walk did not entice him. However, the prospect of another grope did so he smiled and said he'd love to.

Her uncle lived in a townland called Ballygowel. It translated as the town of the fork because the town river and it's sole tributary met there. Gowel in the original Irish had a much cruder meaning, according to O Murchu, referring to a certain part of women's anatomy. This gave women of the area a certain reputation, undeserved in Malachy's experience. It was a bleak and boggy spot.

Most of the walk passed in silence. They walked hand in hand up the boreen that led to the house.

'What happened, I wonder , to women years ago that got in trouble?' Malachy asked.

'I'm sure that river and the bog holes around here could tell a few stories,' Rose said.

Malachy was shocked. 'Do you reckon?'

'What do you think, Malachy? When the John Joyces of this world had their fun and left the women high and dry, what do you reckon yourself?'

Malachy hated it when she used his vocabulary but he had never thought much about what actually happened to women who were pregnant outside of marriage.

'Do you reckon there was much of it going on, though?' he asked her. 'I mean, like, there wasn't as much interest in sex them days.'

'Is that what you reckon, Malachy? I don't think I'm the first girl to come here and be taken in by the beauty of the place and the soft talk of innocent lugs like yourself. I consider myself fairly educated about the facts of life but how close did we get tonight to doing something silly? If it wasn't for the rain that cooled you down, and a cowpat I was afraid of landing in, who knows what might have happened?'

She gave him a long, passionate whopper of a kiss and went inside.

Five minutes later, with well over a mile to go, Malachy was caught in another downpour. Squelching homewards, drenched to the skin, Malachy wondered if th'auld sex was worth it at all.

CHAPTER 27

'So this is where you did the deed with the prieshteen?' Malachy enquired.

Nora was walking away from him.

'Indeed it is, Malachy.'

'And you did better than I did at the lake in the rain. It's hard to believe you guys were at it all those years ago. I always thought my generation invented sex.'

'If yourself and Joyce invented the motor car we'd all be driving Model T's, if your gropings were anything to go by. It was beautiful, Malachy. It wasn't just a once off fumble for us.'

She tried to explain to him what she had felt. She told him how they had challenged every convention of the time and risked everything for one brief spell of passion.

Malachy sat virtually at her feet and marvelled at her courage. He wanted desperately to know how her story ended but Nora stopped talking and walked down the hill, towards the lake. He watched the strange and mesmerising woman, shaking his head in bewilderment at the fact that it was only a day and a half since he had met her. He felt he knew her better than he knew any human being he had ever met, and was also beginning to know himself better. His hangover from the night before had lifted but his long talks with Nora had brought several issues from his own past that he had not spent much time thinking about for years. Forty years ago, he was being touted as a possible priest himself. Now he could reflect on a dozen years or more that he had not darkened the door of a church, except to attend the weddings of people like himself, who in turn would not darken a holy water font until a christening or wedding demanded it. He also realised that he had attended several funerals of his contemporaries in recent years. He watched their children hoist their coffins and wondered who would hoist his and who would essentially give a shite if it was hoisted or not.

He reflected too on the courage of Nora. Alone in a strange town and an almost alien people, she defied the powerful conventions of the time for one throw of the sexual dice. She carried the memories of a time before he was born like they were some kind of sacred pearls while he had discarded his like the brandy boat clubbers pissed over the side of their yachts. A woman of over seventy had more going for her, in her past, present and even her limited future, than he had with all his success and travel.

Malachy smiled in reflection as he found himself wondering was th'auld success worth it at all.

''What's so amusing, young man?' He had been so engrossed in his thoughts that he had not noticed Nora returning.

'I was thinking what a lucky woman you are to have so many memories, old woman,' he said.

'It is a special place, isn't it?' she asked him.

'Remember I told you I spent time in Australia? One office I worked in was managed by a lovely Aboriginal woman called Maggie. We were driving along the south coast of New South Wales one day, going to a branch office. We were passing by a field outside a town called Kiama and she asked me to stop for a moment. She said the field was an Aboriginal sacred site. When we got to the gate she stopped and told me she had to ask the spirits for permission to enter. Maybe we should have done that here, Nora. This is your sacred site, really.'

Nora smiled broadly at him. 'That's a beautiful thought. When am I going to visit your sacred site, Malachy?'

'My sacred site is getting very bloody damp sitting on this peacawn,' he said. 'Come on, we'll see if the restaurants have improved enough in this town to do a decent Sunday lunch.'

Nora offered him her hand and helped him up. They walked slowly around the house, pausing to look through the broken windows. The floor was completely overgrown by brambles and a broken chair was the only piece of furniture to have survived the elements and exposure.

'How come the windows don't face the valley?' Malachy asked. 'The view would have been something else.'

'The view didn't matter much a hundred years ago, Malachy. It couldn't be eaten. But I suppose it's only a matter of time before some cretin builds on it.'

' "Hey paradise, they put up a parking lot", as Joni Mitchell said,' Malachy said.

'Joni who?' Nora asked.

'There's no doubt,' Malachy said as he opened the car door for her, ' but we're divided by a common culture.'

Mass was ending in the church when they reached it. Four wheel drive vehicles vied for road space with ten year old Fiestas. Well dressed people milled around the front of the church. Looking at their faces, Malachy thought many of them were familiar but he knew it was because they were just local people, with the stocky build and etched features he remembered from the country people of his youth. He felt at least some things had not changed. He remarked on this to Nora.

'Tell me what the boys are wearing, Malachy,' was all she said.

Malachy's good humour faded when he realised what she was talking about. Most of the boys were wearing football jerseys demonstrating support for various English, and one Scottish, football teams. The majority sported the word "Vodafone" across their chests and "Keane" or "Beckham" across their backs, indicating, he knew support for Manchester United. A few had "Carlsberg" on their chests, showing they, in turn, supported Liverpool.

'Just when you thought it was safe to go back in the water,' Malachy grumbled, 'Irish country lads supporting an English team, sponsored by a Danish brewery. Sums it all up, doesn't it?'

'Poor Malachy,' Nora said, leaning over to give him a hug, ' never mind, we still have each other.'

There was a time, Malachy knew, when a flash car like the one he was driving would have drawn attention. Now, it was fairly standard. He knew it was for the best, the country had been poor long enough, but still he wondered if some of the baby of values had not been thrown out with the bath water of poverty.

He decided to take a different route back to the town. 'We live on an island' he assured Nora when she asked if he knew where he was going. Though the area they drove through was not as built up as some towns they had passed through, villas and mansions dotted the landscape. Bungalow Bliss had been replaced with tasteless tack. A few renovated farm houses saved the scene from total crassness. Herds of cattle grazing contentedly showed that there was still some agricultural activity around.

They reached the town sooner than he had thought, probably because the town had grown so much over the years.

'How about the Royal for lunch?' he asked Nora. 'If it's still there.'

'Excellent idea,' Nora agreed. 'Did you frequent it in your philandering days?'

'I never collected stamps, Nora, but I did visit the Royal.'

CHAPTER 28

Nora did not know how long she had been crying in Mrs Brown's arms. She cried beyond tears, until it was dry sobs that shuddered through her. The older woman stroked her hair and spoke soothing, soft words. When Nora finally stopped, Mrs Brown made tea for them both. It was dark outside by now so she turned on the light of the standard lamp in the corner. She then retrieved the cigarette tin that held her late husbands letters.

'There are some letters I haven't read for you, Nora. In fact, I have never read them for anybody else this past thirty years and more. The is one I wrote to him but it was returned unopened so he never read it. Getting letters to and from the front was a haphazard process at best. Sometimes, I would receive two or three letters from him at one time and sometimes I'd get one asking me something I'd already told him in a letter written months before. Part of me is sorry he never saw this, part of me is glad.'

Holding the single piece of paper towards the light, she began to read aloud.

'My dear Monty,

I never believed time could pas so slowly. Every day I am without you seems an eternity. Everyone is so proud of you and await your return. I have one piece of news to tell you, and one piece only. I am with child! I did not want to tell you until I was certain but it is true. When you return, we will go through all the names again and pick one for a boy and one for a girl. I have not told anyone here yet. I will try to keep it a secret until you and all your comrades come home. They say it will not be long.

With love from me (and your baby!)

Vera.'

She folded the letter carefully and placed it carefully back with the others. This time, it was Nora's turn to go to her friend and embrace her.

'But the baby, whatever happened?' she asked.

'The same thing that happened many, many babies in Ireland, England, Germany, all over the world. One moment, you are a proud and happy expectant mother. Then, a simple letter arrives that contains the news you've been dreading for so long. The next moment, you are lying helpless and bleeding and alone on the floor. That's another reason the apple trees are special. There's a tiny grave there, Nora. A lot of me and a lot of Monty lie there, a lot of our lives as well.'

Nora felt herself close to tears again. Her friend noticed and stood, taking her by the hand.

'Don't cry, Nora, I've cried enough over the years. Come outside and I'll show you the spot.'

A small mound was barely visible between two of the old apple trees.

'Did you ever tell anybody? Anybody at all?' Nora asked.

'You are the first living soul, dear. Even Thomas, though I have often been tempted to tell him. But it is my pain and I choose to keep it. You have a secret now, what you and Myles did tonight. Is it anybody else's concern, Nora? Is it going to hold you back from every and any chance at happiness, or even contentment? Do you consider that you have done something wrong?'

'Wrong?' Nora asked. 'In the eyes of God, mine and Fr Reilly's, it was wrong. In the eyes of the world, it was wrong. Part of me knows it was wrong. But, the act itself was love. So, it was not wrong, no.'

'Are you still going out to the island with Thomas tomorrow?'

'Yes.'

'Then you need to rest. Off to bed with you now. What's past is past, for both of us. If you decide to tell people, sometime, in the future, then so be it. If you decide to keep it between us, then so be it also. Go now, and I'll call you for Church in the morning.'

Thomas escorted the two women to Church again the following day. As usual, the congregation was sparse and the vicar spoke of past glories and a future that might still be great. Mrs Brown had prepared an early lunch so Nora and Thomas were on the road shortly after noon.

He was again full of stories. One place he told her, had recently been christened "Cabbagetown" by the people who lived there. There had been a raging storm the previous year and they swore that the cabbages in their gardens had been covered in salt by sea spray which had been blown in from the ocean, eight miles away. Nora noticed again how different he became away from the shop, when he was relaxed. Soon, they were descending the hill into Westport. Throngs of people leaving the Church after last Mass delayed them.

'I've lived with these people all my life but if I was to live another life, I would not understand them,' Thomas said. 'They are capable of the greatest loyalty, kindness, courage and decency but the priests still hold them in absolute thrall. I don't understand it.'

Nora smiled to herself as she remembered a priest holding her not long before

'Let's just think about ourselves today, Thomas. I've never had any time alone with you and I want to talk about other things besides the people and their priests,' she said to him.

'I absolutely agree, my dear,' he said beaming back at her.

They had reached the edge of town and were driving by the quays. Large warehouses lined the side and several large boats were berthed along the shore. A little over a hundred years ago, Thomas informed her, these quays had been the scene of some terrible tragedies. The Great Famine had a devastating affect on this corner of Ireland. It was a cause of shame, he said, that his forebears had driven people from their tiny farms because of failure to pay rent. It should not have happened but times were different then. Having said that, he went on, Lord Sligo, whose still owned vast tracts of the town, had been kinder and history and God would judge them all.

Nora began to appreciate more that Thomas was a complex and interesting man. In the shop, he was polite but distant with his staff and customers. He was an outsider in the town but knew it's history. She placed her hand on his arm. 'Thomas,' she said, 'when we are on the island, can we continue the conversation we had on the beach last Sunday?'

Thomas blushed a deep red and Nora noticed that the needle which indicated the speed at which the car travelled, passed the forty mark for the first time. The car wound it's way along the bay, past the holy mountain and through the town of Louisburg. They took a narrow road that brought them to a pier that jutted out into the blue, choppy waters of the Atlantic.

The scene to Nora was like something from a film. The pier was covered with nets, ropes and wooden pots. Three fishing boats were rising and falling on the water. Sea gulls lined the pier wall and the mass of Clare Island nestled on the horizon. A young fisherman sat on an upturned box, repairing nets. Thomas greeted him by name.

'Peadar, are we ready to sail?'

'Indeed, Mr Thomas. It's a perfect day for it. And I'll have a few sacks of mackerel for you when you come back.'

Thomas glanced guiltily at Nora. 'Business is business, after all, my dear.'

Peadar climbed onto a brightly painted yellow boat. He helped Thomas and Nora aboard, then went and started the engine. He expertly eased the boat away from the pier and headed out to sea.

Nora had never been on a boat before. The wind was much stronger than she had expected and blew her long mane of hair behind her. Thomas placed his arm around her. She looked into his eyes, felt his strength and love and knew that everything was going to be fine. She put her arm around his waist and Thomas raised his chin into the breeze, looking like an explorer who has long sought new worlds, and now had conquered them.

Even though it was Sunday, the pier was bustling. The mackerel were running and it was important for the islanders to stock up for the Winter. They, like all islanders, ran the risk of spending long periods cut off from the mainland.

The landing area was dominated by a small castle. Peadar went to great lengths to explain the history and significance of it to Nora. The pirate queen, Grace O Malley, he told her, had ruled these waves in the sixteenth century. She had travelled to the English court as an equal to meet Queen Elizabeth and had never been conquered. Looking at the people on the pier, Nora was certainly struck by the character of their faces. Broad foreheads and features chiselled by an unforgiving sea and unremitting hard work had given them a nobility and majesty in their countenance. Peadar handed Thomas a set of keys, saying, 'She's the black Morris, sir.' 'She' was a car so weather beaten and rusted that Nora did not think it would bear her weight but the interior had been cleaned to a spotless sheen. Despite the best efforts of the cleaners, however, the whiff of fish and salt permeated the car.

The engine started on the first turn of the key.

'These people look after their property,' Thomas said. 'Cars are absolute luxuries here, and expensive. I've noticed around Castlecarraig these past few years that they seem to be getting a little more common. Heaven forbid we get to the point when the roads of this country become dangerous.' They set off on the short journey around the island. Nora had never fully seen and appreciated the grandeur of the ocean before. At the highest point of the island, they left the car and walked along the cliffs. Nora was spell bound by the view. The ocean spread ever westwards, seeming to merge seamlessly with a sky of the palest blue imaginable. Her mind went back to the beauty of the scene Myles had shown her the previous day and she bit her lip as she thought of the choice she had to make.

'Are you alright, my dear?' Thomas's voice was concerned.

'I am simply overwhelmed by the beauty of it all,' she answered.

They then drove back the way they had come, to a small hotel. Here too Thomas was known and greeted deferentially. They were served lunch in a dining room that looked back towards the mainland. Croagh Patrick seemed to rise from the waves to dominate the sky.

'I somehow feel that this place reflects a lot of what we are, Thomas,' Nora said as they sipped tea, gazing through the window.

'That is a very profound remark from someone so young. And beautiful,' Thomas replied, smiling.

'What I mean is,' Nora continued, 'the castle, the mountain. There is the history and the religion. I am not sure if I will ever be part of it. I know it is all beautiful but I feel somehow trapped between the two. Does that sound silly to you?'

Thomas surprised her by reaching across the table and taking her hand. 'I have never felt more at home here than these past few hours. Nor as happy. You are so wonderful that you can climb that mountain and scale that castle and conquer all the history. You are the hope, Nora. My roots are still in the past, like Mrs Brown's, like O Murchu's and all the rest. But you can leave the past, Nora, you can leave it all and build something new.' He stood up. 'Now, we must walk off that lovely lunch.'

He paid for the meal and amid profuse thank yous and blessings, he walked Nora to the nearby beach. It was deserted. The sands were golden and the shallow water at the edge of the strand was emerald.

Thomas coughed. 'As I was saying a week ago,' he began. Nora gripped his arm tightly.

'Yes, as I was saying, I am a man of some maturity.' 'Thomas,' Nora interrupted, 'you are allowed one sentence only!' He took both her hands in his. She looked into his eyes, emerald like the sea and remembered the dark eyes of Myles. She remembered that in those eyes she had seen such despair, longing and passion. In Thomas's eyes, she saw only affection and redemption. He stood in silence and then gazed at the summit of Croagh Patrick as if for courage and guidance. His gaze returned to Nora.

'Am I allowed one question instead?' he asked.

She could only nod.

'Will you do me the honour of being my wife?'

Again she nodded, this time with her eyes tightly closed. 'Yes, Thomas, yes.'

They embraced on the strand. One was the timid and fumbling merchant who had met her off the train. Gone too was the innocent and wide eyed girl who had stepped from the train with such uncertainty. Instead, on the sun kissed beach of the Pirate Queen, there stood a couple forging a bond that had been fired in adversity and would last a life time.

They sat on some rocks and watched the boats as they landed at the pier and the boatmen unloaded their lobsters, crabs and above all, mackerel.

'Are you happy, Nora?' he asked.

'Of course. But I have to be honest with you. You know I brought some trouble to the shop with my innocent chats with Myles. Fr Reilly was quite threatening, I thought.'

'He does have considerable power, that's true'

'Would you live anywhere else? Besides Castlecarraig, I mean?'

Thomas shrugged his shoulders

'It's funny you should say that. Two school friends of mine have been encouraging me for years to join them in a business venture in Africa. In Rhodesia. They have a farm, measured in thousands of acres and want me to go over as manager. I always write back and tell them next year, next year. I could sell up here without any difficulty. No doubt, many would be delighted to see a native, as it were, taking over.'

'But the people respect you Thomas. Some even like you.'

'I suppose. But I've always harboured a secret ambition for adventure. You've brought that out in me. I feel as if I should go to Africa. With you. Everything I wanted right there, adventure and a beautiful woman to share it with. Am I dreaming?'

'No, Thomas, you are not dreaming,' she said and , for the first time, kissed him on the lips.

'I don't expect you to love me, Nora. I'm not that much of a dreamer,' Thomas said as they chugged across the bay in Peadar's boat.

'I could love you,' she said. 'Is that enough?'

Lifting his chin into the breeze again, he said, 'More than adequate, my dear, more than adequate.' They were still laughing as they climbed into Thomas's car to drive back to Castlecarraig.

Mrs Brown knew as soon as she opened the door to them that something had happened. Nora just hugged her and Thomas pecked her on the cheek. Then Mrs Brown shooed him out and brought Nora into the small sitting room..

'So,' she said, tell me all,'

Nora told her of the boat trip and the lunch and the walk on the beach.

'That's all very well,' Mrs Brown said, when she had finished, 'but tell me how you feel about your choice.'

Some of the animation left Nora's face but in it's place Mrs Brown saw a new determination and maturity.

'I chose Thomas because I want a life that I can live with ease and pride. I honestly love Myles, I think, but if I do love him, then I cannot destroy everything for him. I do not want to spend my life making sacrifices and keeping secrets. I can make Thomas happy and be content with him. He told me he has been considering going to Africa. Imagine, Thomas getting bag and baggage together and heading off to the jungle!'

'And what about last night, Nora?'

'Last night is in the past, it's gone, it's yesterday. It's tomorrow that's important now. Three people know about last night, though a lot more will be making a lot of assumptions. Thomas will never hear from me about Myles.'

Mrs Brown took her cigarette tin of letters from the shelf.

'It's not that easy to keep memories locked away, Nora. I'm glad I shared these,' she said indicating the box, 'with you. Maybe some day you'll choose to share your secrets with someone. You'll know when it's time. Now, the wedding.' As she spoke, she placed her letters in a drawer and locked them away.

CHAPTER 29

Rose brought Malachy to the local travel agent early Saturday morning. The travel agency was a cramped and cluttered counter at the back of a hardware shop. Two Aer Lingus posters and a poster of a matador lined the wall behind the counter. The man who served them owned the whole business so dealt with them quickly and efficiently. In exchange for two weeks hard earned wages among the guts and intestines, Malachy got two return tickets from Castlecarraig to London, travelling by rail and boat. He had never been out of Ireland so he felt a surge of excitement. Rose was much more blasé. She had done the journey often enough to know the tedium and exhaustion that went with it.

'I just hope Breege is up to it,' she said. 'It's a tough trip.'

They were due to leave on Monday from Castlecarraig station, then a five and a half hour trip to Dublin. The boat left Dun Laoighre at three and was due to arrive in Holyhead at ten. Then, the train to Euston, another five hours.

'Usually,' Rose told him, 'there is a delay at every stage. If the Dublin train doesn't break down, the boat is late leaving. Lately, as well, the police in Holyhead have gotten a bit stroppy with the bombings and all that in Belfast. So we can expect to be in London Tuesday morning early. Now, you've got to ring that priest and tell him that.'

There was a public telephone outside the travel agency and hardware shop. Rose and Malachy squeezed in. They placed a pile of coins on the phone and lifted the handset. Malachy read out the number to the operator and she instructed him to put another two days wages into the slot. Eventually, he was talking to a man at the other end. He asked if he was a friend of Fr Tommy's.

'I know him, yes.'

Malachy was afraid the operator might be listening in.

'Well, Fr Tommy reckoned you help out , like, as the fellah says, if a girleen was sort of in bother, like, you know.'

A chuckle came through the line.

'That more or less sums it up. When will you be here?'

'Tuesday.'

'Call me.' The line went dead.

'Do you have any idea how much shite I had to shovel to pay for that friggin' call?' Malachy asked Rose as they left the kiosk.

'Money well spent, Malachy,' she said. It had started to rain again.

'Bad auld night for the Reek,' Malachy grumbled.

'I've wanted to climb it for years and we are going to tonight so stop complaining,' Rose said. 'I'll see you later and we'll talk to Marian.'

Malachy got soaked for the second time in about ten hours as he walked home. Halfway through the morning, he began to sniffle. By lunch time, he was sneezing and his mother was fussing over him.

'Surely you're not climbing the Reek tonight. You'll catch your death. Up to bed with you and have a bit of sense.'

Malachy tried to tell him he was fine but was unable to do so because of a bout of coughing and sneezing. He changed his clothes and sat in front of an electric fire in the sitting room. He began to sweat and his nose and eyes watered.. He was utterly depressed. He had visions of having a great court on the side of Croagh Patrick that night. He had climbed the mountain before but never in female company. Several of his friends had told him of the soft heather about halfway up where you could lie comfortably and allow the environment to work it's magic. As he felt his throat swell and temples pound, he knew the soft heather would not yield tonight to the soft impression of Rose's body. At least, he fervently hoped not because he knew he would not be the one leaning over her if it happened. Rose did call in the afternoon. The rain was almost tropical in it's intensity at that stage.

'Oh, my God!' she exclaimed when she saw the state of him. 'You look dreadful.'

'You should see me from the inside,' Malachy joked hoarsely. 'I don't think I'll be climbing the Reek tonight.'

Rose placed her hand on his forehead. He felt it cool and, as usual, erotic.

'You could help me sweat it out,' he said, leering at her with blood shot eyes and a snotty nose.

'Maybe some other time, love. I'll meet you know who and tell her the arrangements for you know what.'

Malachy did not have the energy to understand what she was talking about or to ask her to explain. He nodded weakly and sneezed five times, sending sprays of spittle in every direction.

'Look after yourself, Malachy,' Rose said as she backed away.

After she had left, Malachy finally yielded to his mother's pressure and went to bed. She gave him a glass of sugary , boiled red lemonade and he slept fitfully through the night.

His sleep was troubled by strange, disturbing dreams. He dreamed that Breege and he were walking hand in hand along the crest of Croagh Patrick. He looked towards Clare Island and could actually see the line of silver strand. Then, when he looked back at Breege, it wasn't her but the Lizard who was puckering up. Then, he was lying on a road, and all around him were floods of intestines and crying pigs. He woke up several times during the night, drenched in sweat. He was awake when the rain finally stopped and the first rays of sunshine peered into his room, alive with millions of molecules of dancing dust and Malachy's germs. Dozing again, he was awakened by his mother who was carrying a bowl of soup.

'How are you now son?'

'I'm a biteen weak but the worst of the cold is gone,' he told her.

'Have some soup now and it'll straighten you out. The lemonade made you sweat the badness out of you.'

The soup was delicious, his mothers speciality, a rich broth of vegetables, boiled up with bacon bones.

'What's this I hear about you off to England?' she asked him sternly.

Malachy had to think quickly.

'Rose asked me over so she did. She's going to her best friends party. It's a surprise, so it is.'

'It's a surprise all right. She told me her best friend was in hospital,' his mother said, looking at him with a look that he knew would tolerate no bull. He was shamed and cornered into silence. He slurped his soup noisily.

'Lovely soup, Mammy,' he said, not looking at her.

'Malachy,' she said, 'you've always been a good boy. Are you in trouble? Be honest, Malachy.'

'The only trouble I'm in, Mammy, is I don't know if I'm lying in sweat or something else.'

His mother smiled tightly. 'Your father always got out of bother with a quick word next to him. Don't let the family down, Malachy. We're respectable and that's important for me.'

Malachy did not know if it was the honesty in his mother's face or the fatigue in his bones or the confusion through lack of sleep, but for the first time in his life, he took his mother's hand and said, 'I love you, Mammy. Don't worry about a thing.'

She kissed his forehead, which was another first.

'You're still a bit warm Stay in bed for the day and I'll have your bag ready for your trip to England tomorrow. Enjoy the party. Or the hospital visit.'

He drifted off into a less troubled sleep.

Monday morning brought back the sunshine. Though he was still a bit weak, Malachy was at the station in plenty of time. Rose arrived soon afterwards. They sat in the morning chill without talking. They heard the train whistle about half a mile away.

'Still no sign of Breege,' he muttered.

'She'll be here, She doesn't have any choice.'

The train stopped and the few waiting passengers boarded. Most were men carrying single , battered suitcases. Only a couple of people remained on the platform to bid anyone farewell. Malachy knew these partings were too regular to be taken too seriously and too sad to be experienced too often.

He and Rose had no bother finding an unoccupied compartment. Standing at the door, he watched the guard check the doors. Then he saw Breege rushing through the gate. The guard frowned at her but allowed her board the train. Malachy brought her to their compartment and the train left Castlecarraig.

They travelled in silence, watching as the landscape changed gradually from hilly bog land to flatter, greener fields. Eventually, the train crawled over the bridge, across the Shannon and into Athlone. They still had the compartment to themselves.

'So how did the Reek go?' Breege asked.

'Poor Malachy was too sick to go so Donal had to drag me up, much to his disgust,' Rose laughed.

'What was wrong with you?' Breege asked Malachy.

'Yerrah, I just had a biteen of a cold.'

'He was absolutely dying, be honest Malachy,' Rose said.

'And still you're making this trip for me? Oh, Malachy!' Breege started to cry. Rose hugged her. 'I'm sorry, I just seem to cry all the time, I'm sorry.'

'There's nothing to be sorry about,' Malachy said. 'What's the story at home?'

'Silence. So long as nobody says anything, nothing is happening. Mammy barely looks at me and Daddy spends the night in the pub so everything is normal, really.'

Never having been out of Mayo, Malachy was amazed at how long it took the train to pass through the suburbs of Dublin. Every one of the thousands of houses seemed to have a television aerial. They arrived in Connolly Station and the crowds of people reminded him of the crowds on the Reek. Breege remained totally unmoved by everything that was happening. Rose took charge and led them to another platform where a smaller train was loading. A man in uniform was calling, 'Boat Train, Platform Three.' This train was dirty, smelly and crowded. Most of those travelling were men, with a few families standing on the corridors. Although it was still early afternoon, many of the men were half drunk. One group was in a particularly raucous mood, singing rebel songs and swearing to all and sundry that they had just had the mightiest fucking weekend fucking ever and the craic was fucking mighty. Fair fucks. Malachy wondered what it must be like, to make this journey for real. To leave a small town in Mayo or Galway, or a fishing village or farm, and head off to an alien culture where you were only tolerated because of your brawn and despised for your Irishness. He was going to ask Rose but she was busy trying to get Breege to talk.

'You don't have to make up your mind for another while,' she was saying. 'Whatever you decide, we'll support you. We know it's not easy, Breege but you have to talk about it sometime.'

Breege was silent, dead eyes staring at the floor. Malachy was sure he saw some fellow passengers nod in their direction and pass quiet remarks behind hands that covered their faces. One woman in particular was glancing at them frequently and seemed upset.

When they reached Dun Laoighre, the reality of their situation began to dawn on him. As Rose led them confidently through the main departure hall, his ear picked up a variety of accents from all parts of Ireland. Then, through a long, long window, he saw the white mass of the boat. It seemed to occupy more space than a boat should. Seasoned travellers marched with a purpose, well used to the formalities and hassles. New emigrants looked at the boat, some with excitement and anticipation, most with dread and sadness.

Malachy was pleased Rose was with them She had them marching up the gangway among the first group to board. She led them through a maze of passage ways and stair ways, reeking of diesel and throbbing with the pounding of engines, and brought them to a small lounge.

'Best seat in the house' she said. 'The deck is fine if the weather is hot but freezing otherwise. The bar is only for the brave. You might enjoy a visit there, Malachy, if only to tell your friend what real drinkers are like. Meanwhile, make yourselves comfortable as you can because it's not exactly a cruise ship.'

Malachy went onto the deck to watch as the ferry left port. He leaned on the rail and watched as the crew moved like a well oiled machine to get the ship to sea. He watched Ireland fade from view as the ferry laboured towards Wales.

A woman he vaguely recognised came and stood beside him.

'It's tough, isn't it, leaving?' she said.

Malachy realised she had been on the train from Connolly.

'Have you been back and forward a few times?' he asked her.

'I've been in London two years, this was my first time home. She grasped his arm gently. 'Is that girl your girlfriend, the quiet one?'

'No,' he answered carefully, 'I'm with the English one actually.'

'I think I know what the story is,' she continued. 'I bet there's another dozen girls on the boat in the same condition. I should know. Is she going to keep the baby?'

Malachy was flustered. If it was obvious to this lady, he wondered, did the whole town know?

'Look, the only reason I know is because I went through it myself. I got rid of mine and there is not an hour passes that I don't wonder about it and if I did the right thing. All I'm saying to you is, make sure your friend thinks long and hard before she decides. A lifetime is an awful long time to regret one mistake.'

Malachy felt like a lost child.

'I don't have a fucking clue what to do,' he admitted. 'One lousy, stupid mistake was all she made. She was the most beautiful girl in town you know. I was crazy about her, I still am, but she is so mixed up and confused, she doesn't know what she's doing. Would you talk to her?'

'Believe me. The last thing she needs now is a total stranger giving her advice. I made the trip on my own that time and I'd have given anything for a friend like you. Go on, go back to her. Put your arms around her and tell her you'll look after her.'

'I can't look after myself,' Malachy said. 'I thought Athlone was Dun Laoighre. The water, you see, and the boats.'

She laughed. 'Never mind, you'll learn quick enough. Look after her. You have no idea what's going through her mind. At least, though, she has somebody with her. I was on my own. I stayed in a bed sit after and wanted to end it all. I even turned on the gas and lay down on the bed. I ran out of shillings for the meter, that's how bright I was. Look after her, right?'

Then she left. Malachy wished he had the type of courage she must have had. To go to a strange city, alone, and commit a grievous sin, and have the courage to offer hope to a total stranger , made her the strongest person he had ever met. He wanted to follow her and beg her for some of her courage.

Instead, he went through the bar on the way back to the girls. As soon as he entered the bar section, he knew what Rose had meant when she said it was not for the faint hearted. A fog of tobacco smoke hung over everything and the place reeked of diesel, alcohol and urine. Large men, hard faced and sporting sideburns, lined the bar and sat at every table. Conversation was more subdued but intense. Bottles of duty free whiskey stood on tables covered with pints of beer and porter. One man slept on the floor, the front of his shirt stained with beer, some of which was fresh, the rest of which he had managed to swallow, if only temporarily.

The passage of the boat had been smooth but now the sea became choppier.

Several bodies were bent over the side rail of the deck, puking heartily. Rose was alone when he got back.

'Where's Breege?' he asked her.

'She's been in and out of the loo since you left. She is really suffering, poor thing. And we still have at least two hours to go.'

They were the longest two hours of Malachy's life. Breege appeared a few times and both he and Rose were shocked as each time she seemed sicker and more distraught than before. The sea settled as they approached the Welsh coast. Breege sat beside Malachy and placed her head on his shoulder. Oblivious to Rose, to the dreadful smell of Breege's matted hair, to the other passengers, Malachy hugged her, then raised her chin, looked into the saddest eyes imaginable and kissed her on the lips.

'You can make it Breege,' he whispered, ' and I'll be there all the way.'

She placed her head back on his shoulder and said nothing.

At Holyhead, they thronged with all the other passengers along the maze of corridors. At he entrance to the station, three sets of policemen watched the crowd. People, invariably young men, were selected at random, and questioned. Malachy was one of those.

'Where are you going, sir?' a thin faced, plain clothes man asked him.

'London,' he replied, nervously.

'And what part of London might that be, sir?'

Panic set in. 'I don't know.'

'Really, sir, and what is the purpose of your trip?'

Malachy was tongue tied. He licked his lips nervously.

'As a Special Branch man, I'm entitled to ask these questions, sir, and you are required by law to answer.'

Malachy glanced at the two girls waiting by the wall. The sight of Breege, pale and lost looking, gave him strength.

'I'm going to visit my girlfriend's parents,' he said with a lot more confidence than he felt. 'I'm a bit nervous, officer.'

'I can understand that, sir.' The Branch man stared at him. Then he smirked. 'Enjoy your visit, Paddy.'

Feeling more and more like cattle being herded, they got on the London train. It was getting dark and they saw little of the countryside of North Wales. By the time they reached Crewe, Rose was sleeping soundly.

Breege was staring at her own reflection in the carriage window. She looked exhausted. Malachy thought of the beautiful girl she had been a few weeks before.

'How are you feeling now, Breege?' he asked her.

She shrugged.

'Have you any idea at all what you might do?' he persisted.

'It doesn't matter any more, Malachy,' she said, still looking out the window.

'Of course it matters,' he said, trying to sound reassuring, but feeling totally out of his depth. 'Of course it matters.'

'I mean really, Malachy, it doesn't matter.' She turned and looked at him. Seeing the expression in her eyes, hopelessness and loss, he understood what she was saying.

'Jesus, Breege, what happened?'

'Somewhere, about half way across the Irish Sea, in a filthy toilet of the Holyhead boat, I lost it. I just felt empty. I stayed there for I don't know how long.'

'Jesus, Breege,' was all he could say.

She laughed shortly. 'Jesus. Actually, I prayed for it. I should say her because I knew it was a girl. I prayed for her soul. Do unborn babies have souls, I wonder, Malachy? If you joined the priesthood, you could find out.'

She was so calm Malachy was frightened. He had no idea what to do. Rose slept blissfully on.

'I was going to call her Marian first, then I thought Rose. I wanted to have her sometimes but other times I wanted to get rid of her. I don't know, I honestly don't know what I was going to do in the end. Isn't that an awful thing to have to live with, Malachy?'

He remembered his conversation with the woman on deck. 'I think you'd always be wondering anyway, Breege, whether you kept it, her, or whatever you did.'

'Suppose she was yours, Malachy,' she said looking directly at him. 'Suppose it was you that got me into this. What would you have wanted me to do?'

Malachy could not think of an answer. 'I don't know.'

'But if you had to choose,' she insisted, her voice rising slightly, 'what would you do?'

'May God forgive me, Breege, but I think I'd have said to get rid of it.'

'Why?'

'Because you are beautiful and have your whole life to live and enjoy. Because I've….'

'What? You've what?'

'Yerrah, you know well. According to Marian the whole town knew. I've fancied you for years. If you were pregnant with my child, maybe I'd have feiced off to Australia or some place with you and lived happily after. That's how fairy tails end, anyway.'

'No fairy tale for us then, Malachy.' It was a statement, not a question.

The train sped through the English night. It was almost dawn when it reached the outskirts of London. Despite the tension of their situation, Malachy and Breege were stunned by the vast sprawl of the city. There seemed to be no end to the mass of houses, factories, shops, warehouses, cars, buses, trucks and people. Euston was organised chaos. Malachy had never seen a black person in real life and had to stop himself staring at the Asian and West Indian workers on the platform. Uniformed police stood at the gate. A female constable stopped them.

'Could I see some identification, please?' she asked in a tone that managed to be polite and threatening at the same time. As Malachy and Breege fumbled in their pockets, Rose smiled at the police woman and spoke in a cockney accent that they had never heard before. The police woman smiled and waved them on.

'What did you say to her?' Malachy asked as they rushed away.

'You're a homosexual and everybody knows queers are not terrorists, whatever about vice versa. Now, let's make that phone call.'

Malachy looked at Breege. They had not told Rose yet what had happened. Breege nodded at him.

'Rose,' he said, and was surprised to feel a catch in his voice, 'Breege lost the baby on the boat.'

'Oh no, you poor thing,' Rose said, embracing her. 'We still have to call, though, you need to see a doctor, Breege.'

'I'm fine,' Breege said.

'No, you're not,' Rose told her firmly. 'Make the call, Malachy'

Malachy was looking at the phone. He saw the slots for the money, he saw the receiver and mouth piece but he did not know what to do next. He looked helplessly at Rose. Shaking her head, she held out her hand for the number, then quickly and competently put the call through. She then handed the phone to Malachy. He recognised the voice he had heard the week before.

'I'm the lad who spoke to you last week, Fr Tommy's friend,' he said, looking around as if some neighbour from home might be listening.

'Where are you now?' the voice enquired.

'London.'

'What part?'

'The station.'

'Is that Euston?'

'Indeed.'

'Have you been here before?'

'No.'

'Would you be able to make your way to Fulham. It's on the Tube line.'

'Hold on, please,' Malachy covered the mouthpiece. 'Do you know a place called Fulham?' he asked Rose. She grabbed the phone. A few minutes later, she led them to the Tube station. Malachy clung to the rail of his first escalator while Breege seemed to have reverted to her almost catatonic state. The vastness and the anonymity of the place somehow reassured him. On the tube, he took both Breege and Rose by the hand and they smiled. Soon, he felt, it would be all behind them and they could enjoy the delights of London.

CHAPTER 30

The route they took back to town brought them by the lake. It seemed much smaller than they both remembered.

'I can't believe we used to swim there,' Malachy said, 'look at that algae or whatever that shite on the surface. Unbelievable.'

'Park the car over there, Malachy, outside that new building,' Nora instructed. He did as he was told . The new building was a glass and concrete affair and looked very smart and modern.

'Well?' he asked.

Nora just smiled and nodded to a house across the street.

'Mrs Browns!' he said. 'God, it looks in great nick She must be dead a hundred years at this stage.'

'Poor Mrs Brown lived to be ninety one. We kept in touch for years and then she spent the last few years in a home in Galway. I visited her regularly. When she died, myself and Eileen's sister Michelle were the only two people from outside the home at the funeral. She was a wonderful, feisty old woman.'

'Who has the house now, do you know?'

'A local solicitor, whose father worked for Thomas, actually. He paid her a fair price and that and her pensions kept her in the home. He was also kind enough to visit her now and again, usually on his way to the Galway Races, with his snobby wife. She sniffed around the ward as if she was somebody special while we all knew she was reared on a pig farm. Still, as Eileen used to say, the fly from the mizzen flies highest.'

'Do you want to knock at the door, ask them to let you have a look inside?' Malachy asked her.

'Good God no! I remember it as a beautiful house, full of character and history. I don't want to see it done up in pastel colours, with wooden floors and bidets and shelves full of wine that will be wasted on their uneducated palates.'

'Merciful Jesus, Nora, I hate to think what you'll be saying about me to your posh friends.'

'To be perfectly frank, Malachy, my friends would have little interest in you. I may tell a story or two over dessert about your bumpkin ways and your desperate efforts to act sophisticated, but otherwise, no, you won't really be mentioned.'

'Y'auld bitch, come on and I'll buy you lunch. I know a place that does mean pig's feet and pig's arse and cabbage.'

They drove through the town. The streets were almost deserted. Small groups of men hung around some pub doors, anxiously checking their watches. Malachy looked at them to see if there were any familiar faces from his youth. He was relieved to find there were none. The Frenchman's Bar and Lounge was also a Bistro he noticed. It was not open so he continued until they reached the Royal hotel.

Parking was difficult as the front of the hotel was blocked off by a line of beer barrels, strung with rope. A red carpet led to the main door.

'Let me guess,' Nora said sarcastically, ' a peasant wedding.'

Malachy had been in the hotel years before and it had changed completely. The reception had been a cramped and badly lit alcove. It was now a large bright area, complete with computer and pretty receptionist. She smiled at them and asked them if they had made a reservation for lunch.

Malachy heard Nora draw her breath in sharply and spoke quickly.

'No, we don't have reservations but, sure we'll be in and out before the crowd comes.'

The receptionist directed them to the dining room, which overlooked the park. They took a table by the window and both immediately looked at the view.

'This seems to be much the same,' Nora said quietly, 'though most of the old buildings are gone. That's the very spot I met Myles all those years ago, there in from where the red car is parked.'

'And that bench, right in the middle, that's the one I was on when I heard about Breege,' Malachy said. He looked at the menu. 'Are you hungry?'

'What's on offer?'

'"Soup de jour, carvery, a wide selection of desserts, tea or coffee.'

'How very original. Is there some kind of fish there?'

'Salmon.'

'Probably farmed.'

'How about "fillet of plaice with tartare sauce"?'

'Probably frozen.'

'Well, feic you, I'm going to have medallions of beef chasseur, with a medley of vegetables and selection of potatoes. Followed by homemade rhubarb tart.'

'Probably made in a home for the bewildered. I suppose I could have the rack of local lamb, with a rosemary and garlic garnish. At least if it's local, it's guaranteed to be thick.'

Malachy ordered their meals and was pleased that everything was tasty and the service was top class. Sipping his coffee, he asked Nora, 'What now?'

'I have no idea. I suppose a walk in the park would be a good idea.'

'Sounds alright, ' Malachy agreed. 'How was lunch?'

'The food was passable but this coffee is revolting.'

'God, but there's no pleasing some,' Malachy said, taking a credit card from his wallet.

The park, like everything else, seemed smaller to Malachy. He and Nora linked arms as they strolled through. Some of the benches were occupied and a few other strollers were taking advantage of the warm day. A man in a wheelchair approached, being pushed along by a sturdy and stern faced, middle aged woman. The man was dressed in black. He was leaning awkwardly and one side of his face seemed to have collapsed.

One rheumy eye stared ahead.

'Malachyeah! It is Malachyeah, isn't it?'

Malachy jumped at the sound of the voice.

'It is indeed, Brother. Is it yourself?'

'Malachyeah! I never forget my bys! Oo were a good by, weren't oo? And the udder by, Joyce. He set oo wrong, Malachyeah!' He used a handkerchief to wipe away some drool that was winding from the collapsed corner of his mouth.

'I heard oo were out foreign, is thot the way, Malachyeah?'

'Indeed it is, Brother.'

'Ond who is this ladyeah? She's not oor mother. I wos at her fooneral, Lawrd rest her..' he began to cough, his entire body shaking.

His attendant patted his back with surprising gentleness. When he had recovered, he looked at Malachy again. 'oo should hov been a priesht, Malachyeah! I was wrong about Joyce but I was right about oo. Oo were one of my besht bys. I looked after all my bys, I helped them all when they needed help. I gided them, Malachyeah!'

He seemed to doze. The attendant smiled at them and pushed him away.

'Christ, talk about a blast from the past,' Malachy said.

'That is the ignorant pig of a man who slammed the door of the monastery in my face the day Eileen got married. God seems to have punished him.'

'The bloody Lizard! Of all people. And he's still raving about me and the priesthood.. I'd swear the bastard recognised you too but wouldn't give you the satisfaction.

They managed to walk around the park without bumping into any more ghosts.

'I remember you telling me about O Murchu going on about the cricket here,' Malachy said.

'It's funny, ' Nora said, 'it has to be the most boring game in the world and yet they played it here and were able to keep the peasantry subdued at the same time. I suppose they bored them into submission.'

'As a matter of interest, Nora, do you feel any affinity at all for this country? I mean, you grew up here, live here, your daughter is here. Are you here or are you on holidays or what?'

'I look at you, Malachy, an educated, well travelled young man, well not young any more. You've lived out of this place more than you've lived in it. What are you? Irish? I grew up in this country, yes, but not in your culture. So much of me yearns for the past, Malachy. It's fifty years since those days and I can feel the presence of those people. I can see Myles, there, where the elms used to be. I can see Eileen at the gate, all young. I can see Mrs Brown leaving the church. I can feel them. I can see all these new offices and houses but I can't feel them, Malachy. Is it age, I wonder?'

'I sincerely hope so, otherwise you're doddering.'

She looked at him sharply but then she smiled. 'You're right. It's time to move on. Are you ready to go?'

'Almost, Nora. There's one or two ghosts of my own I need to put to sleep.'

'I need to go back to the hotel to freshen up, as the Americans so delicately put it. Pick me up at the front door in a few minutes.'

Malachy walked back to the car on his own. Looking around, the park was empty. Sitting in the driver's seat, he adjusted the rear view mirror, switched on the engine, flicked on the indicator, farted loudly onto the soft leather and said to his reflection, 'Now who's a peasant, Nora?'

'Where would you like to go?' she asked as she got in beside him.

Malachy did not answer immediately. Despite all the intimate details of their lives that they had shared, there were many details still untold. In his MBA studies, he frequently came across the Praedo Principle, also known as the 80/20 rule. In all negotiations, he was instructed, you never reveal everything, you always keep something back. Mind you, he told his professor at a tutorial one day, we have the same practice in Ireland, called 'playing the cute hoor'. What he had not told Nora was that Marian had filled him in on Breege's life over the years. He and Breege had in fact, exchanged Christmas cards, cars that said nothing other than express greetings for the season but cards that also expressed a shared belief that memories and people matter.

'Where to now, Malachy?' Nora repeated.

'Down another cul de sac on Memory Lane,' he told her.

'Good Lord,' she said, 'just as well we are not staying here much longer. You would regress beyond redemption. We'll be lucky your knuckles are not scraping the ground by the time we pass the speed limits.'

CHAPTER 31

Mrs Brown was thrilled when she heard the news. She immediately dismissed Thomas and sat Nora down to hear all the details. When she was finished, Mrs Brown said, 'First of all, we must contact your family and let them know the news. Then we have to decide on the where and when.'

'I rather fancy going away somewhere, just a quiet celebration. Me and Thomas, my parents. And you, of course. My feeling at the moment is that we should wait a while, until Thomas has his affairs in order here and then go to London and from there to Africa.'

'There is a delicate matter,' Mrs Brown said, hesitantly. 'Though you did not say as much, I gather that you, shall we say, indulged in the passions of the flesh with the would be father Myles.'

Nora blushed, but smiled.

'I see,' Mrs Brown continued. 'My point is, is there any possibility that you might, as they so delicately put it around here, be in trouble?'

'I don't believe so. I won't know for sure obviously for a while but I don't believe so, no.'

'Still, the possibility is there. I suggest, therefore, that you do things a little more quickly than you suggest. A quick trip to London, a registry office and back here as Mrs Thomas Williams. Then, should your clerical companion prove to be as fruitful as most of his countrymen, there will not be as many questions asked. Certainly, the months will be counted but, as I like to think, those who count don't matter, those who matter don't count.'

Nora could see the logic of her ideas. Certainly, she had no reservations about becoming Thomas's wife. He would provide her with security and comfort, things she saw slowly slip from her own family in recent years. He would doubtless prove to be an affectionate, faithful and dutiful husband. She did not believe she was 'in trouble', nor did she believe Thomas would ever know that he was not the only man to know her.

'Nora,' Mrs Brown said, breaking into her thoughts, 'Thomas is the right choice. Only you, Myles and I know what happened. Myles will certainly remain silent, I will never breathe a word and Thomas will be the happiest man in the world. He will be happier than he has ever dreamed he could be. Don't take any chances, Nora, seize the day. Grab your happiness.'

'Is there a chance, do you think, that he might suspect, when we, shall we say, consummate?'

'Nora, dear, forgive me for being blunt, but when stuffy, straight laced, middle aged man finds himself in bed with a beautiful young thing like you, his thoughts are not going to be if he's the first. Rather, he'll be wondering , will he last? So, are we agreed, silence it is?'

Nora's face broke into a broad grin. 'I've wanted to do this since I arrived in Castlecarraig.' She spat on the palm of her hand and extended it to Mrs Brown. She in turn spat on her palm and the two of them shook on the deal of silence.

Word soon got around the small town of the engagement of the attractive young lady and the wealthy middle aged gentleman. Many of the customers in the shop congratulated her and wished Thomas well. One of those was Eileen.

'You are certainly full of surprises, Nora. Still waters certainly run deep. When is the big day?'

'I have no idea, Eileen. Could you meet me after work and I'll tell you all?'

Eileen agreed and was waiting for her as she left the shop.

'Go back to the beginning,' she said immediately. 'Last thing I know was that I had set up you and Myles to sort yourselves out. Next thing, you are engaged to Thomas. Even for you that's a fair leap. From a young and handsome priest to a middle aged Protestant merchant. In less than a week!'

'Actually, Eileen, it took less than a day,' Nora replied.

Eileen looked at her friend shrewdly. 'You have changed. There's a, I don't know exactly, maybe what the old folk call a glicness about you. You seem more calculating.'

'Be honest, Eileen, did you marry for love?'

'Hah! You know well I did not.'

'So, why should I?'

Eileen was taken aback by her forthright manner. 'But you're different. You have style and grace and good looks. Look at me. What do you see? Beef to the ankles. Look at these hands , from doing laundry in cold water for years. Look at where I come from and where you come from. Come on, Nora, don't make a mistake that will haunt you for the rest of your life.'

'So you'd rather I made a mistake that would destroy several lives, would you Eileen? You are the best friend I have ever had. Surely you can see why I am doing what I am doing. Yes, I should run away with Myles. But where would we run to? He has nothing, I have less. We could not stay here, even you would not be happy with that. So I'd make the lives of so many people miserable. So I choose, yes, Eileen, choose, to make one life happy and my own content.'

They walked on in silence. Eileen could not help but admire the steel and resolve in her friend's voice. She linked her arm through hers. 'Can I ask you one question? After that, I'll be behind you all the way.'

'What's the question?'

'Who's the best kisser, old Thomas or young Myles?'

'Thomas' moustache tickles and Myles' breath is a bit funny so it's a draw,' Nora replied grinning. Laughing like little girls, they strolled along the street, arm in arm and content with their destinations in life.

Eileen told her about her short married life. She confided that Seamus was very eager in bed but had a lot to learn and she was looking forward to teaching him and learning with him. His mother was mellowing a bit as well as she began to experience Eileen's cooking and house keeping skills.

As they approached Nora's lodgings, Eileen became serious again. 'Are you going to stay in Castlecarraig?' she asked.

'I don't really think so. Thomas has plans to go away. He says he's been thinking about it for years and now is the time. I think I'd enjoy adventure, Eileen. I don't think I'm meant for life in a small town. I can see myself turning into a dreadful snob.'

'Something tells me you are going to be a snob anyway, Nora, wherever you are. I'll miss you if you go.'

'I'll miss you, Eileen. I don't think I would have lasted this long if not for you. Still, you are going to start producing babies soon, good Catholic babies so you won't have time for thinking about anything else.'

'The way Seamus has been going at me since we got married, like a bull at a gate, you might be right on that score. I will think of you, though, and I'll call my first daughter Nora.'

Nora was touched. 'What about your first son?'

'That's already decided. He'll be Seamus and be either an engineer or a bishop and look after me in my dotage..

They stood and looked at each other. Nora felt a great surge of affection, and also some loss. Eileen had represented all that was good in the strange people Nora had found herself part of. She was kind and helpful and at the same time wedded in every sense to the history of the place. They grasped each other tightly and Eileen walked away.

Later that evening, Thomas called. Nora found that she enjoyed his company and invited him to walk in the garden with her.

The evenings were getting shorter so it was dusk as they stood by the low back wall, looking over the lake. Dark clouds nestled on the horizon, though a redness in the sky behind them promised good weather.

'Are you happy with your decision, Nora?' he asked her.

'Yes, Thomas,' she reassured him. 'I feel sometimes that you are like that old castle on the other shore.'

'Goodness me, you don't mean old and broken down, do you?'

'Not at all. Strong but overcome by history, like the ivy has overcome the castle. You could stay here and be warm and comfortable but imagine the adventures we could have together. I've been dreaming about Africa since you mentioned it. I know nothing about the place except what I've seen in the cinema. But I really believe we could have the most marvellous life together. Do you think so too?'

Thomas regarded her with such adoration she thought her heart would break.

'All my life, Nora, dear Nora, I dreamed of happiness. I was brought up to believe in hard work, and our children will be brought up he same way, mark my words, but always I dreamed of finding someone like you. I had honestly thought I was too late and that my time had passed. Then, you step off a train. Now, here I am, Mr Thomas of Williams and Son, preparing to sell up and head off to the African jungle, not a care in the world. My life may be half over, Nora, but my living is about to begin.'

She stroked his moustache fondly. 'It tickles, you know,' she said, before kissing him gently.

Back in the house, Thomas was all business again. Sitting at the table with Nora and Mrs Brown, he produced a bundle of pages. One contained a time table of events up to the sale of the business. Another, a set of requirements for their marriage. Yet another listed his assets. Looking at this, Nora said, 'I have one of these,' She then produced a sheet of blank paper. 'That's the sum total of my worldly goods, I'm afraid.' Thomas reached over and took the sheet. He put it with his own bundle. 'Now,' he said, ' what's yours is mine and what's mine is yours.'

The next sheet he showed them was far more serious. On it was written the dates of departure of passenger ships from the port of Southampton to Dar Es Salaam. The itinerary of the journey was set down. Exotic names filed Nora with excitement and dread – Naples, Cairo, Mombassa. She knew Thomas was showing her all these for a reason. He was giving her as many opportunities as possible for her to change her mind.

The papers lay on the table before them. Thomas and Mrs Brown looked at Nora.

She picked up all the sheets and tapped them briskly on the table.

The others waited expectantly.

'May I suggest, Thomas,' she said at last, handing him the bundle of paper, ' that you reserve a cabin as soon as possible, for Mr and Mrs Williams?'

CHAPTER 32

Malachy, and Breege followed Rose as she made her way to the address in Fulham. It was an undistinguished detached house. There was nothing to make it stand out from it's neighbours. The door was opened by a man in his mid forties, already grey haired. Even though he was dressed in jeans and tee shirt, Malachy knew straight away that he was a priest.

'Are you Fr Tommy's friend?' he asked him.

'Looks like I'm your friend now, folks, some come on in.'

He led them down a long, cluttered hall way. It was cluttered with card board boxes of every size, and some push chairs. Some of the boxes were open and Malachy could see they were filled with toys and children's clothes. They came to a kitchen that was surprisingly large and even more surprisingly tidy. Two women, girls really, were sitting at a table, silently drinking tea.

'Everybody calls me Paddy,' their host said. 'You two,' he said pointing to Rose and Malachy, 'sit here. You, come with me.' He took Breege by the arm and, with the utmost gentleness, led her from the room.

Without asking, one of the girls at the table got up and got two mugs and poured out tea.

'One of Paddy's few rules,' she said in a Cork accent, ' always have a pot of tea on the stove.'

They sat in silence after that. Malachy felt that conversation with strangers was not something the people in this house wanted. He had never felt such a complete stranger either. He felt as if everything that was happening was beyond his control and yet he felt a strange sense of empowerment. Castlecarraig and all it represented for him seemed far, far away. Joyce and his constant search for sex without consequence, O Murchu and his loathing of all things foreign, the Brothers and their obsession with carrying on stale traditions – as he sat in this corner of London, all these were no longer accepted unquestioningly. Looking at Rose, he knew instinctively that their relationship was over as well. He felt sad about that and rueful that she obviously would not be going to the chemist, at least on his behalf. Soon, he and Rose had the kitchen to themselves. He got up and paced restlessly around the room.

'What do you reckon is happening?' he asked her.

Rose shrugged. 'I imagine there's a doctor on call. Probably check her out, maybe put her in hospital, I don't really know.'

'What do we do so?'

'It depends. If she's OK, bring her home, let her rest there, get over this. If she has to stay, Paddy probably has a bed some place here for you.'

Malachy was not surprised to be getting the brush off, though he was a little hurt.

'So that's it then, for us, me and you, like?'

'I couldn't have put it better myself, Malachy. Look, we had a good time but the Summer is over. I might see you next year but let's be realistic. You're heading off to college, right? I'm going to do the same. Life is beginning for us. You are one sweet man and very loyal, you'll have women chasing you all around campus. You'll graduate and before you know it, you'll be married and settled back in Castlecarraig.'

'Sounds like you have it all worked out for me. It sounds boring.'

'Which would you prefer, Malachy, really? Nice house, nice wife, nice family, a contented life, or chase around looking for the impossible and end up with nothing? Maybe women are a bit more realistic about these things. Prince Charming looks well in the distance but close up, he has a pot belly and sweats a lot.'

'I don't sweat that much.'

'Ah, but you are not Prince Charming. You are Malachy, reliable , loyal Malachy. And I have a dreadful feeling you are going to be heart broken time and time again.'

Paddy came into the kitchen.

'Depending on which way you look at it, it's good news or bad news. We had her checked out by a doctor. She's lost the baby alright. The doc says she's in remarkably good health for someone whose been through what she's been through. They rear them tough in Mayo.'

'So what happens now?' Malachy asked.

'Well, Breege can stay here for a few days and we'll fly her back to Dublin after that. You, I know are Malachy. You might well have saved her life by bringing her here. Girls at home can be driven to extremes when they find themselves in Breege's position. I've picked up the pieces often enough and tried to help put them back together. You're a good lad, Malachy. And Rose, you did a good thing too. London is a big place and a dangerous place if you haven't help, so well done to you as well.'

'Thanks, Paddy,' Rose said. 'I think I'll go home now. It's only a hop on the tube. Malachy needs a kip, though.'

'We'll look after that. What do you want to do, Malachy.'

'I reckon I'll go back tomorrow. I have a room full of animals' guts waiting for me to clean and I hate being away.'

Paddy laughed. 'The gut room! I spent one Summer there myself. Hell on Earth.

Rose, why don't you show Malachy some of the sights for an hour or two? Come back here then for tea and we'll have a pint later if you want.'

'What about Breege?' Malachy enquired. 'I'd like to say a word to her.'

'She's out for the count. The poor child is exhausted, leave her be. She'll be better after a while and you can chat all you want. Go on, now, the pair of you.' He handed Rose a pound note. 'Take him to Piccadilly Circus, into Ward's pub. Have soup and a sandwich. There's a few lads from around home working there. Tell them you're on holiday, say nothing about myself or they'll twig our business. Be back around seven.'

The sights of London cheered both of them up. Malachy was like a child on Christmas morning and his enthusiasm rubbed off on Rose. Lunch in Wards was great craic. He knew one of the lads behind the bar and so he got the biggest sandwich he ever saw. He also drank his first pint of bitter which, even to his inexperienced palate, tasted like ditch water. He was told he could stay while the pub closed for the afternoon but declined. Instead, he walked through Soho. After his first pint of bitter, his first view of a prostitute was equally disappointing. Plastered in make up, she looked sad, bored and desperate. They stood in Trafalgar Square and Malachy watched in fascination as the parade of humanity walked among the pigeons. He was pleased when Rose took his hand and placed her head on his shoulder. 'It's been great Malachy,' she whispered. 'Now, it's time to go.' She led him back to Piccadilly Station. When they reached Fulham, she walked to the train door with him. They had time for a hurried kiss before the door slid shut, leaving Malachy on the platform, watching as Rose faded into the darkness of the Underground.

He found Paddy's house. Inside, Paddy brought him to a sitting room and Breege was sitting on a sofa, watching television. Her smile broke Malachy's heart. He sat beside her and took her hand.

'How're things now?' he asked her.

'I'll live, Malachy. How about you?'

'Never mind me. I've been seeing the sights and drinking pints of bitter. I met one of the Bradys from town in a pub in town. I said nothing, of course, and Rose is gone home.'

'She was very good to me. And good for you, Malachy. Are you seeing her again?'

'Unless by accident, I doubt it. Still, it was good while it lasted. Can I get you anything.'

Breege shook her head. Paddy came in with a tray and handed it to Malachy. 'Best of English grub,' he announced. 'Steak and kidney pie and mushy peas.' Malachy took the tray doubtfully. 'Is it dead, Paddy?' he asked.

'Go on, lad, get it into you. Far from steak you were reared.'

Malachy cleared the plate and brought the tray out to the kitchen. Paddy was talking to another girl, one Malachy had not seen before. Paddy excused himself and took the tray.

'Come out here, and I'll show you where you'll kip,' he said. 'You can crash in my office tonight, there's a couch and a sleeping bag. If you're heading off tomorrow it'll do, if you decide to stay a while longer, we'll organise something more comfortable.'

Passing the sitting room, they looked in and saw Breege was asleep. She looked peaceful. Her hair had regained some of it's lustre and her skin was not as pale.

'We'll leave her be,' Paddy said, opening a door at the top of the hall.

The office was absolute chaos. Files and more files were everywhere. Boxes were stacked against every inch of wall space. An old fashioned desk was barely visible beneath a mass of invoices, bills, bank statements, letters and envelopes. A brand new leather couch took up one side of the room. A sleeping bag was spread out on it.

'Be it ever so humble, Malachy, it's home for tonight. Sit with Breege for a while and I'll come and get you for a pint in a while.'

Malachy sat beside her again and again took her hand in his. A strange man called Hughie was presenting a quiz show on the T.V.. Listening to the soft breathing of Breege and the inane prattle of the strange Hughie, he too fell asleep.

He woke with a start to find Paddy seated where Breege had been. He moved his hands to make sure he was not holding anybody else's.

'You needed a bit of a rest, Malachy. You've been out cold for nearly two hours. Breege went upstairs a while ago. It's a tragedy to see a child like that suffer so much. Anyway, do you want to go for a pint?'

Rubbing his eyes, Malachy agreed. 'Though, to be honest, Paddy, I'm not what you'd call a drinker,' he added. 'Long may that last, Malachy.'

Outside it was dark but only as dark as cities ever get. They strolled for a mile or so and entered a pub called the Fishmonger's Arms. It was crowded and most if not all of the customers were Irish. Even though it was after ten, many of them were still in their working clothes, obviously having come straight from the building site. Paddy was well known and when they reached the bar, the barmaid had a pint waiting for him. 'The same for my friend, Julie,' he said. They sat at the bar sipping their drinks and Malachy felt like a veteran. He said this to Paddy.

'It's the Irish disease, Malachy. The pub and the site. I've been here for years now and

I've seen the finest of men destroyed. Some make it, of course, and if it wasn't for those I wouldn't be able to keep the place open for waifs and strays like yourself and Breege. Paddy in England is a strange creature. He'll look after his own in one way but in another way, he'll destroy them.'

'Are you a priest, Paddy?' Malachy asked. 'I don't want to be rude but I reckon you are.'

'Smart man. Fr Myles Walsh at your service. I know you were not the father of poor Breege's child but I'd say, watching you with her, you care a lot about her.'

'Did you ever care a lot about someone, Father?'

'Stick with Paddy. I get all creeds and colours at the house so we keep the religion thing as low key as possible.' He paused and drank deeply.

'Well before your time, there was a scandal involving myself and a beautiful girl. I was within a year of my ordination, supposed to head off to New York, would you believe. She was the most beautiful woman I had ever seen, or have ever seen since.'

'So why didn't you marry her? Did you really want to be a priest that much, that you'd turn your back on a woman like that?'

'A woman like that, indeed.' Myles looked into his glass as if it was a mirror of his past. 'I can't begin to tell you what she meant to me. I nearly left her like your friend left Breege. In those days, God alone knows what would have happened her but somehow, I think she would have coped. She was a strong, wonderful woman.'

'Where is she now?'

'I'm not sure, somewhere in Africa I think. When all that happened, I knew I could never settle into a wealthy parish in the Bronx or Queens. I felt drawn to helping those people who were victims of circumstances or times or morality or whatever. I did go to America but only to see if there was some way I could learn to set up some place where I could do something positive for the people of home. So there it is, Malachy, my life story. Check me out if you want when you get back. Or, alternatively, do the decent thing and say nothing. Let the hare sit. You'll probably meet other girls along the way and you can send them here, or bring them here. You'll have a lot of secrets in life, Malachy, let mine be one of them.'

Another two pints appeared in front of them. A red faced man with a mop of curly hair winked at them and gave them the thumbs up.

'So what keeps you going, Myles. It must be soul destroying, year after year.'

'What keeps me going, Malachy, is the love of a good woman. I don't know where she is, I haven't seen her for over twenty years, but there is not a day goes by that I don't thank God I met her. What I see most days is a mockery of love, young girls abused and used. What keeps me going is the memory of what true, pure love is. I hope you find it yourself one day, Malachy.'

FINALE

Nora was quietly weeping as Malachy parked her car.

'He said all that?' she asked.

'Word for word,' Malachy answered. 'I went through it a hundred times that night trying to sleep on the leather couch, and on the train and boat the next day. And God alone knows how many times since.'

'Why didn't you tell me earlier you had met Myles?'

'I wasn't a hundred percent sure if they were one and the same for a while. Then, I thought I'd wait for the right moment, then I suppose I decided to be a bit dramatic and save it.'

Nora dabbed her eyes with a tissue.

'Did you not keep track of him through the years, through Eileen or the sister?' Malachy asked her.

'Good God no. You still haven't realised how utterly different times were then. When I left to marry Thomas, I spent the next twenty years in Africa. I did not come back to Ireland once. I didn't leave the farm in Rhodesia for four years, there was so much work to be done. I sorted out the finances, no small achievement in the colonies. Thomas took to farming with the same efficiency he had developed through the years at the shop. We stayed on after the blacks took over and the place became Zambia, then moved to the real Rhodesia. Felicity went to college in Pretoria. Then, Thomas wanted to retire back home to Ireland. After all the years feeling a stranger here, this is where he wanted to call home. So, to answer your question, by the time I met up with Eileen again, a lifetime had passed for all of us. You should be able to understand that.'

'I felt that way when we got back from London. Everything was changed. I suppose, in fairness, if that happened to me overnight, twenty years in the jungle could have changed you as well.'

Nora glanced around her. 'Why have we stopped here?' she asked.

They were on a quiet road on the way out of town, heading West. Once, it had been a well to do area but the years had taken a serious toll. Many of the houses had been converted to flats or let to a transient student population. Most needed to be repainted and the gardens all needed tidying. One house was a cut above the rest, even though the garden was overgrown with weeds. Malachy pointed at it.

'That's where Breege lives.'

'How do you know?'

'Marian told me that time in Santa Barbara. We spent a lot of hours that day wondering about what might have been. But dat's de way, as the Meath man says.'

'Tell me what happened,' Nora demanded.

So he told her. Breege came back from England and took a job in a pub, She went wild, out every night, sleeping around and generally breaking her parents hearts. Her exam results were as bad as expected. She had even taken up with Joyce for a while but dumped him for a married man who had left his wife and children. Then, out of the blue, she began to see Rose's cousin Donal. He had taken over the family farm and was as kind and gentle a man as Breege needed. They got married but whatever had happened her, Breege could not have kids. Still, they were happy until life decided to deal her another heartbreaker. Donal got sick and couldn't keep the farm. They sold up and moved into town. He died of cancer six months later. Breege kept him at home and looked after him to the very end. In the eyes of the town, she went from whoredom to sainthood after that..

'Have you spoken to her or met her in all the years, Malachy?' Nora's voice was gentle.

'Not for a long, long time. I used to meet herself and Donal for a jar now and again. He used to keep me informed about Rose.'

'Ah, yes, your English Rose.' Nora spoke this time with her usual edge of sarcasm. 'What did become of her?'

Malachy laughed. 'My Rose married well, twice and divorced well, twice. Last I heard, she was a leading light in the ex pat community in Spain, good luck to her. I was in Canada when Donal died and didn't hear about it for months. That was five years ago and I haven't seen her since.'

After a moment's silence, he restarted the car and began to do a u turn.

'Are you not going to call?' Nora asked him.

He shook his head. He drove through the town and took the Galway road.

'Why did you not call?'

Malachy glanced at the rear view mirror and saw his home town, small and receding, in the glass. He pressed the accelerator and the car surged forward.

'You know, Nora how you can't step in the same river twice? Same thing. I think I'll leave what's past past.'

'I'll allow that, Malachy, on one condition.'

'What might that be?'

'Could we please travel at least half the journey without such clichés?

'I'll agree to that if you promise not to be so bloody snobbish and stop giving out to me all the time. And I'll expect a major promotion from your son in law for putting up with you for a weekend.'

'Oh, Malachy, your boring life will be back to normal soon enough.'

'Better my boring life than listening to your auld guff for another day.'

And so the bickering continued. The Mercedes made its way through good roads and bad, showers and sunshine. Their journey this time was passed without deep and meaningful sharing of past or present thoughts. That journey was over.

ISBN 1-4120-2418-8